About the Author

Julia Schoonenberg lives in East Sussex. She worked on film screenplays before turning to prose. *Dora* is her second novel.

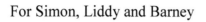
For Simon, Liddy and Barney

Julia Schoonenberg

DORA

AUSTIN MACAULEY
PUBLISHERS LTD.

A CIP catalogue record for this title is available from the British Library.

ISBN 9781785546396 (Paperback)
ISBN 9781785546402 (Hardback)
ISBN 9781785546419 (E-Book)

www.austinmacauley.com

First Published (2016)
Austin Macauley Publishers Ltd.
25 Canada Square
Canary Wharf
London
E14 5LQ

Chapter 1

The children stood forlornly on the platform station, each clutching a brown leather suitcase. The train that had transported them to their destination had left ten minutes before and apart from the porter sweeping up the debris at the far end of the platform, the station was deserted.

"Are you sure we've come to the right place, Tom?" the girl asked the boy.

"Of course we have, silly," said the boy, speaking with more conviction than he felt. He glanced surreptitiously at the piece of paper on which his father had written instructions for the journey and checked the name against the station signpost. "Look, Dora, it says Totnes."

Dora sighed and put down her suitcase. She looked across at a group of people who had just arrived on the platform opposite. A middle aged man and woman were accompanied by two young girls and behind them came a younger woman carrying a small child. The man said something that seemed to make the others laugh and they were all in high spirits. Soon afterward, a train came clattering along the railway track.

"The 3.30 train to London, Paddington, is now approaching on platform 2," rang the booming tones of an anonymous male voice. Several more figures emerged onto the platform, and when the first party climbed into one of the railway carriages, Dora could still hear the girls' high pitched laughter. She watched wistfully as the train started to pull out of the station, longing to be with them in that carriage. The stab of pain below her ribcage reminded Dora of the reason that she and her brother Tom had been sent to this desolate place.

*

Dora's best friend was called Emily Morton and the two of them were bursting with excitement as they skipped down the leafy suburban street. Emily was not only Dora's closest friend but her father Doctor Morton was Dora's family's medical practitioner. Both girls were jubilant because that morning they had learned that each had passed their exams with flying colours which guaranteed them a place at Guildford Grammar School. The war in France seemed far away and was the last thing on their minds as they returned home from school on that sunny June day.

They stopped for a chat at the gate in front of Dora's parents' red brick villa. With a smile and a wave, Emily disappeared up the street. Dora unlatched the front gate, but as she walked up the paved path that divided the neat front garden, she glanced up at the house and stopped short. The curtains at the windows were drawn tight and an eerie gloom seemed to have descended on the house.

From inside the hallway came none of the familiar sounds of a weekday afternoon, in fact the house was eerily quiet. Even the kitchen was deserted. Dora helped herself to a glass of milk from the larder and returned to the hallway just as Tom came out of the parlour, shutting the door after him with unusual care.

"Guess what, Tom! Guess what! I've passed!"

Her brother turned his head and stared at Dora oddly. His face was ashen.

2

"What's the matter, Tom?" Dora asked. "What is it? Where's everyone?"

"There's been a telegram," he said.

"What are you talking about?"

"A telegram's come from the war office. It's Edwin. He's been killed in the trenches," he blurted out.

Dora felt as though two bands of steel had taken a grip around her chest and as they tightened their hold, she gasped for breath. She tried to breathe deeply but it didn't seem to help.

"You'd best go and see Pa. He's in there," said Tom, nodding towards the door he had just closed.

At that moment, Dora could only feel her own pain. It was bad enough when Edwin suddenly went off to enlist in the army, and that had happened barely a year ago. Like so many of his contemporaries, Edwin had been caught up in the patriotic fervour that pervaded the country and responded eagerly to Lord Kitchener's pointing finger; and the ubiquitous message that 'Your Country Needs You'. Dora's own misery at his departure was assuaged by the pride that she felt in him.

With her mother Enid, it was a different story. Dora had never seen her mother betray such emotion but Edwin was her favourite child, the perfect baby son that had been born to her after three miscarriages. He was the apple of her eye.

"But he's barely eighteen," Enid had wailed, over and over again. "He's too young to go and fight!"

There was nothing that Gerald, her husband, could do or say to placate her. He often wished that he could have taken his son's place. But Gerald's age precluded him from enlisting; instead he was forced to stand by helplessly and watch his wife withdraw into a shadow of her former self. It wasn't until Edwin's first scrawled letter arrived in the post that Enid was able to smile again.

Dora needed to see her father and to be told that it was all a mistake. She turned to the parlour door, tapped on it lightly but could hear no response.

The room was in semi-darkness and at first she could only see her father's silhouette, hunched in an armchair by the fireplace. When she put her arms around his neck he barely responded to her presence and she was shocked to witness his vulnerability. Pa had always been such a tower of strength, the one person who could be relied upon to put things right when life got difficult, but now it was Dora's turn to be the comforter.

He felt her tears on his face and pulled a handkerchief out of his pocket.

"Where's Tom got to?" he asked, "He was here just a moment ago."

"I'll go and fetch him," she said, climbing off his lap.

By the time Dora returned to the room with Tom, Gerald had turned up the gas lamp and composed himself. He looked across the room at his two children seated on the sofa.

"This is a very painful time for us all, and particularly for your poor mother, but we have to be brave. We must look after each other and carry on as best we can."

"Shall we go and see her?" asked Dora.

Gerald shook his head. "Not just now. Your mother's in shock and Dr Morton has given her a sedative. I hope she's now sleeping."

Later that night when Tom was asleep, Dora crept into his bed for comfort but listening to her mother's muffled sobbing in the room next door it was impossible to sleep.

The next morning Dora and Tom went off to school as usual. On the surface life continued as before. Their respective schools had been informed of Edwin's death and were sympathetic, though their situation was not unique. As the war took its terrible toll, all too frequently came reports of a father or brother lost in battle.

At the end of the school day Dora preferred to go back to Emily's house instead of returning home directly. She and Tom were glad to accept invitations to tea from their friends' parents, in fact grateful for anything that delayed a return to the melancholy that hung over their home like a shroud. Each day they enquired after their mother, only to be told that she was not yet feeling strong enough to see them.

Gerald had assumed that Enid would welcome the comfort of her two younger children, but each time he suggested she should see them, she wailed pitifully that it was only her little Edwin she wanted to see. Gerald wished that Enid had bonded as closely with Tom and Dora but this had never been the case.

One afternoon, on their return from school, Gerald was waiting for Tom and Dora in the hallway. He took them into his study.

"Now that the summer holidays are upon us, I'm arranging for you to stay with Aunt Hettie in Devonshire," he said.

"Aunt Hettie! But we don't even know her!" Dora exclaimed.

"And it's high time that was remedied. Your aunt is a wonderful woman. And besides, she lives near the seaside, just think of that!"

"Let me stay here with you, Papa," she begged.

Usually Gerald found it difficult to resist Dora's entreaties but on this occasion he was adamant.

"But we won't be a nuisance, I promise you, Pa. You won't even know we're here," said Dora.

Tom dug his elbow into her ribs and muttered that she should shut up. He was ready for an adventure and liked the idea of being near the sea.

Gerald shook his head. "As soon as I receive a confirmation from Aunt Hettie, I'll be putting you both on the train."

Dora was about to protest once more but was silenced by her father's frown though his expression softened when he started to describe his sister's good nature and generous heart. It was of immense regret to him that his children did not know their aunt and that he himself had seen so little of her in recent years. His family's last visit to Hettie's home had been when Dora was very young and it hadn't been a success. Enid disliked what she described as her sister-in-law's Bohemianism and had made no secret of her disapproval.

Dora sat at the kitchen table whilst Lily, the maid, combed out her long brown hair.

"Your Pa's right, you know, Miss Dora. Your aunt's very nice," said Lily.

"Lily, you're tugging!" said Dora irritably.

"Sorry, Miss, but it's ever so tangled," said Lily.

"It always is after it's washed. Here, let me do it," said Dora, snatching the comb from her. "Anyway, how do you know my aunt?"

"She came here once for dinner. It was years ago, in fact I'd only been here a couple of days. It was my first time in domestic service and I was ever so young. I'd never waited at table before and I was really scared. Well, your aunt seemed to know that and was very kind. I thought she was a real lady!"

"Which is more than can be said for some!" interjected Rita, winking at her sister Lily.

Rita was sitting at the table drinking tea. She glanced over her cup at Dora. "Can't think what all the fuss is about! What I wouldn't give for a holiday by the seaside!"

"Have a heart, Reet. She's not been away from home before," said Lily.

Rita grunted. "What about us being sent off to work at barely fourteen? There's some don't know when they're well off."

It was Lily's half day off and Rita, who had come to collect Lily and accompany her home, couldn't wait to be off. In character and appearance, the two sisters bore little resemblance. Lily, the younger by a year, was fair, plump and placid whilst Rita was angular, dark-haired and feisty. What they did have in common was a keen sense of duty to their mother after she was abandoned by their feckless step-father and left alone with four younger siblings to rear. Consequently, the two girls had entered domestic service, and each week they took home their wages to support the family. Rita, however, had disliked domestic work and soon found a job in a factory. Despite the long hours and monotony of the work, Rita had gone into digs with some of the other girls and valued her independence above everything. She couldn't understand why Lily didn't follow her example.

"Come on, Lily. I haven't got time to hang around here all day," said Rita, fetching her coat from the coat rack by the back door.

"We'd best be off now, Miss," Lily told Dora. "And you'd best go and get yourself ready 'cause your Pa'll be

7

here any minute to fetch you and Tom. Your best clothes are all laid out on the bed. You know how your Ma likes you to keep neat and tidy."

*

Suddenly there was a commotion at the other end of the platform, followed by the appearance of a woman dressed in a flowing white dress and an enormous straw hat. She saw the children and waved. A light breeze whipped up her skirt and with it billowing around her, she advanced majestically along the platform like a galleon in full sail.

Beside her, but almost obscured from view, walked a slender middle aged man dressed in a linen suit and a panama hat.

"My dear, dear children!" she exclaimed, opening her arms to embrace them.

"I'm so, so sorry you've had to wait but it was impossible for poor Mr Pickering to get his automobile started. It can be such a tiresome vehicle!"

Dora found that her aunt's warm smile and infectious laughter were as hard to resist as her delicate floral scent.

Hettie turned to the man beside her. "This handsome young man is Thomas, and so like his father, isn't he? And this is my niece Dora, though so grown up I can hardly believe it!"

The man stepped forward to shake their hands. "This is my, husband, Mr Pickering," she announced.

"Or Uncle Alfred, if you'd do me the honour," he said, smiling broadly.

Later, Dora would discover that Hettie's referral to her husband by his surname was one of her many endearing eccentricities. When they met, Hettie had been a widow for ten years and it was only after several years of formal courtship that she finally agreed to become his wife. Dora took an immediate liking to Mr Pickering with his kind eyes, bushy sideburns and big moustache that twirled up into two neat points.

Tom gasped at the elegant motor car. Its chassis was dark maroon and with its roof down, as it was that day, he could see its leather upholstery was of a matching colour. Neither of the children had been inside such a smart vehicle and they were astonished by the speed at which it could travel, exclaiming at the landscape flashing by as the vehicle progressed along the winding country roads.

Mr Pickering, now attired in a driving hat with ear flaps and a pair of goggles that covered half of his face, was focused on the road ahead, whilst Hettie, her hat secured on her head by a wide blue ribbon tied in a bow under her chin, turned to the children at intervals to point out significant landmarks.

They knew nothing about their aunt's home so it was a great surprise when Mr Pickering turned off one of the lanes onto a sweeping gravel driveway and pulled up in front of a small Georgian manor house.

"Here we are, children. Our home Langham Place," said Hettie.

Dora gazed at the house appraisingly, admiring its weathered stone walls and tall sash windows. Surrounding the house was a large landscaped garden, its velvet green lawns interspersed by colourful herbaceous borders. One day I will have a home like this, she promised herself.

A maid and a manservant came running out of the house to greet them.

"This is George and Millicent," Hettie told the children. "They help Martha, our housekeeper, to run the house for us."

The young couple smiled greetings and as George approached to open the car door for Hettie, two Yorkshire terriers dashed out of the house and almost tripped him up. They yelped with joy when they saw Hettie and jumped up onto her lap. Hettie laughed and ruffled the fur on their heads. She turned around to the children. "And these little rascals are Doozie and Willow," she said.

Millicent accompanied the children into the house and up to their bedrooms. Like the rest of the house, the bedrooms were light and airy and decorated in pretty floral wallpapers.

Alfred's car, which was housed in a large barn, was a major focus of attention for Tom. It appeared to be in need of a great deal of cleaning, and every time George came out to fulfil this task, Tom was not far behind, polishing and rubbing at the chassis until it acquired a lustrous sheen. One day Dora came out to the barn to discover what all the fuss was about. The bonnet of the car had been removed to expose its engine, an object of great fascination to George and Tom who listened intently while Alfred explained its mechanisms. It didn't take Dora long to realise that motor parts were of little interest to her and she skipped off into the garden with Doozie and Willow.

Later, as she sat on the lawn playing with them, Tom came up to her. "Uncle Alfred says to tell Aunt Hettie that we're going out but I can't find her anywhere. He's going to give George a driving lesson and I'm going, too."

They had been staying with their aunt for two weeks now and Dora had started to feel conscience-stricken that she could be so happy away from her parents and the family tragedy, but when she mentioned these sentiments to Tom, it was evident that he had no such scruples.

Tom was Dora's senior by two and a half years; and he believed himself to have a superior understanding of how things work in this world. "Don't be so daft, Dora. They're better off without us."

"But poor Pa, I hope Mama's come out of her room."

"Oh, give over, Pigtails. Things'll be back to normal by the time we get back," he said, kicking at a tuft of grass.

"Look, Tom. I'm teaching them to bring back the ball," said Dora, throwing a ball across the lawn.

"They'll never do that!" said Tom, scoffing. "They're not retrievers."

Doozie ran back across the grass with the ball in his mouth and dropped it at Tom's feet.

Dora grinned. "Go on, he wants you to throw it for him."

A little later Dora went into the house to find her aunt. There were six bedrooms on the first floor and one of the doors had been left ajar. Dora peered inside and caught a glimpse of Millicent, or Millie as she was called, in one of the bedrooms. She was humming as she dusted the impressive collection of dolls lined up on a shelf.

"Mind if I come in, Millie?" Dora asked.

"'Course, dear," said Millie, taking hold of a doll and running a cloth over its porcelain face.

Dora looked in awe at the feminine décor. "Oh, what a lovely room!"

"It's Miss Lizzie's old room. Mrs P likes it to be kept clean and dusted," Millie said. "These dolls would be best off in a cupboard to keep the dust off, but this is where they've been since she was a little girl."

She turned to Dora with her merry smile and handed her the doll. Dora thought that Millie was very pretty with her mop of reddish hair and sprinkling of freckles across the bridge of her nose.

"I'm sure Mrs P wouldn't mind if you wanted to play with it."

"So where is she then?" asked Dora.

"Oh, Miss Lizzie, you mean? She got married to an American gentleman a few years back. They're living in Washington now."

At Millie's suggestions Dora went outside to look in the studio, the little dogs following. Originally the building had been part of a stable block that Hettie had converted, installing huge windows along the length of the north wall. She was standing in front of an easel dressed in a paint-spattered overall and completely absorbed in the final stages of a watercolour. Dora watched with interest whilst Hettie applied shades of blue paint to the petals of a delphinium, shaping them with quick, deft brush strokes. Eventually, she stepped back to appraise her work. The little dogs took their cue and rushed up to greet her.

She glanced round at Dora. "What do you think?"

Dora had seen the conception of the painting the previous day whilst she herself was painting an abstract geometric pattern in primary colours. It was a task set by Hettie; an exploration of the fundamentals of working with colour, she had explained. Hettie was a very accomplished artist and her work was often displayed in the local galleries. She had told Dora that for her next lesson she would show her the rudiments of perspective drawing. Dora worked hard at Hettie's well-structured classes, hoping that one day she might be as good an artist as her aunt.

Dora stared at the painting. "I think it's marvellous!"

"Thank you, dear," said Hettie, smiling. "We'll have to see what Mr Pickering has to say. He can be a very strict critic!"

Dora had learned that Alfred used to be a book publisher, and judging by the conversations she had overheard between him and some of the painters who visited the house, he also seemed to know a lot about art. Hettie told her that she had once made some illustrations for a book that he was publishing and that was how they had met.

Hettie noticed the doll in Dora's hands. "Ah, I see you've made friends with Belinda!"

"Yes. I hope you don't mind," said Dora.

"Of course not; when Lizzie was young, Belinda was her favourite doll. My mother gave it to her on her ninth birthday."

Whilst Hettie tidied up her brushes and paints, Dora sat on the floor and undressed the doll, fantasising what it would be like to have a mother like Aunt Hettie. She felt a pang of envy. Had this been the case, she was sure that she couldn't have left her to go and live in America.

"You must miss her," said Dora.

Hettie was now cleaning her brushes and she stopped for a moment. "I do indeed. But what with this dreadful war going on in Europe, it's good to know she's somewhere safe."

Mention of the war reminded Dora of Edwin but Hettie was quick to realise the impact of her words. "Why don't we do something silly and dress up the dogs!" she said. "You could take them for a walk in the pram. Lizzie used to love doing that!"

Doozie looked extremely perplexed to be wearing a pink cardigan buttoned up over his chest. Willow, however, lapped up the attention and clad in a dress with a pink bonnet tied on her head, she sat contentedly in the old pram that Hettie kept in the studio.

Alfred stood staring from the doorway. "Mrs Pickering! Could I have just witnessed a small terrier rushing across the lawn attired in a fluffy pink over-garment or am I hallucinating?"

He advanced into the room and caught sight of hapless Willow seated in the pram. He raised his hand to his head in mock alarm. "And what is that I see in the perambulator! God help me! It's happening again!"

Dinner was served in the dining room and was the only formal meal of the day. It was an event that Dora looked forward to. The dining room was furnished in the new Arts and Crafts style with William Morris wallpaper and complementary draperies from Liberty's and was her favourite room. On warm evenings the French windows were left open and the scent of the lavender would waft into the room. Whether or not guests had been invited for dinner, Tom and Dora were always included. The conversation around the table was often informative and never dull.

Hettie and Alfred always dressed for dinner and each evening Hettie made a grand entrance dressed in a glamorous gown of her own design that often exposed her generous cleavage. On cue, Alfred would exclaim with enthusiasm. 'What a charming gown! What Panache!' In fact, he never seemed to run out of superlatives to express his appreciation, and having delivered his compliment, he would move to her side, kiss her hand and pull out the chair on which she was to sit.

Alfred declared that since children in France were allowed to enjoy wine with their meal, he could see no good reason why Tom should not do the same. His knowledge of wine was extensive. As he poured out a glass for Tom, he discussed its particular merits and the region where it was produced. Sometimes he described how political events had affected those regions, such as the period in the thirteenth century when England had inherited huge territories in

14

France as a consequence of the marriage of Henry 11 to Eleanor of Aquitaine. Alfred had such an uncanny knack of imparting knowledge that he could bring even the most mundane subjects to life. Tom hung on to his every word.

One evening when Tom confided in Alfred about his passion for ships and of his ambition to become a sailor, Alfred exclaimed his shock that Tom didn't know how to swim and insisted that a future seaman must learn that skill. With that in mind, the following day he took Tom and Dora to the beach. They were accompanied by George and Millie and a large picnic hamper. He marched them all down a steep narrow path that led into a sandy bay. The beach was surrounded by huge cliffs that protected it from the wind and Alfred pronounced the calm sea ideal for swimming lessons.

Amongst Alfred's other accomplishments he was an able swimmer, and having decided to teach Tom, he also turned out to be a very able instructor. Tom and Dora giggled together when they saw Alfred walking into the sea in a costume that covered him from his neck to his knees, though they quickly discovered that his strict regime of lessons were no laughing matter. By the end of the summer Tom was a strong swimmer while Dora, George and Mildred could each swim out of their depth with confidence.

All too soon the day came when Hettie had to remind them that a new school term approached and it was time to go home. Having embarked upon that first train journey so unwillingly, Dora was just as reluctant to leave. Tom begged his aunt and uncle to let him stay on.

Seeing the train approaching the railway station, Tom gazed wistfully at the exit sign and considered the implications of refusing to go on it. Dora clung tearfully to Hettie who was herself so overcome by emotion that she felt powerless to act. Eventually Alfred was forced to take each child firmly by the hand and accompany them into the railway carriage.

He and Hettie stood on the platform until the train was well out of sight.

"Thank you, my dear, for taking charge," said Hettie. "I didn't know it was going to be so difficult."

"I've had very little experience with children, but it's my opinion that your nephew and niece are fine young people. In fact, I must confess to have taken a great liking to them," said Alfred.

"I shall miss them," said Hettie tearfully.

Alfred patted her hand and they walked out of the station arm in arm.

Chapter 2

"I can't believe how much you've both grown!" exclaimed Gerald. "Don't they look well, Enid? All that sea air has done them good."

"Evidently Dora forgot to wear her hat. Just look at the colour of her!" said Enid.

He smiled at Dora. "Yes, my little love. You're as brown as a berry!"

"Hmm. A complexion more suited to a peasant," said Enid.

"Well I think it suits her very well indeed!" said Gerald, smiling at his daughter.

As a home coming treat, Dora and Tom were having supper in the dining room with their parents. Enid looked irritable and called out to the kitchen. When Lily appeared in the doorway, she told her that the fish pie was not warm enough.

"How long has this been out of the oven?" she said.

"I took it out just before I served the soup, Ma'am," said Lily.

"Well in future please remember to take it out after serving the soup," said Enid.

At the sight of the fish pie, Dora's heart had sunk. They had been served this same dish almost every Friday evening for as long as she could remember. The gooey tasteless concoction seemed to get stuck to her pallet and was difficult to swallow.

"May I just have a small portion please, Mama?"

"Fish is good for you," Enid replied tartly. "You'll eat what you're given and be grateful for it, young lady."

"We ate a lot of fish at Aunt Hettie's," Tom said. "There was lots of fish we'd never tasted before, stuff like lobster and crab, but it was really nice."

Enid raised an eyebrow. "I'm afraid we can't afford such luxuries here, Thomas."

With the holiday still so fresh in their minds, it took little prompting from Gerald for the children to talk about their impressions and new experiences.

Towards the end of the meal, Enid turned to her husband. "Who is this person called Uncle Alfred whose name keeps cropping up?"

"You may not have accompanied me to their wedding, Enid, but you must remember that Alfred Pickering and my sister were married seven years ago," said Gerald.

"Yes, of course I do. And I didn't come with you because I was unwell at the time, that's no doubt why his name slipped my mind. Actually I don't think that I ever met the gentleman but then the merry widow had so many gentlemen callers!" she said.

Gerald knew how devastated Hettie had been when her first husband died and he disliked hearing her described in this way. "That will do, Enid," he said, putting down his napkin and leaving the table.

Later, Enid sat in her favourite armchair knitting and as she did so, she thought about Dora's description of her aunt's house and looked around at her parlour with a critical eye.

Gerald, who sat in the other armchair, was smoking his pipe and chatting to Tom.

"This room needs to be redecorated, Gerald," she said. "Some new furnishings wouldn't come amiss, either."

Gerald, who was seated on the sofa beside Dora, was chuckling at her impersonation of Alfred when he had witnessed the dogs dressed in the doll's clothes. "It looks all right to me, Enid," he said absently.

"Aren't you a little old to be playing with dolls, Dora? You'll soon be twelve," said Enid.

Gerald turned to Dora. "Ah, yes, it's your birthday next week, isn't it? So what would you like this year?"

"What I'd really like is a dog," said Dora.

"Well, why not?" said Gerald and turned to his wife. "What do you think, Enid? Wouldn't it be nice to have a dog in the house?"

Enid shook her head. "No, Gerald. I don't. Dogs have dirty habits!"

"Not if they're properly trained," said Dora. "You should meet Aunt Hettie's terriers, they're the sweetest, cleanest little creatures imaginable."

"And who's supposed to take care of it while you're at school, may I ask?" said Enid. "I have enough to do running this household."

"How about learning to ride, sweetheart?" said Gerald. "Remember how much you liked the horses at Mrs Jennings stables."

"An expensive hobby," said Enid, doubtfully.

"Since I was responsible for acquiring the licence for Mrs Jennings's riding school, I'm sure we could come to some satisfactory arrangement, Enid," said Gerald.

Enid nodded. "Very well; if that's what Dora wants, I have no objection."

Colonel Henry Jennings and his wife Janet were local gentry and Enid had enjoyed her visit to their farmhouse. Janet was an energetic woman who involved herself in a variety of local activities, notably the local branch of the Women's Institute, of which she was a founder member, and it was at her suggestion that Enid joined the ranks of women who knitted warm clothing for the soldiers at the Front.

Tom, who had been reading his book and only half listening to the conversation, looked up at his mother. "Yes, I'd like a dog, too, Ma."

Enid shot him a quelling look. "If you paid any attention, Thomas, you would know that that subject is closed."

Gerald glanced across at Tom. "What's the book about, Tom?"

"It's about the sea in the days when sailors used the stars to navigate a course. Did you know they could travel hundreds of miles with the stars alone to guide them?" said Tom.

"There's so much rubbish printed these days," said Enid. "I went to buy a copy of Mrs Beaton's cookery book the other day and was shocked by what I saw on display."

"This isn't rubbish, Ma. Uncle Alfred knows about books," said Tom.

Gerald glanced across at his wife. "Alfred was a book publisher before he retired, Enid," said Gerald.

"I wish you'd stop calling me Ma, Thomas, it's really common," said Enid. She glanced at the clock on the mantelpiece. "It's time you two went up to bed."

Dora glanced at the clock. "But it isn't eight o'clock yet, Mama."

"At Aunt Hettie's we never went to bed before ten!" said Tom.

"I'll brook no argument, Thomas. Go to your rooms at once," said Enid.

After the children had left, Gerald picked up his newspaper but the print seemed to swim in front of his eyes. He had been looking forward to the children's return and was disappointed at the way the evening had turned out. He put the paper aside and looked across at Enid. "Don't you think you were a bit sharp with them?"

"I won't accept insolence, Gerald."

"I don't think it was."

"Discipline may be lax in your sister's household, Gerald, but I believe it essential in the rearing of children."

"For God's sake, woman, you expect too much. They've only just come home yet everything you say to them sounds like a rebuke."

Enid got up from her chair, threw down her knitting and glared at him. "I've had enough! Enough of you all! Why should I knit socks for other women's sons when I can't make them for my own child?"

Gently but firmly Gerald pushed her back into her chair, picked up the knitting and put it on her lap. "Our boys at the front are fighting to defend us and they need all the help we can give, and if you don't stop these irrational outbursts you'll make yourself ill again."

Enid became tearful. "I suddenly remember that he won't be coming back and I just can't bear it, Gerald."

"I'll go and fetch your medication, Enid," said Gerald."

Dr Morton had told him that Enid was suffering from severe depression and that all she needed from her family was love and support, but these days she wasn't easy to love, particularly when she kept insisting that the only person who had ever loved or understood her now lay in the earth of a foreign land.

Gerald handed her a small glass and sat down again. "I'm going to increase my hours at the munitions factory, Enid."

She stared at him in dismay. "But you're hardly ever at home, as it is."

"They're very short-handed."

"If you spent more time on your professional work you might get a salary raise and God knows we could do with it."

"Salaries are currently frozen, Enid."

"Well, I don't know how I'm supposed to manage; the price of food has gone through the roof."

"We're not the only ones to suffer the deprivations. There's a war on, Enid, and everyone in the country has to make sacrifices."

Chapter 3

Enid had come to watch Dora's riding lesson and she stood with Janet Jennings outside the fence of the sand school where Dora was going through her paces. In her youth Janet had been a keen huntswoman and nowadays she ran a livery stables as well as her new riding school.

"Look at her," smiled Janet. "She's got a good seat and has no fear at all, that's quite unusual with beginners. She's definitely ready to go out on a hack. In fact, I thought I'd let her go out today; if that's all right with you, Enid?"

"Yes, indeed. I'm glad to hear she's getting on so well," said Enid.

"Right you are, then, let's go in and have some tea and a gossip," said Janet and called to the groom who was sweeping the yard to take over.

Janet was good company. She appeared to know everyone in her village as well as those in the town who were of significance and she was well-informed about all of them. Hugh, her elder son, was at the Front and she told Enid that since the first casualties had been shipped home she had kept busy working as a hospital almoner for the Red Cross.

"As a matter of fact, I do have patients to see today. Would you like to accompany me?"

Enid glanced at her in surprise. "You'd like me to come to the hospital?"

Janet nodded. "That's unless you've got something better to do? Dora won't be back for a couple of hours and there's plenty of mucking out to keep her occupied until our return. Henry's busy and I'd appreciate the company."

Henry's black Ford refused to start and Enid sat in the driver's seat watching apprehensively as Janet gave the engine another cranking. On the fourth attempt the engine began to splutter.

"Pull out the choke now but go gently on the throttle," Janet called to Enid. "And remember what I told you, we don't want to flood it!"

Enid was impressed that Janet knew how to drive the formidable vehicle and dutifully she followed Janet's instructions, wondering how on earth she had been persuaded to undertake this mission. She was greatly relieved when eventually the engine turned over and chugged into life.

"Good show old girl! We did it," said Janet, climbing into the driver's seat.

It was seven miles to the Red Cross Hospital and although Janet drove carefully along the country roads, navigating the potholes with competence, Enid lurched at every bump and clung so tightly to the safety rope hanging from the roof that her hand began to ache.

Before they got out of the car in front of the hospital, Janet handed Enid a pad and pen. "Some of the men will want to write letters to their loved ones but haven't had the schooling to do so," she told her.

The hospital was a converted late Victorian manor house, a huge, austere brick building. Inside the large, wood panelled hall they were approached by a middle aged woman whom Janet introduced as Matron. She was dressed in a navy uniform and white starched cap and her persona exuded efficiency and authority. For a few minutes she talked to Janet about her concerns at the over-crowded wards, lack of facilities and shortage of doctors.

"Every week the number of patients escalates and it's a job to know where to put the more serious cases," she said, her face creased with anxiety. "We have really reached a crisis point here."

Janet listened and nodded. "I'll get Henry to talk to his contacts at the War Ministry, see if they can allocate more doctors and find somewhere else for the overspill. In the meantime, Mavis, you take heart. You're doing a stoic job."

Matron glanced at the watch she wore on her lapel and handed a list to Janet before walking off briskly.

The first ward they entered had formerly been a ballroom and Enid stared in bewilderment at row upon row of occupied beds.

"Most of these boys will be patched up and sent back to the front, poor blighters!" said Janet.

She approached one of the beds. "How are you today, Mr Jones?" she enquired of the patient.

The young man looked up with a smile. "Not so bad, thank you Ma'am. The doctor says I can have this lot off any day now," he said cheerfully, gesturing to his bandaged leg. "But I'd like to let me Ma know that I'm coming to see her, I'm due a few days' leave, you see."

She turned to Enid. "Mrs Jamieson here can write a letter on your behalf."

Enid sat down hesitantly on the chair beside the bed, picked up the pen and pad and carefully notated the message that the young man dictated.

When she finished she nodded to him and got up to leave.

"Excuse me, Ma'am, but you don't have me Ma's address," he said.

Enid blushed in embarrassment. "You're right, Mr Jones. How silly of me," she said, retrieving her pad.

He smiled cheekily. "First time you done this, is it, Ma'am?"

Enid nodded and sat down again. She listened sympathetically as he told her that his mother was a widow and that he had three younger siblings at home. He confided that he had been the family breadwinner and worried about them surviving without him.

"I'm sure that your mother is very proud of you, Mr Jones," said Enid.

The young man nodded modestly. "Thank you for the letter, Ma'am. It's ever so good of you."

Enid felt an unexpected warm glow. "We all have to do our bit, Mr Jones."

As they arrived at the final ward on her list, Janet turned to Enid. "I think I had better warn that you may find this a bit harrowing, Enid. The chaps in here are some of our latest casualties, just brought in from France."

Nothing, however, could have prepared Enid for the appalling mutilation of the patients she saw on that ward and she watched in horror as a doctor attended to a boy no older than Edwin. One of the boy's legs was a stump and most of his head was covered in a blood soaked bandage that the doctor was carefully removing.

Enid's last patient was Corporal Desmond Pearson, his name denoted on a board above his bed. Most of his head was shrouded in bandages and although he could only see out of one undamaged eye, he looked at Enid as though in recognition though when she pulled up a chair to sit by his bedside, he suddenly became agitated and grabbed at her hand.

"You must tell them, Ma. I searched and searched but I couldn't find me unit. Honest to God, it wasn't my fault they copped it!"

Enid looked around helplessly and a nurse appeared at his bedside.

"Shell shock, the poor young man," Janet whispered to Enid as they walked out of the ward. "I told his parents I'd keep an eye on him, they live in Yorkshire, you see. The nurse says they're moving him to another hospital for more surgery tomorrow."

Enid didn't believe she could have endured seeing Edwin in this boy's plight.

"Well done, old girl. You've been a terrific help," Janet told Enid when they returned to the car. "They're crying out for auxiliary nurses, you know. Why not give it a go?"

Enid shook her head. "No, Janet, I'll stick with the letter writing."

*

That evening Enid was still shaken by her experience and when Gerald returned from work they sat together in the parlour before supper and she gave him a detailed account of the day's events.

"I'm proud of you, Enid," said Gerald with a fond smile.

It was a long time since he had seen the caring side of her nature and he was encouraged by her willingness to undertake regular hospital visits and the subsequent improvement in her mood. He had begun to believe that Enid had turned the corner until one evening she informed him that she had decided to resign.

"But why, Enid? Why? The work you're doing is so important," he said.

"It takes up too much of my time, Gerald."

"I don't understand. You've been doing this for almost six months and have managed so well," he said, encouragingly.

"You don't realise how much I have to do here. And the children are becoming unruly, particularly Thomas, he's such a mischievous boy. When I came home today I found that he had tied Dora's plaits to a chair while she was working at her homework. I heard this caterwauling and when I went into the room Dora's chair had just toppled over with her attached to it!" said Enid.

Gerald burst into laughter. "But that was just a prank, Enid. Youngsters are bound to squabble from time to time. I know my sister and I did."

Enid shot him a quelling look. "I didn't find it in the least bit amusing."

Gerald sighed; there were times when he found his wife's lack of humour extremely irksome. "And what about Mrs Jennings? Don't you think you may be letting her down?"

Enid grunted. "What! Janet Jennings? Why should I care?"

"But I thought you liked her."

"She's no idea how hard it is for me; she hasn't lost a son. Every week the list she gives me is longer than the last and I'm tired, Gerald, fed up with it all."

"Then you should discuss it with her, tell her how you feel."

"And you think she'd care!" said Enid with a mirthless laugh. "The way that woman bosses me around you'd think I'm her lackey."

"Isn't that just her manner? Janet Jennings is a big hearted woman."

"Well, I've had enough and I shall tell her so."

Gerald had always kept up a regular correspondence with his sister and these days his letters expressed his concerns for the children. He told her how withdrawn Tom had become at home and of the worrying reports of his bad behaviour and lack of co-operation at school. Sometimes Hettie also received a letter from Dora that usually contained something cheerful like an afternoon spent trekking in the countryside, though occasionally she was tempted to confide about the problems at home. Hettie liked to read these letters to Alfred over the breakfast table.

"What a blessing that Dora has that farm and the riding as an outlet," she said.

"Yes, indeed; but what about Thomas?" Alfred said. "Clearly the boy is unhappy."

He looked thoughtful for a moment. "They should consider sending him to a naval cadet school. It's never too early to embark upon his chosen career."

Hettie nodded. "Hmm, that's an excellent idea. I'll write to Gerald and suggest it."

Gerald had begun to feel the effects of the nervous strain he had been under. He was particularly weary of Enid's constant carping. Sometimes he tried to remember what she was like when he first knew her, recalling how they first met when she had served him in the clothes shop where she worked. Enid was the manager and had helped him to choose a silk scarf for his mother's birthday.

Gerald was then twenty-five years old and had recently found employment in the offices of Hargreaves & Partners, the most reputable solicitors' firm in the town. He had been attracted by Enid's good looks and pleasant demeanour and the fact that she was a few years his senior was of no consequence. He had no idea how hard she had worked to acquire her refined accent and manners. It had required great self-discipline as well as her natural quick wits to achieve her current position.

Enid liked people to believe that she was well born and boasted about the grand household in which she was brought up, and it was several years before Gerald learned that she was the illegitimate daughter of the housekeeper and had lived with her mother below stairs. He admired the way she had overcome these modest beginnings and was aware of her disappointment at not having a home like the one that his sister had inherited on her first marriage. In fact, he often wondered whether Enid believed she could have done better than marriage to a provincial solicitor. It wasn't until Dora was three years old that Gerald had been promoted as a junior partner and they could finally afford a live-in maid.

Beneath Enid's cool reserve Gerald had discovered a depth of sensuality and during the first years of their marriage they had enjoyed a fulfilling sex life. Edwin's birth had followed several miscarriages and the bond that she had with the child was one with which his younger siblings could never complete. During the early years of their marriage Gerald had been able to tease Enid out of her moods but after the birth of Dora her behaviour had become increasing erratic and it was usually the maid or the two younger children who were the victims of her scolding tongue.

Now, twenty-five years later, Gerald thought of his mother's warning that he would not find contentment with Enid. His mother did not make judgements lightly and he should have paid more attention.

One morning as Gerald was walking to work, Enid's reproachful voice at breakfast still rang in his ears and it was shocking to realise that he disliked the woman he was married to. He arrived late and was immediately summoned to the office of Roderick Campbell, the senior partner. Roderick looked up from his desk as Gerald entered and told him to take a seat.

"An error has been made on this tenancy agreement," said Roderick, pushing a file across the desk.

Gerald glanced through the documents and blanched. He remembered handing it over to one of the clerks and suddenly realised that he hadn't checked the details with his usual attention. Gerald was a careful man and in the whole of his career he hadn't made such a careless mistake.

Roderick looked across his desk at Gerald. "These people are valued clients, Gerald. I shall be reimbursing them for their inconvenience from company funds."

Gerald was about to protest that it should be his responsibility but Roderick pre-empted him. "I strongly advise you to take some time off," he said, peering at Gerald over the top of his spectacles. He knew of the family loss and he wasn't an unreasonable man. "I think you need to go home and get some rest, Gerald. And I don't want to see you back here until you are ready."

It was an order, not a suggestion. Gerald knew that he needed a rest but his home was not a restful place to be.

Sometimes, during the late evening, Dora would hover by the banisters at the top of the stairs, disturbed by the raised voices in the parlour. One evening, she saw her father come out of the room, pick up his coat and hat from the coat stand in the hallway and march out of the front door. This scenario happened more and more frequently and Dora would watch his departure in dismay, sometimes staying awake until she heard him return. One morning when she came down to breakfast, her father was absent and it appeared that he hadn't been home all night. Her mother was tight-lipped as she removed his place setting from the table.

Despite her nightly vigils, Dora rarely missed a day at her new school. Standards were high and encouraged by Gerald's pride in his 'little scholar' she worked hard to attain the high marks she achieved. Tom did not fare as well. He was not academic by nature and only enjoyed the hours allocated to sports, a pastime at which he generally excelled. It was now the end of the school year and their school reports had arrived in the post. Enid summoned Dora and Tom to see her in the parlour and they stood in front of her apprehensively.

Enid held Tom's report aloft. "This is disgraceful, Thomas! What's the matter with you, boy? Your brother Edwin always got the top marks in his class. Even your sister has nothing to be ashamed of. You had better take a leaf out of her book or you'll get nowhere in life."

It was rare for Dora to receive any accolade from her mother but on this occasion she cringed from it.

Tom stared down at the floor, his expression inscrutable.

"Don't look so sullen! It's no wonder your teachers complain about your attitude," said Enid.

While she was talking, Gerald had come into the room. He took Tom's report from her hand and glanced over it.

He turned to Enid. "I think we should find a school more suited to Tom's talents, Enid."

"What do you mean, Gerald?" she said.

"I'm talking about a naval cadet college," he said.

Enid stared at him aghast. "You want our son to go off and become a common sailor?"

"No, Edna. Don't be so silly, there's nothing common about it. Undoubtedly Tom will become an officer, but whatever he does, the navy will provide him with a fulfilling and interesting career. I've been looking into it."

Tom was grinning from ear to ear and Gerald put an arm around his shoulder. "If this is what you want, my boy, I'll make an application for an interview at a school in Dartmouth."

"Oh, yes. Thank you, Pa," said Tom.

"Well, off you go now and do your homework," said Gerald. "And work hard at your mathematics. If you need help with it, come and see me."

*

That summer Hettie invited the whole family to come and stay. At first it wasn't possible to over-rule Enid's objections but eventually she and Gerald came to a tacit agreement. Gerald had taken two months of unpaid leave and although he could ill afford the expense, he agreed to Enid's request to have the parlour refurbished. Enid politely declined Hettie's invitation on the grounds that she would be needed at home to oversee the project.

Dora had grown a great deal during the last year which prompted Enid to suggest a shopping trip to buy some new clothes. They took a train to London and headed for John Lewis in Oxford Street. In the girls' clothing department, they selected at least a dozen outfits, eventually paring them down to a choice between five. At this point Enid turned unexpectedly to the shop assistant and told her that they would take all of them. She didn't even wince at the bill. As soon as the clothes were wrapped Enid whisked Dora off to the fabric department to choose materials for her new furnishings. Dora enjoyed the day out, particularly the tea at Lyons Corner House that she was treated to.

Enid did not encourage demonstrative affection but when they reached home she accepted Dora's kiss of thanks with a smile. The redecoration of the parlour had already commenced and Dora hadn't seen her mother as cheerful for a very long time.

"Well, we can't have your aunt thinking of us as the poor relatives who can't afford to buy new clothes, can we now?" said Enid.

"Aunt Hettie's not like that, Mama."

Enid did not like to be gainsaid. "I think I have a little more experience of life than you, Dora."

*

Later, Dora went into her mother's bedroom. She had tried on one of her new dresses and wanted to see herself in the full length mirror.

Enid, who was seated at the dressing table tidying her hair, glanced round at Dora. "That's a very nice frock, it suits you."

Dora was studying her reflection. "Am I pretty, Mama?"

Enid looked at her daughter and felt a pang for her lost youth. Dora had inherited her own green eyes and chestnut hair and was tall for her age. She noticed how Dora's figure was already starting to fill out and acknowledged that her daughter was very good looking. Vanity, however, was not a trait to be encouraged.

Enid got up with a sigh and walked behind Dora across the room. "I dare say you'd pass in a crowd," she said, walking out through the doorway.

Chapter 4

As the train approached Totnes, Tom and Dora hung their heads out of the carriage window and spotted the figure on the platform.

"Look, Tom, there's Aunt Hettie!" Dora called out excitedly.

"But where's Uncle Alfred?" said Tom, turning to his father in dismay. Gerald was seated in the carriage. "He's not with her!"

"Your uncle has been unwell, Tom. We'll see him at the house," said Gerald, getting up to lift their suitcases down from the luggage rack above the seats.

Tom was disappointed not to see George and when he enquired after him Hettie explained that George had recently been conscripted and Fred, their new chauffeur, had taken his place.

"Mr Pickering apologies for not coming to meet you," she said to the children. "But I'm afraid he's recovering from a serious case of bronchial pneumonia and is now convalescing at home."

Though in his usual good spirits, Alfred looked frail. "It's so very good to see you all again," he said, starting to rise from the wicker chair upon which he was seated in the conservatory.

"And it's good to see you too, Alfred," said Gerald, taking his hand. "Don't get up. I've heard you're supposed to be resting."

"Fiddlesticks! Your sister fusses too much," he said with a grin.

"No, Mr Pickering," said Hettie, picking up the discarded rug and putting it back over his lap. "The doctor said you must rest for another week, at the least." She turned to Gerald. "You can't imagine what a difficult patient my husband can be."

*

During the following week Hettie barely left his side, only leaving him when he went to bed in the afternoons. She had no time for her painting but whilst Alfred was resting upstairs she took Dora out to the studio where she set her to work on a variety of drawing projects. Afterwards she and Gerald took long walks together whilst Fred kept Tom occupied in the barn. Fred was a friendly, cheerful man in late middle age who was happy to take Tom under his wing. He had two adult sons fighting with their regiment in France and missed them greatly.

Each evening Alfred joined them for dinner in the dining room and afterwards Dora and Tom played cards or board games with the adults. Alfred often retired early, leaving Gerald and Hettie to talk and they often did so until late into the night. One evening when Dora came downstairs to get a glass of water, she stopped to eavesdrop on their conversation. Gerald was discussing the battle in which Edwin had lost his life and when she heard how his unit had come up out of the trenches to be mown down by machine gun fire, she shuddered and hurried off to the kitchen.

On her return, Dora hovered once more outside the room where they were talking. Her father was pacing up and down and although talking quietly he spoke with intensity. She moved into the doorway to hear him better.

Hettie seemed upset by what he was saying and raised her voice. "But you can't do that, Gerald. It's unthinkable. It would be devastating for the children!"

Gerald was about to reply when he noticed Dora in the doorway. "What are you doing there, Dora? Go back to bed at once!" he said sharply.

Dora was surprised by the unusual severity of his tone and ran off quickly.

George's presence in the household was sorely missed, especially by Millie who confided to Dora that on his next leave she and George were to be married. Dora prayed hard that George would be safe and not suffer a similar fate to her brother. The horrific details of Edwin's death were a shock and her dreams were haunted by nightmares for many months to come.

For Dora some of the most memorable moments of that summer were the occasions when Gerald rented bicycles and took the children cycling through the countryside. Sometimes they cycled to the beach and went to swim in the sandy cove where Tom had the chance to show off his prowess in the water. Years later, Dora could shut her eyes and evoke the sound of Gerald and Tom's carefree laughter as they raced each other along a deserted country lane while she pedalled behind them, feeling the wind in her hair and the warmth of the sunlight on her face.

Enid was furious when Gerald returned from Cornwall without the children.

"School doesn't start for another two weeks, Enid," he reminded her.

"That's not the point. You should have consulted me."

"The children are having a good time and the sea air's good for them."

Gerald was tired after his train journey and weary of his wife's intransigence. He got up from his chair in the parlour and walked to the doorway. "Can't you be satisfied with your new parlour, Enid?"

She threw down the duster with which she was polishing the piano. "But look how shabby this old piano is, it stands out like a sore thumb."

"I see nothing wrong with it."

"It's time to replace it, Gerald."

"I can't afford to do that at the moment, Enid."

Enid's eyes flashed dangerously. "After all I have suffered you'd deny me the one pleasure I have!"

When they were first married Enid had told him how her mother had paid for lessons and how she was allowed to practise on the piano upstairs when the family were out. The piano was the first present Gerald had bought her.

"Then get yourself a new one and leave me in peace!" he said, and stormed out of the house.

Chapter 5

Dora watched her mother polish the mini grand piano and thought of Tom polishing Uncle Alfred's car. So many things reminded her of Tom. He had been away at school for almost a year and she missed him. He rarely came home, even on school exeats, but she knew from Hettie's letters that he visited Langham House quite often. In Tom's absence it was Archie, her piebald pony, in whom she confided. While she brushed his coat and combed out his mane, Dora would tell him about all the things that troubled her.

It was Janet who had been instrumental in acquiring the pony. Archie had been stabled at her livery for several years and when his owner married and moved to London Janet agreed to keep him on at the stables. She offered the pony to Dora and agreed to keep Archie stabled and fed, free of charge, on the condition that Dora would help out in the stables during her free time.

*

One May afternoon after school, Dora was on her way to the farm when Enid decided to accompany her.

"It's a long walk," said Dora.

"And a fine evening for it, too; a little exercise will do me good," said Enid.

Dora was apprehensive. She hadn't told her mother that Janet's son Hugh had recently returned home. When she had met him Dora had been shocked by young man's gaunt appearance but what hit her hardest was the fact that he was the same age as Edwin would have been, had he lived.

Janet had heard nothing from Enid since she had so unexpectedly curtailed the hospital visits but she was not a woman who bore grudges and welcomed Enid in her usual friendly manner. Whilst Dora was out riding Janet took Enid back to the house for tea and when Dora returned later her fears were realised. Enid was pale and tight lipped and they walked home in silence.

That evening as the two of them sat alone at the supper table, Dora wished her father was there. He was so rarely at home.

"Is Papa at the factory again?" she asked her mother.

Enid was picking at her food without interest. "I'd be the last one to know."

"I had a wonderful ride on Archie today, Mama. I'm really grateful to Mrs Jennings, she's been so generous," said Dora.

"With a rich well-connected husband like hers, I expect she can afford to be. Janet is a very fortunate woman, very fortunate indeed. It seems to me that there's very little justice in life," Enid said bitterly.

She pushed away her plate and got up from the table. "I've got a migraine coming on, Dora, I shall go to my room."

Tom arrived home two days before Christmas Eve and Dora was waiting with her father in the hallway to meet him. She was excited and had been counting off the days until his return but when Tom appeared in the doorway he looked so grown up in his naval cadet's uniform that she was suddenly struck by shyness.

Tom grinned and pulled on one of her plaits. "Good to see you, Pigtails!"

She laughed and threw herself at him. "Oh, I've missed you, Tom!"

Enid was sitting in her armchair in the parlour. She looked up when Tom came into the room. "Oh, Thomas, you're back," she said.

"Yes, Mother, I'm back," said Tom and went over to kiss her cheek. "I hope you're keeping well?"

"As well as can be expected, thank you, Thomas, considering all that I have on my plate," she said.

"You know what it's like at this time of year, Tom. Christmas creates a lot of extra work," said Gerald with an encouraging smile. "Your mother and I are very glad to have you back home."

"Perhaps I can be of help, Mother," said Tom.

"There's a good lad," said Gerald jovially, patting Tom's shoulder. "All hands on deck, eh!"

*

Dora stared into the shop window. She had been saving her pocket money for weeks but it wasn't enough to pay for the cut glass vase she wanted to buy for her mother. She turned to Tom with a sigh. "Everything's so expensive!"

"Let's go inside and see what else they've got," said Tom.

"Be careful now. Don't touch! It's all breakable!" ordered Mrs Hancock, the proprietor, a stern faced woman with steel grey hair scraped back into a bun. She looked at them suspiciously, doubting that these young customers could afford to purchase any of her exclusive merchandise.

Amongst a display of glass and china, Tom picked out a vase similar to the one that they had seen in the window.

He turned to Mrs Hancock. "How much is this, please?"

"Fourteen shillings and nine pence," she said.

"We'll take it," he said.

Tom spoke with such adult confidence that Dora glanced at him in surprise.

Mrs Hancock smiled at Tom, gratified to discover that on occasion one could misjudge the customers. "Would you like this wrapped in festive paper, sir?"

Tom nodded. "Yes, we would. It's a Christmas present for our mother."

"Oh, look, Tom. It's started to snow!" exclaimed Dora as they came out of the shop.

Under the amber glow of a gas lamp stood a group of carol singers and for a few minutes Tom and Dora stopped with the other shoppers to listen to their rendition of 'Hark the Herald Angels Sing'.

The snow began to fall more heavily and as she glanced up the street she spotted her father by the kerbside and beside him was a pretty dark-haired woman. The woman's face was laughing up at his as though they were sharing a joke and then he put his arm around her waist and pulled her under his umbrella. Dora was about to tell Tom what she had seen but when she looked again the couple had disappeared into the crowd.

"We'd best go and finish Ma's errands before the shops shut," Tom said, remembering the purpose of their trip.

Later, when laden with shopping, they came in through the back door, Lily was rolling out pastry on the kitchen table.

She glanced up at them. "Ah, there you are, you two. Your Ma's been asking after you," she said.

Tom noticed the bowl of dried fruit on the table. "Making mince pies, eh Lily? Oh, how I love mince pies," he said.

"Never mind them, you'd best get your wet clothes off and be quick about it," she said.

Tom groaned. "Oh, Lord! Is she in one of her moods?"

Enid was waiting by the fireplace in the parlour. She was dressed in a gown of dark blue silk taffeta and her hair was carefully arranged into a flattering chignon.

"Oh, Mama, you look lovely!" said Dora.

Enid ignored her and stared at Tom. "Why are you so late? I told you to be home by five o'clock. Your father's not home either. It seems you've all forgotten that we're going out."

"The town was really busy. We got delayed," said Tom.

"Delayed indeed, I thought that new school of yours would have taught you the importance of punctuality, Thomas," she said irritably. "Off you go now and get changed."

At the doorway Dora turned to her mother timidly. "You really do look nice, Mama. I like your dress."

Enid smoothed a fold in her skirt and gave a satisfied smile. That evening she had taken particular care with her appearance and was pleased by her reflection in the bedroom mirror. Recently Enid had celebrated her fifty second birthday and though her figure had grown more corpulent with age her face was relatively unlined. That evening would be the first time she had attended a social event since the loss of her son and had accepted the invitation because it had come from Dr Morton and his wife. Dr Morton had been supportive and had prescribed the laudanum that calmed her nerves though little did he guess the frequency of her visits to the town's two pharmacists.

The Morton's home was a large, rambling house in which each of the five Morton children had been born. Apart from the separate wing that housed the doctor's surgery, that evening the house was crammed with friends and neighbours and an air of jollity prevailed, not only were they celebrating the festive season but also the promise of an imminent end to the war.

When Dora and her family arrived they joined the throng of people singing carols around the Christmas tree. Mulled wine was served to the guests and afterwards they dispersed themselves amongst the three reception rooms.

At almost seventeen Tom was as tall as his father and had inherited Gerald's fair colouring and easy charm. Dora was amused to see that Emily couldn't take her eyes off him though when he addressed her she blushed and was tongue tied. Unfortunately for Emily, Peter and Harry, her nine year old twin brothers, had picked up on her reaction and hovered around giggling that their sister was in love with Tom.

Emily hissed at them to go away. "If Ma had to have more babies, I wish they'd been girls. Those two should have been strangled at birth!" she said to Dora.

"Best to ignore them, Em; the more you react the more they'll do it," said Dora sagely.

"It's just so embarrassing!" said Emily.

"Talk of embarrassing, just look at Ma over there with your Uncle Reggie," said Dora, gesturing across the room to where Enid was chatting to Richard Morton's good looking younger brother.

He and Enid stood apart from the rest of the group in the drawing room and, judging by their body language, their

44

conversation was intimate. As he spoke Reggie reached out a hand to stroke back a loose strand of her hair, a gesture that she responded to coyly.

"Daddy says Uncle Reggie's an incorrigible flirt. He thinks it's time he found a good woman and settled down," said Emily.

"But look at Ma! She's lapping it up," said Dora, wincing at her mother's coquettish smile.

"I suppose even old people get crushes," said Emily with a shrug. "Come on, Dor, let's go and get something to eat."

Dora followed Emily into the dining room where they helped themselves to the buffet supper on the sideboard and then took their plates to sit down at the table.

"How are things at home, Dor?" Emily asked.

"There aren't as many rows but then Pa's hardly ever home," said Dora. "Do your parents ever have rows?"

"Not that we're supposed to know about," said Emily with a grin. "When there's a disagreement they go off somewhere by themselves."

"You're lucky! I can't remember a time when mine didn't. Pa was really placatory after Edwin died but then the rows got worse than ever. Sometimes Ma flies into a rage for no real reason at all. It can be quite scary," said Dora.

"Perhaps your Ma's going through the change; that's when women's hormones are all over the place."

"The trouble is you can never gauge her moods, one minute she's quite normal and then she turns into a virago."

Emily looked thoughtful. "Maybe she suffers from schizophrenia, I read about it in a medical book."

"What's that?" asked Dora.

Emily was too distracted by Tom's appearance to respond. He came through the doorway after Emily's two elder brothers. Donald, the eldest, had been invalided from the army due to a shrapnel wound and after his recovery he had secured a desk job at the foreign office. Ian, the second son, had been exempted from enlistment due to poor eyesight and was currently studying theology at Cambridge.

Dora stared at the striking young woman who accompanied them. "Who is that with them, Em?"

"That's Glenda Stanton, she got a place to read history at Oxford, you know. I overheard Mrs Stanton telling Ma that Glenda's been actively involved with the Suffragettes and it got her suspended from college. She also said how much she worries about the dangerous exploits Glenda gets involved in and how they could lead to arrest and imprisonment."

Dora stared at Glenda in awe. "Oh, my! She must be brave!"

Emily nodded. "The other day Pa was saying that public opinion has changed in their favour and the government will have to capitulate. Pa and Ma believe their cause is just, you know."

"You mean they'll get to vote?"

"Absolutely, and about time, too!"

"Ma doesn't approve of them. She thinks that too much education is detrimental to a girl!"

"Well, I hope that won't stop you applying to university. You've got the brains, Dor."

"I know that Pa won't mind, actually I think he'd be pleased."

Emily had already decided that she was going to study medicine. "Well, nothing would stop me and I think you'll regret it if you don't."

Dora glanced down the table to where Tom now sat with Glenda. Like the rest of the group seated nearby, she and Emily listened intently as Glenda held forth, speaking with authority and eloquence.

"Women have taken over the men's jobs while they've been off fighting and have proved themselves just as capable. It's time for men to admit that we're not just domestic half-wits and accept our equal status!"

"Oh, here, here!" intoned Tom, clapping vigorously with the others. It was doubtful that Tom had ever given a thought to women's rights thought Dora with a wry smile.

Glenda glanced around at her audience and smiled. "One day soon they'll come to appreciate our abilities and welcome us into the professions without any quibble."

After supper Emily coerced her elder brothers and Glenda to join her and the other children in a game of sardines. At first Ian held back. He was a serious young man of nineteen and made it clear to Emily that he did not have the inclination to take part in such a juvenile activity.

"Don't be so stuffy, Ian. Donald's going to play! It's Christmas!" said Emily. She glanced towards Dora, knowing of his soft spot for her friend. "Well, Dora's expecting you to join in, aren't you, Dor?"

The twins knew all the best hiding places though there was so much giggling that they were also the easiest to be found. Donald and Glenda did better; they were some while alone in the broom cupboard before being detected. When Dora's turn came she decided to venture into the cellar, a room she had not entered before. She squeezed into a murky corner behind some packing cases and a few minutes later she heard the twins open the door at the top of the staircase. Peter peered down into the semi-darkness. "Nah. She'd never come down here, it's spooky!"

The door slammed shut and Dora shivered, wishing she had chosen a spot less dank and cold. Should someone decide to turn the key in the cellar door she could be trapped there but as she was about to leave she heard the door open softly, followed by a footfall on the staircase. She crouched in the dark corner, holding her breath.

There was silence for a few moments as Ian adjusted his eyes to the semi-darkness, then spotted the hem of Dora's yellow dress peeping out behind the boxes. He pretended to make a thorough search of the cellar but Dora was so relieved to be rescued that she jumped up and almost fell on top of him as he struggled to squeeze in beside her.

Ian helped her to right herself. "But Dora, you're freezing!" he said, taking off his jacket and wrapping it around her.

Dora snuggled into its warmth and crouched down beside him. It was almost ten minutes before Tom found them and in the meantime they chatted quietly. Ian was reserved by nature and of all the siblings he was the one Dora knew least well. Curious to know him better, she asked him whether he intended to become a parson like the Rev. Palmer, the vicar in their local church. Much to her surprise she learned that Ian had loftier ambitions; his intention was to work at a mission station in Africa.

Later that evening, when they returned home, Enid was in a skittish mood. When Gerald went into the parlour to check on the lamps he didn't hear her footsteps following him into the room and turned in surprise.

"Gerald," she said softly, her arms reaching out to him.

His body went rigid. "No, Enid," he said, and gently removed her arms from around his neck. "I'm tired."

She stroked his jacket lapel. "Perhaps you'd prefer me to take a lover!" she said teasingly.

Gerald backed away. "If that would make you happy, you should do so, Enid."

"Come on, Gerald. You must see that I'm not being serious, though there are certain gentlemen who find me desirable."

"Well, you certainly made a spectacle of yourself tonight."

The amber lights in her eyes glinted dangerously. "How dare you say that, Gerald? I think this must be jealousy!"

"What, of you and Reggie Morton? Don't be ridiculous."

Dora heard the raised voices downstairs and seeing that Tom's light was on she went to his room and opened the door.

"Can I come in?" she asked.

"'Course you can, Pigtails."

Tom made a space and she climbed into his bed. "Em's got a crush on you, Tom. You must be kind to her, she is my best friend," she told him.

Tom chuckled. "I wondered why she was being so odd!"

"And what about you ogling Glenda Stanton?"

"I wasn't!"

"You were hanging on to her every word. Oh, Glenda. Here! Here! Everything you say is amazing!"

Tom threw a pillow at her head and told her to shut up.

Dora picked up the book that lay on the bedside table and began to leaf through it.

"So what is a cumulus nimbus cloud?"

"That's a heavy dark grey cloud. It often means that a thunder storm's coming."

"Like Ma's face before she erupts into a rage!"

They burst into giggles and didn't see Enid standing in the doorway.

"You disgusting children! Get out of that bed at once, Dora!" she shouted.

Tom and Dora stared at her in astonishment then Dora rushed out of the room and crashed into Gerald on the landing outside.

He caught her in his arms. "Whatever's the matter?"

"It's Ma. She came into Tom's room and screamed at us."

They could hear Enid shouting at Tom. "At your age, you should know better Thomas. How dare you let your sister come into your bed?"

"I think you're mad!" Tom shouted back at her.

Gerald went into Tom's room and took Enid by the arm.

"That boy's a rotten apple! He's no son of mine!" she screamed at him.

"That's enough, Enid, enough I tell you," Gerald said, grabbing her bodily and removing her from the room.

Once he had her inside her own bedroom he leaned against the door and stared in disgust at the figure sprawled across the bed. He wondered how he could ever have loved this woman.

"It's you who are disgusting, Enid. I think Tom's right. You are mad!"

At that moment Gerald made a decision that would change all their lives, but it was many years later that Dora learned the truth of what took place over the following weeks.

Chapter 6

Janet opened the front door and found Enid standing on the threshold.

"I hope you're not too busy, Janet," said Enid apologetically. "But I need to talk to you."

Janet had seen little of Enid in recent months and was surprised by her unexpected visit. "Come in," she said and took Enid into the drawing room.

She poured out two glasses of sherry and handed one to Enid. "So what's up, old girl?" she asked, sitting down.

Enid sat tensely on the edge of an armchair. "Well, I'll come straight to the point, Janet. Gerald has gone."

"Gone where?"

"That's the problem. I don't know. He left ten days ago."

"You mean he isn't at the office?"

"No. I went there yesterday. They've got a new receptionist who doesn't know me and she told me that Gerald no longer worked there. She asked whether one of the other partners could help me!"

"That sounds rather odd. Didn't he tell you that he had resigned?" said Janet.

"No, Janet, he said nothing. A few days after Christmas we had a row and I told him to get out. He looked at me in a very odd way and said that there was nothing he'd like to do more, then he went upstairs, packed up some clothing and when he came down he bundled some papers into his briefcase and left."

"Has he ever done anything like this before?"

"No, never; and of course I didn't really mean him to go."

"No, of course you didn't, my dear. We all have our disagreements," said Janet, nodding sympathetically.

"Dora will be home in a few days. What will I tell her?"

"She's still staying with her aunt, is she?"

"Yes. Gerald put both the children on the train the day after Christmas. I objected of course but Gerald over-ruled me. He said he had telephoned his sister and she was expecting them."

"I did receive a telephone call from Gerald telling me that Dora would be away for the rest of the school holiday."

"Well, I know nothing about that," said Enid, shaking her head. "But then Gerald has changed so much recently that I hardly know him at all."

For a few moments Janet was silent. "I don't like to speak out of turn, but there has been some gossip."

"Gossip? What kind of gossip?"

Janet looked at her uncertainly and bit her lip.

"For God's sake, Janet, if there's something you know you must tell me."

"They do say the wife is usually the last to know," said Janet, taking a moment to clear her throat. "I don't know how to put this delicately but Gerald's been seen around with a certain young woman."

Enid blanched. "What?"

Janet nodded. "Yes."

"Are you saying he's involved with another woman?" Enid asked. This was something she hadn't considered.

"Don't be too alarmed, Enid. A few years ago Henry had a brief affair with some silly young thing but he soon came to his senses."

"But Gerald has resigned from his job, Janet."

"Yes. That does put a different complexion on things."

Enid drained her sherry glass. "Please tell me what you know, Janet."

"All I know is that Gerald has been seen with Marian Holmes."

"Never heard of her; do you know this woman?"

"Yes, as it happens her parents-in-law are friends of mine. We used to belong to the same hunt."

"But where is her husband, what about him?"

"Her husband Richard was one of the first casualties of the war. Marian is a widow with two young sons."

"Why didn't you tell me, Janet? I had a right to know!"

"Because it could be idle gossip. There might be nothing to it."

Suddenly this other woman took on the shape of a real threat. "Oh, I think there is. It all makes sense now. He was so often absent."

Janet topped up their glasses and Enid swallowed the sherry in one gulp. Her initial concern for Gerald's welfare had turned to anger.

"What a swine! I'll make him pay for this."

"There, there, old girl, it might not be as bad as it seems. There could be some perfectly reasonable explanation for his disappearance. Handle it right and you'll get him back!"

When Enid returned home, she found a letter from Gerald lying on the hall table. He had written to tell her that he would not be returning and suggested they met. The letter was written on the stationary of the guest house where he was staying and included a telephone number. That evening she phoned him and they agreed to meet in Regents Park two days later.

Gerald waited for her by the bandstand and led her across to a bench by the lake and sat her down. She watched him as he sat down a few feet away, noticing his new shirt and tie and thinking how handsome he looked. She looked at him carefully and gave a small smile.

"You look well, Gerald."

He nodded. "Well, I'm not going to beat about the bush. I want a divorce, Enid," he said.

She turned ashen. "A divorce! You want a divorce, Gerald?" she said feebly.

"Yes, Enid, I want a divorce."

Enid clutched at the arm of the bench. "But, Gerald, the stigma!"

"Is that all you care about, Enid?"

She stared at him in fury. "A man who abandons his wife after she loses a son... I would think you'd care about your reputation, if nothing else!"

"There are more important things in life."

"But what about the children, I think they'll care!"

"Yes, I was coming to that. I'd like Dora to come and live with me."

"That's unthinkable! A mother is the only person to bring up a growing girl."

"That depends upon the fitness of the mother."

"How dare you insinuate that I haven't been a fit mother, I've always done my duty by the children."

"Duty, maybe, but I don't think that's enough."

She looked back at him and suddenly the fight went out of her. "Perhaps I have sometimes been a bit harsh, but Gerald, I can change, in fact I promise you I will, you'll see. Just come home and let's forget about all this."

"I can't live with you any longer, Enid. My mind is made up."

"It's that woman, isn't it, that woman Marian?"

"I won't have Marian brought into this."

"Oh, yes, you will. How do you think the children will like the idea of their father being an adulterer? They won't be able to hold up their heads up for the shame!"

"Now you're being ridiculous, Enid," he said and glanced at his watch. "It's time I was going; I need to get back to work."

"So you have a new job, Gerald?"

He nodded. "You can of course stay on in the house, but I'll be coming to see Dora as soon as she returns from Devonshire."

"Oh, no, you won't, Gerald. If you insist upon this divorce, you will not see either of the children again."

Enid clutched at her handbag and got up from the bench. "Those are my terms, Gerald. The decision is yours."

*

Dora got off the train and followed the other passengers towards the exit barrier. The station was unusually busy with pedestrians moving in all directions. Amongst them were several soldiers being reunited with family members and now that Dora had come to terms with her brother's death she was glad to see the return of those soldiers who had survived the carnage. She searched the faces of the people on the other side of the barrier but could see no sign of her father.

"Dora, my dear girl," said Enid, hurrying forward and taking Dora in her arms. "It's good to have you home."

Dora was taken aback by this unusual display of affection. "Nice to see you, Mama," she said and looked around for her father. "Isn't Pa with you?"

"No, your father couldn't come," she said, taking Dora's arm. "Now come along. Let's go and find the tramcar."

During the journey home, Dora chatted animatedly about Willow's litter, describing how the terrier had given birth to three puppies but only two of them had survived. By the evening her bubbly mood was more subdued due to her father's continued absence and at supper her mother's vague explanation about a business trip didn't ring true.

"Well, my dear, since it's the last day of your holidays tomorrow why don't you go over to the stables to see Archie," said Enid. "I expect you've missed him."

Dora's spirits lifted. It was exactly what she was hoping to do.

Early the following morning when Dora came down the stairs she overheard her mother talking to Lily in the hallway.

"I'd like the post brought directly to me when it arrives, please Lily," said Enid.

Lily nodded. "Very well, Ma'am."

"And the same applies with the second post. So much unsolicited stuff is sent these days and I don't like it cluttering up the hall table."

What Dora didn't know was that a letter from her father had arrived for her the previous day and, having recognised the handwriting, Enid had opened it and read that he would be coming home to see her on the day after she returned from Devonshire. Enid tucked the letter into the back of a drawer.

"Would you like to take the day off tomorrow?" she asked Lily at breakfast.

Lily almost dropped the toast she was carrying. "The day off, Ma'am?" she said.

Enid nodded. "Miss Dora will be back at school and I shall be out for the day."

"The whole day?" said Lily.

"Isn't that what I said?" said Enid.

"Yes, Ma'am, thanks ever so much," said Lily. "I'll go over and see Joe and the children."

Dora glanced at her mother, surprised by the generous offer.

After Lily left the room Enid turned to her. "Lily has an admirer, you know. Last week he took her to a party in his local village hall; it was held to celebrate the end of the war."

"I hope Lily had a nice frock to wear?" said Dora, having rarely seen Lily dressed in anything other than a black dress and white apron.

"Yes, indeed she did. I advanced her money from her wages and she bought some material from the market. Her mother helped her make it," said Enid.

"Oh, good for Lily. I hope Joe is nice."

"The man's a widower with three small children. He's farm manager over at the Stubbs' place. I only hope she doesn't get any silly ideas in her head and decide to leave us. It's taken me so long to get her trained," said Enid with a sigh.

*

Janet was out in the stable yard when Dora arrived. "Good to have you back, Dora," she said with a welcoming smile.

As they walked towards the paddock where Archie was grazing, Janet turned to Dora. "Is everything all right at home then?"

Dora was puzzled by the unexpected enquiry. She nodded and assured Mrs Jennings that her mother was well.

Gerald arrived promptly at eleven o'clock and instead of using his door key, he rang on the bell.

Enid greeted him at the door, wearing a new dress and her face carefully made up. "Well, Gerald, this is a nice surprise."

He followed her into the parlour and sat down. "Where's Dora? I sent a letter telling her I was arriving at eleven."

"I think there are some things we need to discuss first, Gerald," said Enid, taking a seat opposite.

"Very well, Enid," he said.

"About this extraordinary idea of a divorce..."

"Yes?"

"Have you really considered the implications?"

He nodded. "I have, Enid."

"Well in that case, as I said to you in the park, you won't be seeing Dora. In fact, she was so shocked when I told her about her your intentions that she said she had no desire to see you at all."

"What? Dora said that?"

It didn't sound like Dora at all and he frowned, thinking of her anxious expression on Christmas day as she glanced between her parents. He had done his best to create a festive atmosphere but Enid's mordant mood put them all on edge.

Dora and Tom's gift went barely acknowledged until Gerald went to pick it up. "What a charming vase; how very thoughtful."

Enid glanced at Dora. "Yes, it's very nice. Thank you."

"It's from Tom, too. He paid for most of it, Mama," said Dora.

"Then thank you, Thomas," said Enid.

Enid's attitude to her second son had irked Gerald for a long time. He knew that neither Tom nor Dora had shared the close bond she had with Edwin but it recent years she had picked on Tom constantly. It didn't take Gerald long to realise that Tom's blameless presence rarely failed to remind Enid of Edwin's absence. On the one occasion he had confronted her about the injustice she had denied it and flew into a rage.

"Oh, yes, Gerald," said Enid. "You have to understand that Dora is growing up and she has a mind of her own. When my daughter learned that you intended to abandon us for a new family, she was adamant."

Gerald's face turned ashen. After a few moments he got up and handed Enid a piece of paper. "This is the name of my solicitors. You can contact me through them."

That night, on her way up to bed in the attic Lily passed Dora's bedroom door and heard her crying. She went into the room and took Dora in her arms.

"Oh, Lily. Why has he left me? What did I do wrong?" said Dora, sobbing in Lily's arms.

Chapter 7

It was six weeks into the new school term when Enid received a phone call from the school secretary to arrange a meeting between her and Miss Pritchard, the Headmistress. Enid was nervous. She had been too ill with grief to accompany Gerald when he had attended the preliminary meetings at the school and this summoning by the Headmistress was daunting.

As Enid was shown into her study Miss Pritchard got up from her desk and came across the room to shake her hand. "Ah, Mrs Jamieson, it's good to meet you at last."

Miss Pritchard was a tall, stately woman with a formidable reputation for the high standards she expected of her pupils and Enid looked at her nervously. "I understand you wished to see me, Miss Pritchard."

"Yes, Mrs Jamieson. We need to talk about your daughter. Please be seated."

Miss Pritchard returned to her chair and opened the file on her desk. "Your daughter Dora was awarded a scholarship to gain entrance to my academy, was she not?"

"Yes. That's correct, Miss Pritchard."

"Well, I'm afraid that this term Dora's work has fallen behind, badly behind. I have a report here of her recent performance in class and it really isn't up to standard."

"Oh? But Dora's always been so conscientious about her studies."

"Yes, so I have understood but that unfortunately Mrs Jamieson no longer appears to be the case. My teachers have told me that she is listless in class and not exhibiting the potential I expect of my students. I have spoken to Dora myself and found her attitude most unco-operative."

"I will talk to my daughter, Miss Pritchard."

"Very well, Mrs Jamieson; but I do expect to see a vast improvement in Dora before the end of term. Otherwise, well...I am sure you understand. We would be very disappointed to lose her."

That evening Enid confronted Dora. "What is the matter with you? Do you want to be expelled from the school?"

Dora shrugged her shoulders.

"Well?" said Enid.

Dora had never been a rebellious child and Enid was baffled by her attitude. "Do you really want to lose your place at the school, Dora? Don't you think that your father's departure is enough humiliation for me?"

Dora's pent up emotion burst to the surface. "Well, it's your fault he left us!"

Enid rose from her chair in fury. "How dare you!" she said and slapped Dora's face hard.

Dora burst into tears and fled from the room.

She refused to come downstairs for supper and did not emerge from her bedroom the following morning. Lily left a breakfast tray outside the door but reported to her employer that it had not been touched.

"What am I to do with the girl?" said Enid in exasperation.

"Maybe you could talk to that aunt she stays with by the seaside," said Lily tentatively.

Enid frowned at Lily's audacity though later, when she sat down in the parlour and picked up her knitting, she thought over the suggestion.

Dora remained closeted in her room and not until the third day of her self-imposed exile did she venture out. From downstairs she heard the commotion of a visitor's arrival and assuming her mother would be entertaining her guest in the parlour, she crept down the stairs and headed for the kitchen to fetch a glass of milk. Lily was sitting at the kitchen table drinking tea with a man and when he turned around Dora gasped at George in disbelief. She knew that he was back from the war because she had seen him on her last visit to Aunt Hettie's, but what was he doing here?

"George!" she shrieked in delight.

George got up and gave her a hug. "Hello, Miss Dora. Good to see you."

"What are you doing here?" asked Dora.

"I'm here with Mrs P. We've just driven up from Devon," he said.

She stared at him in amazement. "Aunt Hettie is here?"

He nodded. "Yes. She's chatting with your mum."

Dora drank down the glass of milk that Lily pushed into her hands and dashed into the parlour. She was so pleased to see her aunt that she burst into tears.

Aunt Hettie got up and held her tightly. "I'm so happy to see you, sweetheart, and look, I've brought you a small companion," she said, gesturing to the furry bundle abandoned on the chair. "This little fellow is to be yours, Dora."

Dora eyes widened. She looked from Hettie to the puppy. "Mine?"

"Yes," said Enid. "This puppy is the reason your aunt is here."

Dora cradled the little dog in her arms and gazed down at him in adoration. "His eyes were still closed when I last saw him and look at him now!" she babbled excitedly.

"You may remember I named him Wilf after his grandfather but you of course can call him whatever you like," said Hettie.

She turned to her aunt, laughing. "Oh, Aunt Hettie, Wilf is the most gorgeous creature I've ever seen!"

Enid smiled indulgently. "Why don't you take him to meet Lily? I daresay he needs a drink of water."

"Oh, what a sweet child!" said Hettie, dabbing at her eyes with a handkerchief.

"You know, Hettie, I believe that puppy may be a life saver," said Enid. "It's the first time I've seen her smile since I told her that her father had left."

"Oh, the poor lamb!" said Hettie. "I'm so very glad you telephoned me, Enid."

"I was at my wit's end, I can tell you," said Enid, going to the cupboard and taking out the whisky decanter. "I just didn't know what to do."

"Let's hope that this is the solution."

Enid poured a measure of whisky into two glasses and handed one to Hettie. "I really don't understand, Hettie. I've given Gerald the best years of my life, taken care of his home and brought up his children and this is the reward I get, a divorce!"

"I want you to know Enid that I don't approve of what my brother's done."

"I'm glad to know that."

"I think it's disgraceful and I've told him so," said Hettie. She paused and took a drink from her glass. "I care for my brother a great deal but I believed it my duty to tell him that unless he came back to you and Dora, I would have no more to do with him."

Enid decided that Hettie was a woman of principle after all and was sorry she had misjudged her. "Thank you, Hettie. It's good to know that I have your support," said Enid.

Hettie blew her nose. "Have you heard from Thomas?"

Enid shook her head. "No. Not since Christmas when Gerald decided to send them off on the train to visit you."

"Well, Tom came to see us after receiving his father's letter. He was certainly upset by the news but he accepted the situation with great maturity. Afterwards he talked about his wish to join the merchant navy."

"Oh?"

"Alfred could be of some assistance with that. He has connections with Houlder Brothers, a reputable shipping line, and with your approval, Tom could apply to them. It's a career with good prospects, Enid. Tom would get the opportunity to see the world."

"If that's what he wants, I have nothing against it. I have sometimes found Thomas difficult, you know, but I'm glad to hear he's doing well."

Hettie could not imagine how anyone could find the boy other than amiable. "Alfred and I think that Tom is a credit to you," she said, hoping that the compliment would elicit some maternal pride but there was no change in Enid's expression.

She cleared her throat. "I understand that my brother is determined upon divorce."

Enid nodded.

"Whether or not he believes he has grounds to sue for divorce, you are the aggrieved party here, Enid," said Hettie levelly.

"Yes, most aggrieved!" said Enid, her voice raised a notch. "I would never have believed Gerald to be capable of behaving as he has. Oh, the stigma of divorce! The humiliation! You just can't imagine it, Hettie."

Hettie looked at her sister-in-law's angry face. "Yes, it's very unpleasant and I do sympathise with your feelings, Enid. But please don't get upset," said Hettie, taking another drink from her whisky glass. "The best thing now is to be practical."

"Practical?"

"Yes, Enid; you will need to consult a solicitor."

"About the divorce?"

"Yes. Someone discreet who will fight your corner."

"Yes, I see."

"If you wish, I could ask Alfred to make a recommendation."

Enid nodded. "Would you accompany me to see this person, Hettie? I don't think I can do it alone."

Hettie was taken aback at the unexpected request and for a moment her loyalties were conflicted. She recalled her brother's recent visit, his description of Enid's psychotic behaviour and the events that had led him to leave. She had listened to her brother with sympathy. However, when he had told her of his intention to divorce Enid and marry Marian she had been appalled.

"Unfortunately, Enid, it's rather bad timing because we're going away very soon. Still, we'll see what can be arranged."

"Yes. Dora mentioned that you planned to visit your daughter in America."

Hettie's face brightened. "Yes, we are indeed. It's almost four years since I've seen Elizabeth and now that she's expecting a baby, our visit can't wait any longer. As soon as we heard that the travel restrictions were lifted we booked ourselves on the first passage available."

"When's that?"

"The Queen Mary sails in three weeks."

Enid looked at Hettie thoughtfully. In the circumstances, might she not postpone this visit? Wouldn't that be the action of the caring aunt she professed to be? Better still, Hettie could invite Dora and herself to accompany them. Gerald could pay for it. He owed her that. The idea of a ship board romance wafted through her mind, she had heard of that happening. It would serve Gerald right. Enid was ready to ask outright when Hettie spoke.

"I realise the timing is unfortunate, Enid. But my daughter is expecting us. We've had the passage booked for months and the berths are entirely filled. Lord knows when we might get another."

Chapter 8

The settlement that Enid received from Gerald was modest though with wise management it could have provided a reasonable livelihood. Her solicitor advised Enid to invest the money for the future but she was enjoying the novelty of having such a sum at her disposal too much to pay heed.

It was a year after Enid had received the divorce settlement that she was summoned by Mr Handley, her bank manager. At the meeting in his office Mr Handley cautioned Enid on her extravagance and warned her that if she continued to spend at her current level there would be no money left in her account.

The news was such a shock that as soon as she arrived home, Enid dismissed the new cook and gardener on the spot. Having refused their request for a week's salary in lieu of notice, she watched their angry departure, thinking wistfully of that smart motor car she would now be unable to purchase. The installation of electricity and a new bathroom had been costlier than she had realised and was astounded by how quickly her settlement could be depleted.

With Mr Handley's admonitory tone still ringing in her ears, she turned her thoughts to her former husband. She would eradicate all traces of him from the house; the blame for her situation lay squarely at his door. It took her, with the help of Ivy, Lily's replacement, the best part of a day to empty Gerald's study, remove his clothing and the possessions he had left behind. Anything of value was locked away in a cupboard.

When Dora returned from school that afternoon she noticed the neat piles of her father's clothing stacked up in the scullery and she stared at them in misery. His favourite old tweed jacket lay on top of one pile, the one he liked to change into after he came home from work. Dora picked up the familiar garment and took it up to her bedroom, then lay on the bed and buried her face in it, inhaling the slightly sweet smell of the tobacco that her father used to feed into his pipe. When Wilf jumped up and licked her tears she wrapped him in the jacket and cuddled the bundle to her chest. This brought about another fit of sobbing and that was when her mother came into the room.

"What on earth are you crying about now?" said Enid.

Dora untangled Wilf and hid the jacket behind her.

"And what are you doing with that?" said Enid, taking hold of the jacket but Dora wouldn't let go.

"Give that to me at once," said Enid, wrenching away the garment and cuffing Dora across the head.

Wilf gave a low growl and Dora put her arms around him protectively. Enid stood there with the jacket in her hand and stared at the little dog. "That dog can go, too."

Dora jumped off the bed and confronted her mother. "If he goes, I go and you will never see me again!"

Dora's hazel eyes flashed dangerously, her expression uncannily resembling her mother's when similarly aroused and for a moment Enid lost her composure. She took a step backwards and stared at her daughter's angry face. Much to her own surprise Enid had become quite attached to the little dog and hadn't intended to carry out her threat.

"The dog can stay. But you must come to your senses, Dora; your father is a feckless man. If he cared about you at all, he would be here with us today."

It was at Janet's suggestion that Enid took in lodgers. At first it was a difficult adjustment to accept strangers into her home and their presence entailed a great deal more cooking, cleaning and laundry. Apart from an appearance at meal times, the three male lodgers kept much to themselves and after a while the household settled into a new routine.

At the commencement of Dora's last school year one of the lodgers left and his place was taken by a middle aged woman called Mrs Stanley. It was then that life at home began to deteriorate. Enid's short temper did not improve and nor did her health. Dora blamed that on Mrs Stanley and her insidious influence. Sometimes Enid forgot herself and would snap at the lodgers for what she deemed their unreasonable demands. As a consequence, two of the lodgers handed in their notice and after a few months the third also left, leaving Mrs Stanley as their sole lodger. The embittered war widow enjoyed nothing more than commiserating with Enid about the unreliability of the male sex and the injustices of life in general.

One afternoon when Dora came into the kitchen, she was shocked to see the two women drinking gin at the kitchen table. Enid glanced at the half empty bottle standing on the table and looked up guiltily. "Dora! I wasn't expecting you back so soon."

Dora stood staring from the doorway. "The exam finished early."

Enid looked befuddled. "What exam?"

"My finals, Mother. Don't you remember?" said Dora.

Enid turned to Miss Stanley. "My daughter is very clever, you know; one of the best students in her year."

It wasn't the first time Dora had seen her mother drunk in recent months and she turned to leave.

"Dora, don't you want your tea?" asked Enid.

"I'm taking Wilf for a walk," said Dora.

"Don't be long, girl. Your mother needs you to help with the supper," said Mrs Stanley.

Dora stared coldly at the woman, barely able to disguise her dislike. Mrs Stanley had been a poisonous influence on the household ever since her arrival.

She turned to her mother. "Where's Ivy?"

"Gone off in a huff," said Enid.

"Why? What happened?" said Dora.

"Oh, the silly girl took umbrage at something Mrs Stanley said to her. It was just a storm in a teacup," said Enid.

"Do you mean Ivy has left?" said Dora.

Enid shook her head. "She'll be back."

"That idle little slut knows which side her bread is buttered!" said Mrs Stanley with a smirk.

With Wilf at her heels Dora marched furiously along the pavement. She was fuming in rage and needed to walk it off. She crossed the road, intending to go to the park but before reaching it, she changed her mind and took the road that led to Janet Jennings's village.

The maid opened the front door and a few minutes later Janet appeared and ushered Dora and Wilf into her sitting room. By now Dora was calm but as soon as Janet enquired after her mother, Dora's anger returned and she described the distressing situation at home in the most vehement of terms.

Janet nodded thoughtfully. "Hmm. I did bump into your mother last week. In fact, I invited her to come over for tea but she never turned up."

"Mother's very absent-minded these days."

"That often happens when one is under stress. Running a boarding house can be hard work."

"Mother says we can't manage without the money the boarders bring in but she just let them go, all except for Mrs Stanley. As far as I know, she's made no attempt to replace them.

"Perhaps it's time to move to a smaller property. You should get a good price for your house."

"I doubt that Mother would hear of it."

"Perhaps she may consider it when she realises that without such a large household to run there'd be no need of lodgers. She could make sufficient money on the transaction to put some aside, invest it even. That could produce a reasonable income."

"Oh, yes, Mrs Jennings What a joy it would be to have no lodgers!"

Janet felt a great deal of sympathy for Dora. In her opinion the girl had been forced to grow up much too quickly. "I'll have a word with your mother, Dora, see what I can do."

On the last day of her exams Dora came home to find Mrs Stanley absent and her mother in a much better mood. Enid made a pot of tea and as they sat drinking it in the parlour, she informed Dora of her plan to move to a more modest property.

"That's a really good idea," said Dora with a smile.

"I went with Mrs Jennings today to view a terrace house a few streets away. It's a bit on the small side but I think I could manage it without a maid and Mrs Stanley was good enough to say she'd help out."

Dora frowned. "Mrs Stanley?"

"I'm afraid poor Margaret was rather put out and I had to assure her that she didn't need to look for alternative accommodation."

"That's the whole point of moving to a smaller property, isn't it?"

"What do you mean, dear?"

"Surely the sale of this house will leave us with money in the bank. We won't need to take in lodgers."

"But Margaret would be so disappointed. And she has such a trying job, you know, Dora."

Mrs Stanley worked as a daily companion to Lady Bingham, an elderly widow, who lived in one of the large Georgian properties on the other side of town. From what Dora had heard, Mrs Stanley's most onerous task was to read the latest chapter of a favourite novel prior to her employer's afternoon nap.

"Imagine having to spend your day in the company of a testy old lady with failing eyesight," said Enid.

"I don't imagine that to be too difficult," said Dora sharply.

"Oh, Dora; where is your compassion?"

Dora had heard enough. "Mrs Stanley is a vicious, conniving and manipulative woman. What about all that booty she brings home with her? Do you think it is out of generosity that Lady Bingham lavishes these gifts upon her? Or, could it be to keep Mrs Stanley sweet?"

"Dora, how can you say such things about Margaret?"

"I say it because I don't trust the woman and I believe you have been taken in by her. I was shocked to see my father's silver cigarette box on her dressing table. I had gone into her room with the laundry and when I demanded to know what it was doing there she told me you had offered it to her. Is that true?"

"Yes. Margaret really took a fancy to it; she has so few nice possessions of her own. The poor woman has had a hard life, you know."

"Oh, poppycock!" Dora exclaimed. She stared at her mother in exasperation. "Mrs Stanley is a trouble maker – and she drinks!"

Dora refrained from adding that she also believed Mrs Stanley encouraged her mother to drink. She had seen the empty gin bottles left out with the rubbish.

Dora got to her feet, her jaw clenched in determination. "I will not live in the same house as that woman a minute longer!"

Enid sighed in resignation. "Very well, Dora. If you insist?"

Dora had expected her mother to put up more of a fight and wondered whether, deep down, she too, would be glad to see the back of Mrs Stanley. However, it soon became clear to Dora that her mother was intimidated by the woman because a week passed and nothing appeared to have been mentioned regarding her departure and once again it fell to Dora to consult Mrs Jennings.

Two days later Mrs Stanley and her belongings were gone and straight away Dora visited the farm to report the good news.

"That is indeed fortunate," said Mrs Jennings, feigning surprise.

Dora gave a sly smile. "I don't know how you managed it but I'm very grateful."

75

Mrs Jennings smiled conspiratorially. "All I will tell you is that neither you nor your mother will ever be bothered by Mrs Stanley again."

*

Leaving the home she had grown up in was a terrible wrench for Dora and clearing it out was like disposing of everything she cared for.

"Look, Dora. I don't like this anymore than you do," said Enid. "How do you think I feel about leaving the home I have lived in for over twenty-five years? Well, I can tell you. I don't like it one bit. But I'm putting on a brave face and I think you should be doing the same. I'm tired of your sulking."

Dora stood at the kitchen table packing the china into a box. She glanced at her mother who was emptying the cupboard of saucepans. "I'm not sulking. I'm just sad," she said.

"Well, cheer up then. Think of all the fun we can have choosing the new furnishings; do you remember the last time we did that?"

When Dora didn't respond Enid glanced across at her. "Dora?"

"I'm sorry, Mother. I don't feel well."

"Then go upstairs and lie down."

As Dora left the room, Enid called after her. "And don't come back until your mood has improved!"

Dora's lack of enthusiasm was disappointing and unhelpful. Enid had expected better of her.

There was a reason for Dora's listless mood but it was not one that she could share with her mother, not yet anyway. It was on the day they had begun packing up that she had found her father's letter at the bottom of a drawer and for almost a week it had been burning a hole in her pocket. She was glad to know that her father had not abandoned her willingly but her mother's duplicity was a bitter pill to swallow.

She had recognised her father's distinctive hand writing on the envelope at once. The letter had been written on company paper with a London address, a telephone number printed at the top. She had read it over several times, then slipped out of the house and headed straight to the telephone booth in the post office.

A female voice had answered. "Tompkins and Partners Solicitors; may I help you?"

Tentatively, Dora had given her father's name and asked whether she might speak to him.

"Hmm. Mr Gerald Jamieson, you say? I'm afraid Mr Jamieson left us some while ago."

Dora's voice was urgent. "How long ago?"

"It must be close to three years now. Mr Jamieson wasn't with us for long, only about eighteen months I believe. Perhaps one of our partners could be of assistance?"

"No, I don't think so," said Dora. "Could you tell me whether Mr Jamieson left a forwarding address?"

"Yes, I did have one," said the voice. "If you would be good enough to hold the line for a moment, I will enquire."

Dora stood in the telephone booth, feeding more coins into the box and biting her nails. It was a long time until the voice came back on the line, the minutes passing like hours.

"I've just had a word with our senior partner and I'm afraid it appears that Mr Jamieson is no longer at the address we have on file."

"You have no idea at all?"

"I'm very sorry I can't help you, Miss. Mr Jamieson didn't move locally, he and his family went to live in Montreal."

Dora gasped. "He went to Canada?"

The office had been quiet that morning and there was something about the caller's young voice that had made the receptionist curious. "Yes. Mr Jamieson's wife was French Canadian, you know," she said chattily.

"His wife?"

"Yes. They took the two boys with them, of course. I understand that Mrs Jamieson has relatives there."

"Oh, I see," said Dora. She had wanted to tell the receptionist that there must be a mistake. She and Tom were his family.

"Is there something else I can help you with?"

"No. Thank you very much," Dora had answered, her voice no more than a whisper.

Dora didn't confront her mother about the letter until they were settled into their new home. It had resulted in an angry exchange during which Enid defended her actions vehemently.

"Everything I have done has been in your best interests, Dora," she said.

"So your lies and deceit were for my sake?"

"I'm your mother. How dare you question my actions, you ungrateful child!"

Dora stared at her mother's bitter face and wondered whether she could ever forgive her.

Chapter 9

Enid decided to make a fresh pot of tea. She carried the kettle over to the sink and as she held it under the tap, she watched the pretty blue tits eating up the bread that she had left on the bird table and smiled, thinking how odd it was that she had never noticed the birds in their former garden. Perhaps she hadn't had the time in those days. It was over two years since they had moved and she no longer thought as much about the past.

The bacon and eggs in the pan were cooked and she put them onto a plate and carried it over to the table. She put aside the copy of the Daily Sketch she had been reading and sat down to eat her breakfast.

Dora came into the room dressed in a smart frock and sat down opposite her.

Enid poured her a cup of tea. "Are you going out?" she asked.

"Yes, I've arranged to meet Emily," said Dora, helping herself to a slice of toast.

"Don't you want some bacon and eggs?" Enid asked.

"No, thanks; I don't have time," said Dora.

"Did I tell you I saw her mother the other day? She told me that Emily wants to be some kind of doctor. I was so surprised."

"Why should you be? Emily's been studying medicine for the last two years."

"Studying medicine is one thing, but the idea of a woman doctor seems a bit strange to me. Before you know it, we'll be having women priests."

Dora grinned. "And why not?"

She finished off her toast and took her plate to the sink.

Enid looked up at her. "Is that a new frock?"

"It's the one I bought in the summer sale. Feathy altered it for me."

"It looks nice," said Enid, bending to feed a scrap of bacon to the Yorkshire terrier who sat by her feet.

"Yes. Feathy's very clever."

Miss Featherstone or Feathy, as she was known by the staff, was the seamstress at the dress shop where Dora was employed. Feathy's domain was the large work room at the back of the shop and there she was responsible for the alterations of the clothes that were purchased in the shop and also for fashioning the custom made orders. Dora loved to watch Feathy deftly cutting the materials from her cleverly improvised patterns and then sewing the garment in her tiny meticulous stitching. For Dora it was the most interesting part of her day.

Dora had assumed that the sale of their former home would alleviate her mother's financial difficulties but there had been debts to be repaid that Enid hadn't mentioned and Dora had realised that she needed to find a job. The first advertisement that she had seen was for a trainee salesgirl and having recently matriculated from school, she didn't have the qualifications to apply for anything more ambitious. By coincidence, the job offered was at the same couture establishment where her mother had once been employed but as the business was now under different ownership, Enid saw no point in mentioning it.

The proprietor was Madame Morel, a small, plump woman with a sharp featured face, was a stickler for discipline and punctuality. Should any of her employees have the misfortune to arrive late for work, a sum of money was deducted from their pay packet. Brenda Watson and Priscilla Gates, the two sales assistants who worked on the shop floor with Madame were middle-aged and viewed Dora with distrust. It wasn't because she was young and attractive but because any newcomer could pose a threat to their coveted jobs. The men who returned from the war had reclaimed the jobs the women had filled in their absence and nowadays, employment for women was scarce, even in the factories.

Madame Morel had scrutinized Dora carefully at the interview. It was important to her that her employees were well spoken and looked tidy. The girl who stood in front of her appeared suitable and she had taken her into the office to write down her details.

Madame Morel looked up from the notes on her desk. "I assume you can sew. There are occasions when you will be needed to assist my seamstress in the workroom."

Dora had little sewing experience but it was fortunate that her mother had allocated her the task of turning the sheets, one of the many economies they were obliged to make. They didn't possess a sewing machine and the sheets had been sewn by hand.

Dora nodded modestly. "Yes, Madame."

"Very well," said Madame. "You may start next Monday, 8.30 sharp.

Madame's origins were obscure. When she conversed with her customers her speech was accented, suggesting her French roots. However, there were the odd occasions when her carefully enunciated English vowels had a habit of straying into cockney. This was of no consequence to her employees, by them she was addressed as Madame though, in private, the epithets applied to her were less respectful.

"So where are you meeting Emily?" asked Enid.

"There's a Fabian Society meeting in the Municipal Hall," said Dora, picking up her gloves.

"Why on earth should you want to go there today? It's Whit Monday, a public holiday. Haven't you girls got anything more exciting to do?"

"Emily's an ardent member of the society. Last week the speaker talked about a universal health care system that Em said was really interesting."

"Hmm, those people are socialists, Dora. Mark my words; if things go on as they are we'll all end up being murdered in our beds!"

Dora laughed. "What on earth are you talking about, Mother?"

Enid put down her slice of toast and gave a small shudder. "Those evil Bolsheviks who murdered their own royal family; that's what happens when socialists get control."

"Emily says that all the Fabians want is a fairer, more just society."

"Oh, twaddle! I'm amazed at the Mortons allowing their daughter to get mixed up with such subversive types. Too much education isn't natural for a girl."

"Well, today Mr George Bernard Shaw is the speaker."

"Ah, yes, Mr Shaw is a playwright," said Enid, nodding in approval. "I once went to one of his plays in the West End. It was called Pygmalion and was about a flower girl who got transformed into a lady. Your father and I often went to the theatre before the war, you know."

She picked up the scrap of bacon that was left on her plate and handed it to the little dog at her feet.

"Please don't give Wilf so many tit bits, Mother. He's getting fat!" said Dora, smiling down at the little dog.

Wilf was now seven years old and had been living with them since his first appearance as an eight week old puppy. The little terrier had brought back light after those dark days of grief that had followed her father's departure and Dora loved him passionately.

She bent down beside him and nuzzled the fur on his head. "I'll see you later, sweetheart," she whispered.

Dora picked up her gloves from the sideboard and looked across at her mother who was carrying her plate across to the sink. Enid's shoulders were stooped and Dora was shocked at how fragile she looked. Enid had aged a great deal in recent years. She no longer took the same care with her appearance, nor took much interest in any of her former pastimes; but it was her growing memory lapses that caused Dora most concern.

The first time it happened Dora had come home to find Enid seated in her favourite armchair, one of the two that had been brought from the old house, her hands passive on her lap and her eyes staring vacantly into space.

She had looked up startled when Dora asked whether there was something the matter.

"No dear, I'm just waiting for your father to get home; he must have got delayed again."

"There are many things that can cause memory loss," Dr Morton had told Dora. "But unfortunately there's nothing we can do about it."

Dora turned in the kitchen doorway. "Isn't it your evening for the Women's Institute?"

"Oh, yes, I'm glad you reminded me. Did I tell you that Janet has arranged for Mr Armstrong to collect me in his auto mobile?"

"That's very kind of her."

"I only agreed to go to stop the woman nagging."

"Well I'm sure that Mrs Jennings values your participation."

Enid lifted her head, a glimmer of her former spirit returning. "Yes, indeed. I believe I still have some standing in this town."

*

After the meeting Dora and Emily went to the tea house and took seats at a table by the window.

"So what did you think of Mr Shaw, Em?" said Dora, looking across the table at her friend.

"He's a brilliant orator, isn't he?" said Emily, adjusting the position of the teacup in front of her.

"Oh, yes. But isn't he an odd looking man! What with his great height and that long, straggly beard, he looks so eccentric."

"Mr Shaw is pretty remarkable for a man over seventy; he's got the energy and enthusiasm of someone half his age."

"I didn't know he was a political activist."

Emily raised her eyebrows. "But Mr Shaw is always in the press."

"I don't have much time to read newspapers, nor much else these days, Em."

She omitted to mention the fashion magazines she read so avidly. New editions appeared regularly in the salon, arranged on a table for the benefit of the clientele and Dora

84

took every opportunity to scan their pages, paying careful attention to the latest trends.

"No, I suppose you don't, working all hours in that dress shop," said Emily. "How are you getting on?"

Dora gave a rueful smile. "I'm still the lowest in the pecking order!"

Emily looked at her with sympathy. "It's a blooming shame you didn't try for university."

Dora shrugged. "No good crying over spilt milk!"

A lack of finance had squashed any hope of furthering her education and it had been a bitter blow for Dora at the time. At school she had scored high marks in the arts subjects though she had never considered herself to be in her friend's academic league. Emily had a sharp, analytical brain and the ability to find a solution to any mathematical or scientific question that was set in front of her.

"Why not show some initiative then? Let Madame see that you have a brain!"

"It's not easy to get enthusiastic about the frumpy stuff we sell. If it were my shop, you know, I'd throw it all out and replace it with modern, up-to-date styles."

Emily glanced around at the matrons who patronized the tea shop and chuckled. "And within three months you'd be bankrupt," Emily chuckled.

"Corsets are a thing of the past, Em. Fashion has undergone a radical shift."

"Hmm, I dare say."

The whims of fashion were of no interest to Emily. "I thought Mr Shaw's lecture was really inspiring. We were very privileged to have him as our speaker today."

Dora nodded. "Em, Is Mr Shaw a revolutionary socialist?"

"Good Lord, no! Mr Shaw is a Pacifist, Dor. Were you really listening today?"

"Some of it was hard to follow."

"I'll give you some of the pamphlets Mr Shaw writes for the Society so you can understand his philosophy."

As she was talking a man stopped at their table, "Miss Morton! How are you?"

Emily looked up and smiled at the man. "I'm very well, thank you, Mr Armstrong."

He glanced across at Dora. "Oh, this is my friend Dora Jamieson."

"Jack Armstrong. A pleasure to meet you, Miss Jamieson," he said, taking Dora's hand and appraising her with interest.

He was a tall, well-built man with a square jaw and strong features. Dora smiled back shyly.

"Was he a war casualty?" said Dora, noticing his limp as he walked out of the teashop.

"Yes, I'd imagine so. Makes him rather dashing, don't you think?" said Emily with a giggle.

"I suppose it does."

"Actually, Dor, Mr Armstrong's my optician He supplied me with these new spectacles."

Dora looked across at her. "They suit you, Em."

"They're lighter than the last ones, much more comfortable, too," said Emily, pushing the steel rimmed spectacles higher on her nose.

She glanced down at the bill and told Dora to put away her purse. "You can treat me once you get that promotion."

As they walked out of the teashop Emily turned to Dora. "Look, why don't you come back with me? Everybody's home for Whitsun and they'd all love to see you, Ian especially."

*

Dora sat beside Emily on the squashy, comfortable sofa in the Morton sitting room and glanced around the familiar room. Donald and Ian were lounging in armchairs, listening to Emily's account of Mr Shaw's lecture.

"I heard him once in Hyde Park. George Bernard Shaw is an impractical visionary, he'd like to create a Utopia here on earth," said Donald.

Emily frowned. "His ideas are not impractical, Donald. You should understand him better before making such statements!"

Donald turned to Dora. "And what did you make of him, Dora?"

"Dora thought him a revolutionary!" Emily chuckled.

Ian saw Dora's embarrassment and turned to his sister. "I think that's a fair enough assumption."

"And how would you know, Ian?" said Emily. "I didn't think your reading extended beyond the bible these days.

Donald turned to Emily reprovingly. "Do put a sock in it, Em. Time you stopped being such a tiresome brat."

"I'd rather be that than a pompous, middle-aged stuffed shirt!" said Emily, picking up a cushion and throwing it at him.

Donald ducked and the cushion hit the standard lamp behind him. Mrs Morton came into the room just as it crashed to the floor. She stared at the lamp and then at Emily, her eyebrows raised.

"Sorry, Ma," said Emily, hurrying across the room to pick up the lamp.

Mrs Morton turned to Dora with a smile. "Dora, it's good to see you. How are you?"

Dora stood up and smiled back at her. "I'm well, thank you, Mrs Morton."

"I hope you'll be staying for supper?" said Mrs Morton, pushing Donald's feet off the table. "We see so little of you these days."

"Thank you, Mrs Morton, but I have to get back to Wilf. My mother's going to a W.I meeting this evening."

"Well, bring him back with you," she smiled. "You know the little fellow is always welcome here."

Enid was upstairs changing when the doorbell rang and she called down to Dora to answer it.

Dora stared in surprise at the man standing on the doorstep. "Mr Armstrong!"

"Miss Jamieson. How nice to see you again," Jack smiled. "I'm here to collect your mother."

"Yes. Please come in," said Dora, stepping back.

As he walked into the small hallway Wilf gave a low growl and was about to nip at his ankle when Dora made a grab for him.

Dora showed Mr Armstrong into the parlour and immediately his large masculine presence seemed to fill the small room.

"Well, fancy meeting you twice in one day, Miss Jamieson," he said, taking a seat in one of the armchairs. "That's serendipity!"

Dora hovered by the fireplace. "It's very good of you to take my mother to the meeting tonight."

"Oh, that's no trouble; I'd arranged to take my mother anyway."

Enid came bustling into the room. She wore a smart frock that hadn't been out of the wardrobe for months and with her hair neatly waved and face made up, Dora thought she looked much more like her old self.

"Mrs Jamieson, what a pleasure to see you again," said Mr Armstrong, rising from his chair.

It was clear from Enid's expression that she didn't remember him. "Good evening," she said with a polite smile.

He reached out his hand. "Jack Armstrong. We met when you were with your husband at a charity event."

"Oh, yes indeed," Enid smiled. "That was some while ago."

"And if I may say so you haven't changed one bit, Mrs Jamieson."

"Oh you flatter me, Mr Armstrong!" said Enid, relishing the compliment and primping her hair.

Later that evening at the Morton dinner table Dora chatted to Emily about Jack Armstrong's visit to her house. "I don't know what got into Wilf. He's usually so friendly but didn't like Mr Armstrong one bit!"

"Jealousy, I expect," said Emily, with a grin. "A man like Jack Armstrong could pose a threat."

Dora laughed. "He's old enough to be my father!"

"Well, I'd have an older man any day," said Emily.

Mrs Morton glanced across at the girls. "Is that Jack Armstrong you're talking about?"

"Yes, Ma; we met him in the teashop," said Emily.

"Such a charming man, don't you think? It's a mystery to me that he's still a bachelor," she said.

That evening Ian was much less reserved than usual. He had just returned from a teacher training course set up by the Church Commission and was full of enthusiasm about his impending trip to their mission station in Kenya.

"At the moment we've only got a large room at the back of the Mission but the Alliance of Protestant churches have just purchased a plot of land and once we've raised the capital we're going to build our school there."

"Where exactly is it, dear?" said Mrs Morton.

"A place called Kikuyu, about twelve miles from Nairobi," said Ian.

"So you'll be teaching at the school will you, Ian?" said Dora.

"Yes, Dora, I will. We intend to open an elementary school, you see."

"That must be exciting," she said.

He smiled at her across the table. "Yes, it's very exciting. The children who come to us can't read or write and the school will be life changing."

"At least the little heathens won't just have Jesus crammed down their gullets!" Emily chuckled.

Mrs Morton looked at her daughter reproachfully. "Emily, show some respect. A little more church going would do you no harm."

"But Mother, you know I'm an atheist!" said Emily.

Dr Morton looked down the table at his daughter. "That's enough, Emily," he said firmly.

Dora regarded him challengingly. "But Pa, you've always told us to be true to our beliefs and not be afraid to express ourselves, haven't you?"

"There's a time and a place for everything, Emily," said Dr Morton.

It was a fine, warm evening and after supper Dora took Wilf outside and sat on the garden bench, her mood reflective as she watched him scamper amongst the undergrowth. The events of the last year had left her with a great sense of loss, in particular the death of Alfred Pickering in January. After a short illness he had succumbed to bronchial pneumonia and Dora had taken the train to Cornwall to attend his funeral.

At the reception that had followed the funeral service Dora and Tom had been reunited with their cousin Elizabeth who had come over from America with her five year old son Michael. She had inherited her mother's charm and warmth and young Mike was a lively, fun-loving child, his antics providing a welcome respite from the solemnity of the occasion. The death of Uncle Alfred had been a bitter blow and Dora was further distressed to learn that Hettie would be closing up the house and going to live in America with her daughter.

That evening in the Morton garden Dora was conscious of yet more change; the dispersal of the big happy household that had been such a fixture in her life. Emily was living in digs and the twins were now away at boarding school.

The bench faced away from the house and Dora didn't notice the approaching figure.

"Oh, Ian!" she said, suddenly seeing him standing beside her.

"May I join you?" he said.

Dora moved along the bench to make room for him. "Wilf loves this garden," she said. "Ours is no bigger than a postage stamp."

He gave her a sideways glance and thought how lovely she looked in the half light. "Are you still working in that dress shop?"

"Yes, I'm afraid so."

"Wouldn't you like to do something more with your life?"

"Yes, of course I would."

"You could come out to Africa and work at the Mission. They offer assisted passages to volunteers."

Dora shook her head and grinned. "I doubt I'd have much to offer."

"That's nonsense, you've got a great deal to offer, you're just not aware of your strength."

He longed to put his arm around her but his innate shyness prevented it. "You've always struck me as the kind of girl who likes a challenge."

"Hmm, I suppose I do."

"You know I've always been very fond of you, Dora."

"And I'm fond of you too, Ian, all of you."

"My hope is that your feelings for me might grow stronger," he said, and suddenly emboldened he took her hand. "You see, Dora, I think you'd be well suited to the life I'm embarking upon."

She was alarmed by how earnest he was. Ian was a gentle, sensitive man and she was searching for a response that wouldn't hurt his feelings when Emily came out of the house and called to her.

"So what's been going on?" said Emily, walking along the pavement beside her.

"Nothing really," said Dora.

"I saw you holding hands, Dor."

"It was awkward."

They stopped for Wilf to lift his leg against a lamp post. "Oh God! He didn't propose to you, did he?"

"I think he was about to."

"Oh dear, poor old Ian! I know he's always held a torch for you and the way he was looking at you at supper did make me wonder."

"I had no idea."

"Well, never mind, he'll get over it. Soon he'll be too busy converting his little heathens to have time for earthly desires!" said Emily with a chuckle.

Dora giggled. "Oh, Em! You're' wicked!"

That night she lay awake for a long time replaying the evening in her head and for a moment she speculated on the idea of escaping to a new life. Wilf snuggled up against her on the bed and she kissed the top of his head, swearing that they would never be parted. When eventually she fell asleep she dreamed that she was in the African jungle being chased by wild animals. With the predators at her heels she ran for her life through the undergrowth and just as they were upon her she felt herself grasped by a strong pair of arms and Jack Armstrong was smiling down at her.

Chapter 10

After the long Whitsun week-end the town was busy and in Madame Morel's shop business was brisk. During the afternoon a customer called Mrs Cavendish, one of Madame's most valued clients, arrived with a gown she wished to have copied.

"Unfortunately, one of the maids used too hot an iron, the wretched girl. As you will see it's left a nasty brown mark on the skirt," she told Miss Gates.

As soon as her customer had selected her purchase Madame beckoned over Miss Gates to complete the transaction and approached Mrs Cavendish with an ingratiating smile.

"Please let me assist you, Madame," she said, removing the gown from its wrapping and spreading it out on the counter top.

The gown was unlike anything she sold in the shop. Madame was almost fifty years old and still favoured the corseted bodice, but this glamorous gown had a low, daring neckline and lacked any bodice at all.

"The frock is from Paris and a particular favourite of my daughter's," said Mrs Cavendish.

"Oh, so chic! How stylish!" cooed Madame. Paris was, after all, the world's fashion capital.

"As you can imagine, my daughter was devastated," said Mrs Cavendish.

Madame Morel hung the gown on a hanger with reverence. "Well, Madame, I can assure you that you will not be disappointed with its replacement."

The following day the oyster silk for the new gown was collected by Miss Gates from the wholesalers and Feathy set to work on the pattern. Dora watched her arrange it on the outstretched fabric and attach it with pins.

"These panels have to be cut on the bias, you see," said Feathy, cutting along the curved lines, her scissors gliding through the silk as though with a life of their own.

What most impressed Dora was Feathy's ability to cut without waste and one day when Madame was out of the shop, she practised on a length of material from the oddments box. Cutting fabric was by no means the effortless task that it appeared and Dora consigned her efforts to the waste bin.

*

When Miss Laura Cavendish came for her first fitting, she arrived alone, entering the shop with curiosity. Her mother had been a customer for as long as she could remember but this was Laura's first visit. The front of the double windowed shop displayed a selection of dresses, skirts and tops for day-time wear. They were of a high quality but one glance was sufficient to persuade Laura that the merchandise was too conservative to be of interest to her; and was therefore surprised when Madame escorted her through the wide archway into the salon at the back where Feathy's creation was displayed on a mannequin.

"Oh, how gorgeous! It's perfect!" said Laura, clapping her hands in delight.

Later, when dressed in the gown, Laura stood in front of the tall mirror and appraised her image. The sleeveless dress had a low V-neck, skimmed over the bust and waist and the fluted skirt reached mid-calf, brushing lightly against her legs when she moved. Feathy, who knelt at her feet, had to beg her to remain still as she adjusted the hem line. Dora was standing by, waiting to assist, when they were startled by the voice of a customer popping her head through the archway.

"Jemima!" said Laura, turning in surprise. "What are you doing in here?"

"I've come with Mama. She's collecting an alteration," said the girl, her eyes were fixed on the oyster silk dress. "Is that being altered?"

"No. It's been made by Miss Featherstone here," said Laura, making a twirl. "What do you think?"

"It's absolutely stunning, Laura," said Jemima, her eyes now swivelling around the room. "Well, I'm looking for something for the hunt ball, perhaps I might find a gown here."

She turned to Dora. "Do you have something you could show me?"

"This gown is a made to measure order, Madam," said Dora.

Jemima looked disappointed. "I looked in Selfridges the other day and couldn't find a thing. They had plenty of frocks with the new dropped waists but either they didn't fit or they just didn't hang well," she said.

Dora took a deep breath. "Our dressmaker could make up any design that you chose, Madam," she said. "Miss Featherstone is a genius."

Feathy glanced up and almost swallowed the pins in her mouth. Madame was attending to Mrs Templeton, Jemima's mother, and on an impulse Dora picked up the copy of Vogue that lay on a table beside the sofa. She flipped through the pages until she found what she was looking for.

"There are some designs here that might interest you," she said.

A few minutes later Madame appeared with Mrs Templeton and by the time they left the shop two hours later three new orders had been placed and Madame was smiling smugly. Her commissions were extremely lucrative.

By now, Madame Morel's employees had left for the day and she looked around her emporium thoughtfully, her eyes resting on the two-piece suit that was displayed on a mannequin. The long, unstructured jacket and straight skirt had been one of similarly designed suits that she had ordered from one of her favourite fashion houses. In her opinion the garments would have benefited from more tailoring but the fact that only one remained in the shop was testament enough to their popularity. The younger generation might prefer to go without stays and now it seemed that even some of the middle aged matrons she dressed were prepared to put them aside, though she herself would not follow their example. However much she might regret the loss of the last era's elegance she had to accept that tastes in fashion were undergoing a radical shift. From the faster pace of life to the blare of car horns in the streets it was a busier, rapidly changing world.

One morning, a few days later, Madame asked Dora to see her in the office. Nothing had been mentioned about Dora's intercession with a customer and she assumed that she would now be reprimanded for her temerity. Worst of all, her employment might be terminated.

As Dora stood in front of Madame Morel's desk she felt her stomach churning just like it did when summoned to the headmistress's study. Madame, however, had something entirely different on her mind.

"I'm making some changes, Miss Jamieson," she said, looking up at her. "It's my intention to modernize, you see. A successful business must move with the times," she said.

"Yes, Madame."

"I intend to purchase a typewriter and the purpose of this innovation is to create a more efficient administration, particularly in relation to our account customers. Sometimes it's necessary to correspond with the clients regarding a quotation or a late payment of an invoice."

Dora looked puzzled. It usually was Brenda who took care of the invoices.

"And it is therefore my intention for you to take a course in typewriting. Well? What do you have to say, Miss Jamieson?"

"Thank you very much, Madame."

"I have here a note of the hours and address of the secretarial college you will attend," she said, handing Dora a sheet of paper. "You may be interested to know that they also offer classes in book keeping as well as Mr Pitman's shorthand. Knowledge of book keeping could be an asset to an ambitious young woman."

Later, when Dora went into the work room for her tea break Feathy was bent over the cutting table outlining a pattern. She looked up as Dora came into the room.

"She expects me to have this order ready in two weeks and I haven't even finished making up the patterns. On top of that I'm supposed to make two tea dresses for the shop!" said Feathy, standing upright and stretching her neck.

"She wants to display them in the shop? I thought you only did the made to measure orders?" said Dora.

"Not anymore," said Feathy. She looked at Dora and gave a wry smile. "So much for my genius!"

"That's exploitation!"

"Not much I can do about that, is there?"

"But Feathy, you could find employment in one of the London fashion houses any time you chose."

Feathy shook her head. "And do all that travelling?"

"You could move house."

"And leave my old dad? I've lived with him in the same house all my life and now that Mum's passed on, he needs me to keep him company. Dad would never move away."

Dora boiled the kettle on the Primus stove and as she made a pot of tea she told Feathy about the typing classes.

"I hope it won't put Brenda's nose out of joint," she said.

"Never! She'll thank her lucky stars. Try writing your best copper plate with Madame breathing down your neck and not even 'a thank you', let alone an extra few shillings in her wages."

Feathy perched on a stool by the window to drink her tea. "I've known Brenda a long time, you know. She used to live on the same street as me. Brenda was such a pretty girl, always smiling, and clever with it. All the boys down our way were after her."

Dora was surprised. It wasn't easy to reconcile this image with the careworn woman of today.

Feathy took a drink of her tea. "I always remember how envious I was that first day I came back from my job at the factory and saw Brenda playing hopscotch out in the street with the other youngsters. Not a care in the world she had then and next thing you know she's supporting three kids and a husband invalided out the army."

"What happened to him?"

"His unit was blown to bits at Passchendaele."

Dora nodded. "1917."

"Thought you'd be too young to remember that."

"My brother was killed at the Somme, two years before. I followed the war very carefully."

"I'm sorry to hear that, Dora. There can't be many a family as wasn't affected, one way or another. Terry got half his face smashed in and lost most of his hearing, too. Brenda says he won't speak about it, not ever. Terry was the only survivor."

"Oh, poor Brenda. I didn't realise."

"Well, why should you? It's not like we get the time to get to know one another…"

"I don't pay you to sit gossiping here all day," said Madame, glaring at them from the doorway. "Dora, back to work."

She turned to Feathy. "The woollen fabric has arrived. Let me know as soon as those patterns are ready, I want to take a look before you start cutting."

Dora attended the typing classes three evenings a week and unless it was one of her mother's bad days, supper was usually waiting when she arrived home. What troubled Dora was to witness Wilf's doleful expression when he watched her leave again so hurriedly afterwards. She was on the point of giving up the classes when help was at hand.

Mrs Simmons was a kind hearted neighbour and since Dora had first gone to work she had come each day to check up on her mother. One afternoon when Dora had come home Mrs Simmons was just leaving the house. "I think you'll find your Mum in better spirits today, Dora. I've been teaching her how to play Patience and I think she's finally got the hang of it," said Mrs Simmons with a chuckle.

Upon hearing about Dora's predicament Mrs Simmons suggested that her daughter Sarah could walk the dog after school. "To tell you the truth, Sarah often pops in with me when I visit. She likes the chance to play with the little fellow," she said.

Sarah, a gentle natured thirteen year old, accepted responsibility for the little dog with enthusiasm but accepted the payment of a six pence coin that Dora handed over with reluctance.

Chapter 11

Feathy had been off work for three days. During the years she had worked in the shop she had rarely taken a day off and Madame was flummoxed by the unprecedented situation. On the first day of her absence a neighbour had arrived with a message that Feathy had succumbed to influenza, but there had been no further news since.

"This really is most tiresome. There are two orders promised for next week. What am I to tell my clients?" she said. "I should like you to visit Miss Featherstone on your way home and tell her I need her back at work," Madame told Dora.

The terraced house where Feathy lived was similar to Dora's though the modern extension at the back included a bathroom instead of the usual outdoor lavatory. She was met at the door by an elderly man who introduced himself as Bert, Feathy's father. Bert took her into the kitchen and as he shuffled about making a pot of tea, she looked around the homely room. Two easy chairs were set before the open range stove and a folded newspaper lay on the small table set between them. Something that smelled very tempting was simmering in the pan on top of the stove.

"I was ever so worried about my girl the first couple of days," said Bert as they sat at the well-scrubbed kitchen table drinking their tea.

"We lost her mother in the flu epidemic in '19. I was afraid I'd lose my daughter, too."

"Is there anything I can do for you, Mr Featherstone?"

"No, Miss, thank you," said Bert. "The doctor says the best thing now is lots of bed rest, but I know my girl. Soon as she can she'll be fretting to get back to work."

"Tell her that she's not expected back for at least another week. Say that Madame and the doctor insist on a period of recuperation," says Dora.

"Madame says that, does she?" he said with a wink.

Dora smiled at him. "By the time your daughter returns Madame will be so relieved she'll quickly forget about the length of her absence."

As Dora was leaving she turned in the doorway. "I'll try and ensure that her wages aren't docked."

"We don't need no charity, Miss."

"No, Mr Featherstone, just what is owed to her."

First thing the following morning Dora walked purposefully into Madame Morel's office and her report on the grievous state of Feathy's health was so harrowing that Madame was disturbed.

"Perhaps Madame, you'd be good enough to allow me to take over her wages to pay for the doctor and the medicines she needs, maybe some nourishing food, too. Her poor father is an invalid, you know and he's utterly distraught."

Madame sniffed. "I don't run a charity, Miss Jamieson."

"The doctor believes that Miss Featherstone's been overworking."

"She's not complained to me," said Madame irritably.

She looked at Dora hovering in the doorway. "Is there something else, Miss Jamieson?"

"I'm just hoping that Miss Featherstone does come back."

Madame stared up at her sharply. "Why wouldn't she?"

"Seamstresses of Miss Featherstone's calibre are so much in demand."

"But she works in the most superior establishment in this town."

"Of course, Madame; but Bond Street and Mayfair are only a train ride away."

Madame frowned. Feathy's continued loyalty was something she had taken for granted but perhaps the girl knew something she didn't. "Please inform Miss Featherstone that I am concerned for her welfare and you may collect her wages at the end of the day. I will have an envelope waiting."

The week before Feathy's return a new employee called Kathleen Sullivan arrived at the shop, having been employed to assist Feathy in the workroom. Kathleen was a tall, gangly redhead of nineteen who, during the war, had worked as a machinist making uniforms for the troops, but having had no experience as a seamstress she was soon in difficulty with the fine sewing required of her. Brenda and Dora helped out as best they could and were both immensely relieved when Feathy returned and took the girl under her wing.

Whenever the shop was quiet, Dora was allowed to practise on the new typewriter which was now set up on a desk in Madame's office and within a few months she was sufficiently proficient on the keyboard to take care of the paper work. Madame nodded in approval as she read over the correspondence that Dora had typed. It was clear from the accuracy of the spelling and punctuation that the girl had received a good education.

Every Tuesday at the same time Madame Morel put on her coat and hat, saying that she would be out for the rest of the day. Miss Gates, being the employee of the longest standing, was left in charge. One afternoon when her employees were drinking tea in the work room their speculation on Madame's destination caused a great deal of ribaldry.

"Maybe she has an assignation with a gentleman friend?" said Miss Gates.

"You know your problem, Miss Gates," said Feathy, chuckling. "You spend too much time with your nose stuck in those bodice rippers!"

Miss Gates blushed crimson to the roots of her hair. She liked to read on the bus during her journey to work and there was usually a novel of that description secreted in the depths of her bag.

"The French are Catholic, aren't they?" piped up Kathleen unexpectedly.

Feathy glanced at her. "Yes. That's right, Kath."

"Well she might go to see the priest and make her confession, mightn't she?" said Kathleen, who was herself obliged to do so each week."

"Doubt his other customers don't get a look in, come Tuesdays!" said Brenda, laughing.

"To tell the truth, I reckon Miss Gates's got it right," said Feathy.

"What, Madame and a fancy man? Pull the other one!" said Brenda.

"Well look how she gets herself all dolled up, bet you she's wearing her best bloomers, an all," said Feathy with a chuckle.

Emily was on one of her rare visits home when she popped over one evening and suggested to Dora that they meet at the teashop the following day.

"I'm sorry, I always seem to be late," said Dora, breathlessly. "We went over to see Archie and I had to take Wilf home."

She took a seat and looked across at Emily. "I like your hair, Em. It really suits you."

Emily frowned. She was glad the dratted perm had almost grown out. It was a reminder of Roger and her appalling lapse of good sense. Looking at those unworn frilly blouses languishing in her cupboard each day was enough admonishment.

Dora glanced at Emily's book. "What are you reading?"

"Freud and Yung, a comparative analysis."

"Interesting?"

"Enlightening," she said, pushing the book into her bag. "And how are things with you?"

"Oh, much the same; this morning Madame brought up the book keeping course again."

"So why don't you do it?"

"And give up my afternoon off?"

"It wouldn't be for ever. Do you really want to remain a shop assistant for the rest of your life?"

Dora shook her head. "What I'm tired of is the constant scrimping and saving."

"Then you'll have to find yourself a rich chap, won't you?"

"Chance would be a fine thing!" Dora laughed.

"Well, I shan't ever get married."

"What about those dashing doctors you work with?"

Emily winced. "No, Dor, I won't."

Emily had inherited her father's angular frame and as an adult she took little interest in her appearance, not until she fell in love. During that last summer Emily's world had been turned topsy-turvy when she met a man called Dr Roger Timmins in the hospital where she was working. He was a clinical psychologist and head of the department to which she had been assigned.

Roger, a bachelor in his late thirties, was a thoughtful man with a talent for enthusing his students with his own passion for clinical research. He had been impressed by Emily's intellect and, as the top student of her group, he had taken a particular interest in her. At the end of the working day they had often spent time talking in his office and sometimes on a fine summer's evening he had joined her for a stroll in the park. Emily was disappointed when other students accompanied them and had contrived occasions to spend time alone in his company.

Beneath his earnest demeanour Roger had revealed the kind of ironic humour that Emily could relate to and though their discussions revolved around abstract topics, rarely straying into the personal, Emily had hoped that their friendly rapport could develop into something more intimate. One day during the week prior to her transfer to a different department Emily had been in his office when the conversation took on a more personal note.

"Your work is extremely promising, Miss Morton," he had said, looking up from her essay on his desk. "You have a real aptitude for clinical psychology. What first ignited your interest, might I ask?"

When she described the extensive library of research books in her father's study that she had devoured as a girl, he chuckled. "You must have been an unusual young lady. I have two sisters and the only books they had their heads into were of a rather more romantic nature!"

"My father is a doctor, a family practitioner, and it's he who encouraged me, you see."

"Then your father is a very enlightened man, it's time there were more women in the profession."

Emily had smiled proudly, thinking how much her father would enjoy meeting Dr Timmins.

When she had confided her regret at having to leave his department Dr Timmins had smiled warmly. "And I'll be sorry to lose you, Miss Morton, I shall miss our enlivening chats."

"Well, we don't have to lose contact, do we?"

"Absolutely not, my dear, you always know where to find me, don't you?"

Emily didn't set sight on Dr Timmins for several months and that was not until she bumped into him at the hospital's Christmas party. He had been standing out in the corridor chatting to another doctor when Emily was on her way out.

"Ah, Miss Morton, how good to see you," he had smiled before turning to introduce her to his companion. "This young lady is one of the brightest students I've ever had the pleasure to teach."

After his companion had walked away he and Emily had begun chatting and he listened with interest as she told him of her decision to major in psychiatry.

"And I thank you Dr Timmins for being such an inspiration," she had said.

He had smiled a bit tipsily. "Well, my dear Emily, I think you should know how much I enjoyed those stimulating discussions of ours."

His use of her Christian name for the first time was all the encouragement that Emily had needed and suddenly she stepped forward and kissed him on the lips. His arms had then enfolded her and he kissed her back but after a few moments he had pulled away, looking embarrassed.

His former companion had just reappeared with two glasses of wine and Dr Timmins had glanced at Emily with a shamefaced smile. "I er…look forward to seeing you again, Miss Morton."

There was nothing to be done about the absence of feminine curves but Emily decided that a permanent wave might be flattering and the following week she had gone to the hairdressers where her straight, mousy hair was transformed into flattering waves. Immediately afterwards she had put on her coat and headed straight to the hospital.

Roger had looked up from his desk with a small frown. "What can I do for you, Miss Morton?"

"I thought I'd drop by to say hello," she said, smiling shyly.

"I'm afraid I'm just on my way out, I'm meeting someone and already running late," he had said, pulling on his coat.

Emily had stepped back as he strode through the doorway.

"Maybe another time?" he had said with a nod before hurrying off.

That evening Emily had been chatting with Sally, a student in her year, when Roger's name had come up. Sally had referred to Roger's latest research paper and was singing his praises.

"Yes, he's such a clever man, really quite brilliant," Emily had said. "Actually I went to see him this afternoon but he was rushing to meet someone."

"Probably off to see his fiancé," said Sally.

The colour had drained from Emily's face. "Fiancé?" she said.

"Haven't you heard? Dr Timmins has just got engaged," said Sally. "She's a real looker, they say."

Dora looked at Emily quizzically. "There's something you're not telling me, isn't there?"

"Nothing that won't keep," she said and went on to gripe about the injustices of the establishment. "Some of the brightest students throw in the towel and submit to a life of domestic servitude because they make it so difficult for women to gain entrance to university, let alone to enter the professions. Take my advice, Dor, and grab whatever qualifications you can. It takes guts for a woman to succeed in this male controlled world."

Chapter 12

The book keeping course turned out to be more rewarding than Dora had anticipated. She had studied the rudiments of the single-entry system during her last year at school and the columns of figures in the journals held no mystery; and it wasn't long before she progressed to the ledgers.

One evening, she was on her way home after a class, her books in a satchel on her shoulder and her head full of balance sheets, when a car pulled up on the kerb beside her. The driver wound down the window and Jack Armstrong put out his head. "Miss Jamieson, may I give you a lift?"

Dora didn't pause for long, her satchel was heavy.

As the car turned into the high street he suggested a stop at the coffee house. It was Dora's first visit and she stood in front of the shop's counter staring in surprise at the vast array of coffee jars that lined the shelves behind. From the labels on the jars it seemed that the coffee beans had been imported from every corner of the globe.

"Well, what would you like?" he asked.

"I've no idea. Please would you make the choice?"

They took a seat at a corner table and when the waitress came to take their order he asked for a pot of the Kenyan blend and a jug of cream to accompany it.

"I think you'll like it," he said, turning to Dora. "It has a mellow but fulsome flavour."

Dora sat back in her chair and looked at him across the table. The reason she had accepted the lift was not just the weight of her satchel, it was the fact that Mr Armstrong had known her father.

"Did you know my father well, Mr Armstrong?"

"Let's not be so formal. Please call me Jack."

"Then you must call me Dora," she smiled.

"Well, Dora, I should tell you that I hadn't realised the connection until I came to your house and recognised your mother. I've got a good memory for faces."

It was years since Dora had spoken with anyone about her father and it was difficult to restrain her impatience.

"What about my father, Jack?"

"I can't say I knew him well but it was your father who drew up the agreement when I took over the lease on the shop. That was how we met."

Dora thought about that Christmas when she had seen her father with the pretty dark haired woman. Maybe Jack had known her, too. The waitress put a pot of coffee on the table and Dora watched Jack pour it.

"Were you acquainted with my father's friends?" she asked.

"Only those I met at the club. He was good enough to get me a membership."

"Did you know that my father married again?"

"No, I knew he'd left town but I didn't know he'd re-married."

Aunt Hettie wouldn't discuss her father after he left them and Dora felt thwarted again but as she half listened to Jack discuss the two shops that he owned it suddenly occurred to her that Mrs Jennings was the person she should question.

The following Sunday when she went over to the farm Janet was out in the yard with a groom. They walked together to the field where Archie was grazing and when Dora whistled the pony pricked up his ears and trotted over to the fence. While he crunched on the apple she handed him, a young piebald pony appeared beside him, reaching out her head expectantly.

Mrs Jennings laughed. "This is Dolly, she's new to the livery and she follows him everywhere. Archie pretends to ignore her but I think that secretly he loves the adulation. He's been very perky since she arrived."

Later, as they sat at the kitchen table, Dora asked Janet whether she had known her father's new wife. Janet, who was packing eggs for Dora to take home, looked across at her thoughtfully. Dora was an adult now, she had every right to know about the step-mother she had never had the chance to meet.

"Marian Holmes was a war widow and left with two young sons. I met her once or twice when I went over to see Helen and Gordon, at her parent-in-law's home; we used to belong to the same hunt. Marian was a charming young woman but she wasn't a rider. Helen and Gordon were very good people and they did their best for Marian and the boys after Anthony was killed."

"It must have been hard for them to lose their grandsons, too."

"Yes, that was very sad."

"Do you know whether Marian keeps in touch with them?"

"Unfortunately, Helen died a few years ago and since then Gordon's been a recluse, he doesn't encourage visitors."

Chapter 13

Spring had come around again and Feathy was blooming like the bursting pink blossom on the cherry trees. She chose to ignore the curious stares from the other employees, waiting until Madame's afternoon off to disclose the secret she was nursing.

"You've been grinning all week like a Cheshire cat, Feathy!" said Brenda, drinking her tea with the other employees in the workroom. "Come on; now tell us what's going on."

Feathy smiled around at them. "I'm to be married."

"You are a dark horse, Daphne," said Brenda.

Miss Gates looked thunderstruck. "Married!" she gasped.

Feathy then told her astonished audience that she and Arthur, her fiancé, would be celebrating their engagement the next Saturday and they were all invited to join them at the George Inn. In response to the barrage of questions that followed, Feathy told them that she had known Arthur Burgess since school days but hadn't seen him again until they met at her cousin's house the previous year.

"You mean that bloke who became a bobby, he lived down our way, didn't he?" said Brenda.

Feathy nodded. "Yes, Bren, that's Arthur."

Kathleen's eyes were agog. "And he's been holding a torch for you all these years, just fancy that!"

"No, Kath, not exactly," said Feathy. "Arthur's a widower. His wife died during that flu epidemic a few years back. He'd moved up to London after he was married but now he's moving back."

"What, back here?" said Brenda.

"Yes, to be nearer his boys. They've been living with his in-laws, you see," said Feathy. "Arthur used only to see them on Sundays but now he's been transferred to the local constabulary that will all change."

Once the excitement died down Brenda turned her attention to Dora.

"You know what, ladies, our Feathy isn't the only dark horse around here, is she now?"

"What do you mean by that?" said Miss Gates, turning to Dora. "You're not getting married, too, are you, Miss Jamieson?"

Dora shook her head and laughed.

"Just a bit of courting then, you and that gent in the coffee shop, was it?" Brenda teased.

"Oh, Miss Jamieson; do tell," said Miss Gates.

"There's little to tell, Miss Gates," said Dora. "It was just Mr Armstrong from the opticians. He was kind enough to give me a lift home after my book keeping class."

"Best watch yourself, love," said Feathy. "Jack Armstrong could charm the birds from the trees, if he's a mind to."

Miss Gates looked peeved. Since his arrival in the town the good looking optician had been the focus of her romantic fantasies. "Mr Armstrong is a very respectable gentleman!" she said primly.

Brenda grinned. "And not half a bad catch, eh, Miss Gates?"

It was only two days ago that that Dora had accompanied Jack to a pub on the outskirts of town but she kept that to herself. It had been an unseasonably warm day for early spring and after spending two hours bent over ledgers Jack's proposal of an escape to this rural retreat had been too appealing to refuse.

The King's Arms public house was situated in a valley and the garden behind was even prettier than Jack had described. It was planted with borders of tulips just coming into flower and ahead of where she sat under the boughs of a flowering magnolia was a steep bank of daffodils swaying lightly in the breeze.

"Not a bad spot, eh?" said Jack, placing two tall glasses on the rustic table in front of the bench.

"It's lovely, Jack," she smiled.

"Well, I got us Somerset cider. They say it's very good," said Jack, sitting down beside her.

Dora took a drink from her glass. "Hmm, yes, very nice."

Jack turned to her. "I made some enquiries about your father, by the way."

"Oh?"

"Yes. I talked to some of the older members at the club. One of them mentioned he was living in Canada. I suppose you knew that."

Dora nodded. "That's about all I do know."

He took a drink from his glass. "My father left when I was a youngster, you know. The fact is my mother threw him out."

"That must have been hard for you."

He shook his head. "No, I was too young to even remember him."

Dora looked wistful. "Sometimes I find it difficult to remember what my father looks like."

"You still miss him?"

"I do, it's left me with a big hollow inside."

He rested his hand on hers for a moment. "One day a man will come along who'll fill up that hollow, you wait and see."

An attractive young couple had come into the garden and seated themselves on the terrace. Dora had watched them, struck by how happy they looked. The young man had said something funny that made the girl laugh and then had taken hold of her hand and raised it to his lips. The girl's eyes had followed him when he had left to go back into the pub as though she couldn't bear him out of her sight. Dora had tried to imagine what it would feel to be so in love.

"Do you have a boyfriend, Dora?" Jack had asked.

"No."

"Well, either you're rather picky or the blokes around here are short-sighted," he had chuckled.

"I did once have a kind of marriage proposal," she had said with a giggle. "I could now be living in Africa as a missionary's wife!"

Jack had laughed. "I can't quite imagine that!"

The strong cider had made Dora light headed. "What I'd really like is a career in fashion."

"I thought that's what you did."

"No, I mean couture. I'd create my own designs and sell them to the rich and famous."

He had smiled indulgently. "Well, you never know what fate has in store."

When Jack had stopped at the kerb outside Dora's house he had insisted on carrying her satchel to the front door. She had enjoyed the excursion and turned in the doorway to thank him.

"It's been a great pleasure and I hope we can repeat it."

Enid had been watching through the window and turned to Dora as she entered the parlour. "Are you and Mr Armstrong courting, Dora?" she asked.

"No, Mother. He's just a friend."

"Well, you could do worse. Mr Armstrong is very well set up."

Chapter 14

Dora re-read Tom's letter and smiled to herself. From his infrequent correspondence she had learned of his promotion to second officer though his description of the countries he visited were invariably sketchy and he rarely mentioned his friends or the people he met. This letter was different; Tom was in love. He wrote that for the last few months he had been working on a ship that ferried coal to the Channel Islands and it was here that he had met Kitty, a girl from St Helier in Jersey. He described her as perfect in every way and he couldn't believe his luck when this paragon of virtue accepted his proposal of marriage.

"Mother, Tom's got engaged," said Dora.

Enid had just come into the kitchen and was pouring herself a cup of tea. "What, Thomas is to be married? Good gracious, isn't the boy a bit young to be thinking of that?"

"Tom's almost twenty-three," said Dora, getting up. "Well, I must get off to work."

She turned in the doorway. "Remember, I'll be out for a couple of hours this evening."

"Where are you going?"

"To meet Feathy's fiancé."

"What, Miss Featherstone is getting married?"

"Yes. It seems that romance is in the air!" said Dora with a grin.

"Romance, huh! More like an excuse for you to go gadding about."

"That's not fair. I don't get much of a social life."

"But what about me; how am I supposed to fill my evening?"

"That's really up to you," said Dora, putting on her gloves.

"Well, where is my piano then?" said Enid. "You know how I like to play in the evening."

"We didn't bring it here when we moved. Perhaps you've forgotten but it was sold with the rest of the contents."

Enid stepped across the room and glared at Dora. "You mean you sold my piano without even consulting me?"

"It was your decision, Mother."

"That's a lie, I would never have agreed to part with one of the few things that give me pleasure; but that's typical of you. I suppose you sold it and pocketed the money, is that what you did?" said Enid, her eyes flashing dangerously.

"What you're saying is crazy, do try and calm down."

"You are the one who is crazy and wicked too, you heartless ungrateful child! You deprive me of everything that makes me happy!" Enid shouted shrilly.

Wilf pawed at Dora's leg and she scooped him up in her arms. "I'm going to take Wilf round to the Simmons, I shan't leave him here with you in this mood."

As suddenly as it had erupted Enid's temper left her and she turned tearful. Dora put Wilf on the floor and helped Enid back to her chair, then took the laudanum from the cupboard, poured a measure into a glass and added water.

"Now drink this up and you'll soon feel better," said Dora, handing her the glass.

"I don't think you know how lonely it is here, Dora. I want to go home."

"Yes, yes, I know," said Dora, patting her shoulder. "Now why don't you play a game of Patience?"

She fetched the pack of cards from the sideboard and handed them to her, waiting until Enid began arranging them on the table.

Miss Gates had declined Feathy's invitation on the grounds that a public house was not a place for respectable ladies so Dora and Brenda arranged to go together. At first Dora didn't recognise Brenda as she approached down the street. Her hair had been cut into a flattering bob and she was wearing a dress in a shade that emphasised the blue of the eyes; some carefully applied lipstick, powder and touch of rouge completed the transformation.

"Brenda, you look lovely!" said Dora.

Brenda smiled shyly. "I've just been to the hairdressers."

Dora took her arm and they walked off along the pavement. "My Terry's ever so much better now he's working at his carpentry again and he's stopped paying attention to them that like to stare."

"Who is he working for?" asked Dora.

"For himself. A few months ago a neighbour asked him to repair a doll's house and now he's started making them from scratch, his own designs and all. You really must come and see them, Dora, they're ever so lovely."

The George Inn was formerly a coaching house and although now lit by electricity it retained the features and atmosphere of a bygone age. The oak beamed room thronged with people and Dora couldn't see Feathy but she spotted her father chatting to two young boys by the fireplace. Bert was just introducing Dora and Brenda to Arthur's boys, when Feathy appeared with a stout, middle aged man on her arm.

"This is my Arthur," she said proudly, her brown eyes sparkling.

Arthur had a broad, open face and ready smile, the kind of man you felt you could trust. In response to Brenda's interrogation Arthur told them that he was employed as chief constable at the local constabulary and later, when Feathy was showing them her engagement ring, she confided that a promotion was in the offing. Sergeant Bingley, the officer currently in charge at the station, was soon to retire.

*

At Madame's request Dora had inspected the shop's ledgers and afterward suggested how the accounts could be kept more efficiently.

"Then what about you taking over the books, Miss Jamieson?" said Madame.

"I wouldn't like to put Mr Higgins out of a job," said Dora, looking up from ledger she was reading.

"High time the old bloke was retired," said Madame.

"Er... would that... mean a wage raise, Madame?"

Madame was taken aback by Dora's boldness and thought for a moment. "I might remind you that I shelved out a lot of cash for them classes."

"Even so, it's a lot of extra work."

Madame was beginning to realise how stubborn the girl could be. "Very well, let's say an extra half crown in your pay packet."

Dora worked diligently on the accounts, implementing innovative cost effective measures that improved the business turnover and earned Madame's respect. Dora told no-one of her salary raise and each week she stowed away the extra cash in the post office.

One day, Madame came into the office when Dora was working on the ledgers and complained that Feathy was behind with the orders.

"What's got into her and made her so workshy?" she asked in frustration.

The fact was that Feathy had abandoned her old habits and was no longer willing to spend extra hours in the workroom. Charlie and Tim were now living with their father and went to Feathy's house after school where her father took care of them until his daughter's return. Madame Morel might sigh and look aggrieved but Feathy paid no attention. 'I'm off to make tea for the boys' she'd say, leaving promptly at five thirty each day.

In his latest letter Tom had invited Dora to come to visit him in Jersey and by a happy coincidence, the shop's two-week closure in August was at the same time as his leave. Dora was excited to be going on her first trip away since those days of visiting Aunt Hettie in Devon and dipped into the savings to pay for traveling expenses and new clothing. Feathy cut out patterns from the fabrics obtained from the market stalls and Dora stitched them on the sewing machine after work. Occasionally she found useful remnants in the oddments box, one of them sufficient to make into a bolero and others into scarves and decorative trimmings.

She had thought long and hard about making the trip and it had taken the reassuring voice of Mrs Simmons and the support of Dr Morton to persuade her that her mother would come to no harm in her absence. On the day before her departure, Enid watched Dora pack her clothes into a suit case.

"I can't imagine why you'd want to travel abroad on your own. You could encounter all kinds of dangers," she said.

"Jersey is in the Channel Islands, Mother. It's part of the British Isles."

"Well, whatever, it's still foreign," said Enid petulantly. "In my day no well-bred girl would travel alone, it's asking for trouble!"

Though her request to accompany Dora had been refused point blank; Enid was convinced that Dora would relent and watched tight lipped as she closed the suitcase and fastened the latch.

Chapter 15

Tom was waiting on the quayside as Dora came off the ferry. Beside him stood a petite girl with bobbed blonde hair and wide blue eyes. Kitty Beaumont stepped forward and reached up to kiss Dora's cheek. She was little over five feet tall.

"Oh, at last!" she laughed. "I've heard so much about you."

Kitty reminded Dora of one of Lizzie's dolls and it was easy to see why Tom had fallen in love with her. Wilf, waiting patiently beside Dora on a lead, looked up at Kitty quizzically and as she bent down to pet him Dora turned to Tom anxiously. "You did say the landlady doesn't mind having him, didn't you?"

"No need to worry, Dor, there's a perfectly good kennels down the road."

"Take no notice, Dora, it's all arranged. And you just behave yourself, you horrible tease!" said Kitty, thumping Tom playfully on the chest.

After the taxi took Kitty home Dora and Tom were driven to the guest house and after depositing her suitcase there they took Wilf for a walk.

"We've been invited to dine with Kitty's parents," said Tom as they strolled along the seafront.

"What, this evening?"

"No need to get jittery, Dor. You'll love them. They remind me of Aunt Hettie and Uncle Alfred, though without the eccentricities. Just don't mention anything about Kitty and me. Our engagement isn't yet official."

"Oh?"

"I haven't talked to Kitty's father yet, you see. To tell you the truth, I'm a bit apprehensive. A second officer in the merchant navy isn't the best catch in the world, Kitty could do much better."

"And she could do a lot worse, Tom," said Dora, "Kitty looks like the kind of girl who knows her own mind."

The Beaumont home was a large Victorian villa situated high up in the hills and when Dora and Tom climbed up the steep lane that evening he told her about Kitty's brother.

"Lucas died in the war, his battalion got blown up in the trenches and his body was never recovered."

Dora stopped for a moment to catch her breath. Such stories were all too common yet never failed to shock.

Tom took her arm and they carried on walking. "I thought it best you knew before meeting the family."

Rose and Hugo Beaumont received Dora with a genuine display of pleasure, including her in the affectionate welcome they bestowed upon Tom.

"It's so lovely to meet you, Dora," said Rose, kissing Dora's cheek and fussing over her with motherly concern, inquiring about her journey and general well-being before taking her arm and leading her into the drawing room.

"Now you must come and meet our neighbours, Clarissa and Charles Ainsley," she said, gesturing to the well-dressed couple chatting by the window. "They have a house on the island."

Charles, a tall good looking man in his early sixties, took Dora's hand in a firm handshake. "Welcome to Jersey, my dear," he said, with a friendly smile.

Clarissa's greeting was more reserved; a cool appraising glance and brief handshake before turning her head to address her hostess.

Charles had just begun describing the highlights of Jersey to Dora when a tall, fair haired young man came in through the French windows.

"Ah, here's Nicholas, my son," he said, turning to introduce him. "Nicky can tell you everything about the island. He's been coming here since he was a boy."

Nicky's striking good looks took Dora off guard and an annoying flush crept up her neck but he had such a winning manner and unaffected charm that she quickly regained her composure. When Tom spotted Nicky he came over to speak to him and Dora noticed the familiarity of their greeting. She watched Tom and Kitty slip out through the French windows.

"You know my brother then?" she asked.

"Yes. We met at a party at the yacht club last summer. It was the same evening that Kitty met him. She saw me chatting to Tom and asked me to introduce them. She told me later that it was love at first sight!" he said with a chuckle.

Dora laughed. "She seems a very sweet girl."

"Oh, yes. I've known Kitty since she was small, her brother and I were good friends."

A manservant appeared with a tray of cocktails. "Let's take these outside," said Nicky, picking up two glasses. "You really must come and see the view. Dinner's served late here, they follow the French tradition."

Dora followed Nicky out to the terrace and saw Tom and Kitty seated under an apple tree, gazing at each other and talking intimately. Nicky put down their drinks on a table and they took seats on the wrought iron chairs. The terrace offered a spectacular panorama of St Auben's Bay, the low sun on the horizon bathing the water in a bright orange glow and for a few minutes they sat in companionable silence.

"That castle belongs in a fairy tale," said Dora, looking across at the medieval building that nestled in the bay.

"That's Queen Elizabeth castle, Sir Walter Raleigh named it for his queen."

He told her how Raleigh had once been Governor in Jersey and prompted by Dora's interest he related other noteworthy events, peppering them with racy anecdotes.

"If you have an interest in history, you've come to the right place, Dora. These islands are full of antiquity and legend."

Following dinner, the males of the party remained at the table whilst the ladies retired to the drawing room where Dora took a seat next to Kitty and observed the two older women seated opposite. Rose and Clarissa were an incongruous pair with nothing in common except for the fact that their husbands belonged to the yacht club and regularly went sailing together. Rose was a plump, fair haired matronly woman whilst Clarissa was dark-haired and slender with a well preserved complexion enhanced by her artfully applied cosmetics. From the top of her perfectly coiffed head to the tips of her stylish shoes Clarissa exuded sophistication.

While the girls were chatting together Dora overheard Clarissa discussing her son Nicky and pricked up her ears.

"Will Nicky be here for the whole summer, Clarissa?" asked Rose.

"Yes, I believe so, Rose. Nicholas doesn't return to university until the autumn," said Clarissa.

"The academic life seems to suit him," said Rose.

"If only his studies hadn't been interrupted by the war Nicholas would have embarked upon a career by now. Time's slipping by and it's high time he took his place in society."

Rose poured out coffee and handed a cup to Dora. "That's a very pretty frock you're wearing, Dora," she said.

"Dora works in the business, Mama. She was just telling me she designed it herself," said Kitty.

"What a clever girl you are, Dora," said Rose.

Clarissa looked across at Dora with a cool, appraising eye. "So you work for a living do you, Miss Jamieson?"

Dora nodded. She could imagine the haughty woman's disdain if she told her how she had haggled over the price of the green silk fabric on the market stall and had no intention of letting her know that she worked in a shop.

"Weather permitting, we're heading for the Isle of Sark tomorrow," said Tom as he walked with Dora back to the guest house.

"Is that one of those tiny islands you can barely see on the map?"

"Uh huh, Sark is only about two miles wide and allows no motor cars; Kitty says we'll love it. I think she's got something planned for every day of your visit!"

"How very kind of her."

"By the way, Kitty's invited Nicky along tomorrow."

Dora's heart missed a beat. "Oh?"

"Kitty insists he knows the island well and will be an excellent guide. I hope you don't mind, Nicky's a good chap."

"Yes, I'm sure he is."

Seabirds wheeled overhead as the little boat skimmed across the turquoise bay and with the wind whipping at her hair, Dora gazed at the dramatic spectacle of towering cliffs and verdant land that lay ahead.

"Welcome to the most peaceful spot of earth, the Isle of Sark," Nicky announced.

It was his suggestion to hire one of the horse-drawn carriages to tour the island and as the little horse trotted along the winding lanes he pointed out places of interest and commented on the ragged coastline's ever changing rock formations. However, Pierre, their French speaking driver, insisted upon regaling them with his own commentary in a dialect so guttural and jarring that no-one could understand.

As the little carriage approached the high narrow causeway that led to Little Sark at the southernmost point of the island, Kitty stood up and, addressing him in French, she asked Pierre to desist. Muttering something indecipherable he jerked on the reins and the little horse shot forward, jolting the carriage and unbalancing Kitty. Tom gasped in horror at the deep ravine below them and grabbed at Kitty.

She fell into his lap and burst into laughter. "I'm afraid Pierre prefers things done his own way!"

Kitty's enthusiasm and laugher were infectious and an hour later, when they went to collect their rented bicycles, the little party were in high spirits though the peddle up the steep lanes was a sobering experience and only Wilf, running alongside, was undaunted by the challenge. At the ascent to the cliffs they dismounted and wheeled the bicycles up to a flat patch of scrub land. Below lay the sea and quickly stripping into their swimsuits they clambered down over the rocks and plunged into the water.

The sea was clear and calm and the four of them swam out for several hundred yards, then Tom and Kitty disappeared into a cave and Dora followed Nicholas out of the water. As he reached down a hand to help her over the rocks she saw a long deep scar across his left shoulder blade that she hadn't noticed before.

As she settled down on the picnic rug damp tendrils of hair cascaded down to her shoulders.

Nicky smiled down at her. "You look like a mermaid who's lost her tail!"

"I'd never be that careless!" she laughed.

Nicky's body was lithe and tanned and she eyed him covertly as he bent to take a drink from the hamper. She had never seen a man undressed and was astonished by such masculine beauty. He handed her a glass of lemonade and when he came to sit down beside her they began chatting and she discovered he was studying for a PhD in archaeology at Cambridge.

"Your mother said you went back after the war," said Dora.

He nodded. "I was one of the lucky ones, Dora, a lot of my chums weren't so fortunate."

"You were wounded though?"

"You mean this old scar," he said, glancing at his shoulder with a shrug. "If you didn't get killed they patched you up and sent you back. But let's not talk about the war, not today, I'd rather talk about you and those glorious copper highlights you have in your hair."

Dora laughed. "That must be a trick of the light, my hair is brown!"

"You are a very beautiful girl, Dora, and that is no trick of the light!"

*

Kitty stared into the shop window. "Oh, look, Dora. Isn't that elegant! No froth and frills. That's exactly what I have in mind."

Dora stared at the bridal gown displayed in the window of the departmental store and nodded in approval. It was in heavy cream silk that hugged the body and fluted out from just below the knee. The simplicity of the style would suit Kitty's small frame perfectly.

"To let you into a secret, Tom's speaking to Papa after lunch today."

"Ah, so that's why you wanted me out of the way, is it?"

Kitty laughed and shook her head. "No, of course not! It was Nicky who proposed taking you to Guernsey," she said, glancing at her watch. "We'd best get down to the ferry now else he'll think you've stood him up!"

Since their meeting Dora had seen Nicky daily but until they began strolling along the paths of Guernsey's pretty inland scenery it was the first time they had spent time alone since that brief interlude on Sark. The rugged coastline paths were not as easy to negotiate and as she followed him down one of the steep tracks she tripped on a rock and he reached out to catch her. Afterwards he kept hold of her hand and she was surprised at how natural the intimacy felt.

They stopped for lunch at a seafront restaurant and during a long leisurely meal they discussed a variety of topics and made each other laugh, exchanging memories of childhood holidays, Nicky's of Jersey with his sister and Dora's of Devonshire with Tom.

Nicky talked with such eloquence about his studies that Dora, who knew nothing about archaeology, discovered how engrossing the subject was.

"Dora, you're like a breath of fresh air!" he laughed. "When I get going on my hobby horse, I see eyes glaze over, especially girls', but you don't do that."

A waiter appeared and left the bill on the table. "We've got over two hours until we take the ferry so it's time we planned our afternoon," said Nicky, taking out his wallet.

"I'd like to see the house where Victor Hugo lived. I noticed a hoarding by the quayside; it said the house was open to visitors."

"Great idea! They say that Hauteville House is worth a visit," he said. "You know, I suspected you might have a literary bent."

"I read Victor Hugo in sixth form."

"I can imagine you as a blue stocking."

"I did once have hopes of applying to university but instead I ended up working in a dress shop."

"No shame in that, is there?"

"Perhaps not, though I doubt you're in the habit of taking out shop assistants!" said Dora with a rueful laugh.

"And aren't I fortunate to be in the company of the most intelligent and enchanting young woman a fellow could ever wish to meet."

Tom and Kitty's engagement was now official and on the last evening of Dora's visit Rose and Hugo held a party to celebrate the event, inviting a host of family friends and relatives. Tom's guests were some of the people he had made friends with since coming to the island, including Sammy Park, the harbour master. Sammy was a retired naval man with a ribald humour that Tom and the other men appeared to enjoy. As Dora watched Tom laughing at one of Sammy's risqué anecdotes it struck her how much he resembled their father.

When she went out to the terrace with Kitty and some of her girlfriends she saw Rose seated under the rose arbour chatting to her sister Diana. Rose beckoned her over and Diana left them to talk.

"It's a lovely party, Mrs Beaumont," said Dora, sitting down.

"Yes. But such a pity your mother couldn't be with us this evening," said Rose. "I do look forward to meeting her."

Dora nodded.

"Tom doesn't talk about her very much but I suppose that's men for you," said Rose. "Though of course he does sometimes mention his father."

"My father and Tom were close."

"Yes. It's very sad that your father left when you were both so young. It must have been hard for your mother, particularly when she had also lost her eldest son. I feel that I can empathize with her. I, too, lost a son in the war."

"I'm afraid my mother took little solace in her two remaining children. My brother Edwin was her favourite, you see."

"Grief can do funny things to a person," said Rose, giving Dora's hand a gentle squeeze. "You know, Dora, when Kitty first became so attached to Tom we did have some reservations. Kitty can be impetuous and she's still very young but the more we got to know your brother, the more we liked him and came to appreciate his steadiness."

"I'm glad to hear that," Dora smiled.

"I've been hoping to have a chat with you, Dora, because I wanted you to know about a proposition that we intend to put to Tom."

"Oh?"

"You see, we need a new manager for the dairy farm and Hugo believes that Tom has the right aptitude."

Dora glanced at her in surprise. "Oh, gosh! Tom would have to resign from his job."

Rose nodded. "That's entirely up to him but whatever his decision we plan to give them the farmhouse as a wedding gift... It's where Hugo and I lived when we were first married."

Dora could not begrudge Tom his good fortune but she did feel a sharp twinge of envy. Tom would be part of a loving and prosperous family, his future secure and full of promise.

Dora glanced up as Nicky came out to the terrace and walked over to them. She thought he looked exceedingly handsome in his formal cream suit.

Rose stood up. "Well, I'm sure that Nicky will keep you entertained," she said with a wink. "I must go and see how Cook is managing. We're having a buffet supper in the dining room."

"I'm so glad to find you on your own at last," he said, sitting down on the chair that Rose had vacated. He turned to face her. "I can't bear the thought of you leaving tomorrow."

"Nor me."

"Couldn't you wangle a few more days?"

Dora shook her head. "My mother's expecting me."

"You could send her a telegram and tell her you've been delayed?"

"I also have a job to go back to, Nicky."

"Yes, of course. Forgive my thoughtlessness."

He leaned forward and took one of her hands in both of his. "So when can I see you again?"

Dora hadn't dared speculate on the future. Nicky took his privileged background for granted and he seemed to have no conception of the yawning gap between them.

"Well, Dora, is there a lover at home; someone I don't know about?"

"No, Nicky, there's no-one," she smiled.

"Well, that's a relief!" he laughed. "I suppose you realise that you've stolen my heart."

Dora tingled with happiness. She loved this man with every fibre of her being.

"Oh, do say something, sweetheart, even if it is that you don't return my feelings."

Dora had never felt rush a rush of emotion. "Oh, but I do."

He had taken a diary from his pocket and was jotting down Dora's address when Kitty approached them.

"Oh, sorry, am I interrupting...?" she said.

"Could it wait, Kitty?" said Nicky.

"It's just that there's a chap who's been dying to meet Dora all evening. I promised him I'd find her."

"Then he'll just have to wait a bit longer, won't he?" said Nicky.

Kitty rolled her eyes and left.

"Look, sweetheart, I'll be back on the mainland by mid-September. Could we meet in London?"

Dora shook her head. "I work a five and a half day week, Sunday is my only day off."

"In that case I'll drive down to you. I'll be staying with my parents in London so it shouldn't take long and if I can get away earlier I shall, without you here the days will seem endless."

Chapter 16

The new autumn fashions had arrived and Dora was dressing the shop window when Jack Armstrong passed by. He stopped and doffed his hat to her.

"May I have a word?" he mouthed through the glass.

Dora stepped back into the shop and seeing that Madame was not around, she went outside to speak to him.

"Dora, it's good to see you again," he said, smiling.

She smiled back at him. "You, too, Jack."

"I trust you enjoyed your holiday."

"Oh, yes, it was amazing."

"Let's meet at the coffee shop after work. You can tell me all about it then."

Miss Gates stared at them through the doorway. She nodded to Jack and he doffed his hat to her. "I'll see you later, Dora."

It was less than a week since her return from Jersey but her days had been so busy that it felt like much longer. The household chores had piled up and after a day of cleaning the house from top to bottom Dora had returned to work.

"Well, well, what a whirlwind romance!" said Jack as he sat with Dora in the coffee shop later.

"Let's hope for your sake that the fellow is genuine."

"Yes, I think so."

Jack added sugar to his coffee and stirred the cup. "What do you know about his family?"

"His parents are Charles and Clarissa Ainsley, I met them, too."

"Hmm, that name rings a bell. Yes, I remember now, Mrs Charles Ainsley is often featured on the society pages. She works for charities, organizing events, gala affairs, that sort of thing."

"I can't imagine Mrs Ainsley working," said Dora with a smirk.

"Not work as we know it, Dora. Those events are all about social interaction. It's how women of that class fill their days."

"I can't say I cared for her much."

"Most of those society women are dreadful snobs so if you intend to see the son again you'd best be on guard."

"Yes, Jack. I shall."

"The upper classes have very little idea of how the rest of us live, you know, and when it comes down to it they stick to their own."

He topped up their coffee cups. "It sounds as though your brother has fallen on his feet; your mother must be glad."

"The only person she cares about is herself!" said Dora, her resentment spilling out before she could stop it. "I'm sorry, but Mother can be difficult."

Enid had taken the news of Tom's good fortune with her usual acerbity. "Hmm, it sounds like Thomas has been ingratiating himself with these people. The boy's got his father's gift of the gab," she had said.

"Oh, for goodness' sake! Tom is your son, surely you must wish him well," Dora had replied.

"Fat lot of help that boy has been."

"But he sends us money whenever he can!"

"Huh! And how often is that? For all he cares we could starve!"

"You aren't alone there, Dora," Jack said with a wink. "I love my mother dearly but sometimes her possessiveness drives me to distraction!"

"Well, you are her only child; I suppose that makes you special!"

"That's better," he said. "You look lovely when you smile."

A few days later Dora received a letter from Tom but the longed for letter from Nicky did not materialize. Tom's letter was longer than usual and she scanned it quickly, there were loving messages from Kitty and her parents but no mention of Nicky. Days passed and when still no word came she began to question his sincerity. Had the spark between them existed in reality? These thoughts were passing through her mind as she walked down the high street and bumped into Jack coming out of his shop.

"Ah, Dora, I was hoping to catch you. A client has just offered me some theatre tickets for a West End production he's involved in and I wondered whether you'd accompany me?"

"Yes. Thank you, Jack. I'd love to."

"Good. I'll see if I can get them for next Saturday week."

Dora had been returning from an errand for Madame and didn't have time to stop and chat. "Sounds lovely; sorry, Jack, I've got to go," she said and hurried off down the street.

That evening when she entered the house she was met by an acrid smell. "Mother, where are you?" she called and hurried into the kitchen, an agitated Wilf at her heels.

The room was filled with smoke and it took a few moments to locate the blackened pan of potatoes on the gas stove. She grabbed at the pan and the smouldering tea towel beside it, threw them into the sink and opened the window.

She found her mother dozing in the parlour. "For goodness sake, Mother, have you lost your sense of smell?"

Enid looked up in bemusement. "Whatever's the matter?"

"You could have set fire to the kitchen."

"Oh, yes, I thought I'd make a start on the supper."

"But you left the potatoes to burn," said Dora, glancing around the untidy room in irritation.

It took Dora the best part of two hours to clear up the mess and then she took Wilf out for some exercise. The day had been sultry and the air was hazy with midges and the left over heat. Beyond the park the late summer sun hung low in a muted pink sky, reminding her of that other sunset the evening she had met Nicky. The puzzle of his silence was becoming a torment, she had after all known him for such a short time and without a yardstick it was impossible to gauge his intentions.

By the time they returned home Enid had retired to bed and, with an unexpected surge of energy, Dora decided to tidy up the parlour. She picked up the magazines and papers that littered the floor and as she stacked them up with those on the sideboard, she came across an envelope addressed to her. The elegant sloped hand writing was not familiar and she ripped it open with trembling hands.

'Dearest girl,' it said. 'You have only been gone for twenty-four hours and already I'm missing you. It is as though a light has gone out on this island. Please write and tell me how you are. I plan to come home a week early as I must see you soon.

Yours ever, Nicky.'

Dora didn't believe that her mother would have hidden the letter deliberately, she had no reason to. Nevertheless, she decided that she could save herself any future heartache by fitting a lock to the post box.

On Monday morning of the following week Jack was standing outside the shop as Dora arrived for work. It had just begun to rain and Miss Gates opened the door.

"Oh, Mr Armstrong," she smiled. "Do come in out of the wet."

"Just for a moment, thank you," said Jack.

He turned to Dora. "I just came to tell you that I have the theatre tickets for Saturday."

Dora stared at him blankly. She had forgotten all about his invitation.

"Oh, what is the production, Mr Armstrong?" asked Miss Gates.

"The Revue at the Criterion, it's supposed to be good," said Jack. "Well, if you'll forgive me, I'm in rather a rush. I have to be at the Hammersmith shop this week."

He walked to the door. "Well, good day to you, ladies."

Miss Gates gazed after him; doe eyed then turned to Dora with a frown.

Two days later a telegram arrived. Enid hadn't handled a telegram since receiving the one that had related the news

144

of Edwin's death and she held it out to Dora with trembling hands.

"The boy from the telegraph office brought it this morning. I didn't dare open it."

Dora patted her shoulder. "There's nothing to be worried about, Mother. Look, it's addressed to me."

Enid was wringing her hands as she waited for Dora to read the contents.

"Oh, it's wonderful news! Nicky will be in London tomorrow and he's coming here on Saturday."

"Who's coming?"

"Nicky. I told you I met him in Jersey."

"Yes, of course I remember, you mean that young man you met on holiday."

"Yes, Mother, Nicky!" Dora laughed.

"Well, I'm glad for you, love. It's high time you had a nice beau," said Feathy in the work shop the next day."

"Keep it to yourself, Feathy, would you?" said Dora.

"My lips are sealed, Dora, but hang on a minute, don't you have a theatre invitation for Saturday?"

"Oh God, of course! What on earth am I going to tell Jack?"

"Tell him the truth. In the circumstances I'm sure he'll understand."

After work Dora went round to the opticians and met Ernest Humphries, Jack's partner, a short grey haired man with a kindly face. He took Dora's note with a smile and as she turned to leave a tall, heavy set woman appeared from the back.

"Oh, it's Miss Jamieson, if I'm not mistaken," she said, eyeing Dora suspiciously.

Dora stared a moment before realising that she must be Jack's mother. "Yes," Dora nodded. "Good evening, Mrs Armstrong."

"I hope that Mr Humphries has been able to assist you."

Dora was aware of the woman's exacting eyes scrutinizing her as she explained the purpose of the visit.

"I will ensure that my son receives your message, Miss Jamieson," she said coldly.

"Thank you very much. Well, I won't take up any more of your time," said Dora and hastily retreated.

Earlier that day Emily had dropped by the shop to tell Dora that she was back for a few days, and after returning home to collect Wilf, Dora took him with her to visit the Morton house.

"So you've finally bagged yourself a toff!" said Emily, chuckling.

Hilary Morton held the tea pot mid-air and glanced across the kitchen table at her daughter. "Emily, don't be so uncouth."

She poured out the tea and handed a cup to Dora. "I think your friend Nicholas sounds very charming and we all look forward to meeting him."

"Why don't you bring him for supper on Saturday, Dor?" said Emily.

"Yes, that's a good idea," said Mrs Morton. "Uncle Reggie's coming and Donald will be here with Glenda so the evening promises to be lively."

"You remember Glenda Stanton, don't you, Dor? You met her at that Christmas party," said Emily.

"What, Glenda, the suffragette?" said Dora.

Emily nodded. "Donald's been seeing her on the quiet all these years, would you believe it? He's such a dark horse."

"We've plenty of room if Nicholas would like to stay over-night, Dora. The twins don't have an ex-eat until next month," said Mrs Morton.

Dora was relieved that the nagging problem of how to entertain and accommodate Nicky was now resolved. With her habitual thoughtfulness Mrs Morton also included Enid in the dinner invitation, instructing her brother beforehand to pay her especial attention. She seated them together at the dinner table and Reggie rose to the challenge so admirably that Enid was in her element. Dora could never predict her mother's mercurial moods but that evening Enid had her wits about her and responded to Reggie's playful banter with the kind of enthusiasm that Dora hadn't witnessed in years. Enid had always been enlivened by a man's company and Dora, astonished at her transformation, wondered whether she might have benefited from more of it.

Around them the conversation buzzed, with Nicky a lively participant. Donald, who took a keen interest in archaeology, talked to Nicky at length, particularly in relation to Egyptology, a subject that had been brought to the public's attention by the extensive press coverage of the recent discovery of the tomb of Tutankhamen.

"I read that it's probably one of the most important finds ever," said Donald.

"I do believe so," said Nicky. "What makes it so extraordinary is that the tomb was found almost entirely intact. I plan to go out to Luxor to see King Tut for myself."

"Imagine that! A visit to the Valley of the Kings!" said Glenda.

"Yes, it's very exciting," said Nicky. "With any luck I'll be out there in the New Year."

Donald turned to Glenda sitting beside him. "What about us taking a tour there next year?"

"Oh, yes, Donald. That would be wonderful!" Glenda smiled.

Dora, who was seated nearby, saw her eyes light up when he murmured that they might make it their honeymoon destination.

Dora was gratified to see how well the Morton family had taken to Nicky. Even Emily appeared to find him a worthy conversant.

"I was just telling Nicky about a Roman villa I read about in the National Geographic," she said, turning to Dora. "Apparently they've excavated some amazing mosaics there. I believe it's a popular tourist destination."

"Yes, Bignor Palace is a place I've been meaning to visit, just haven't had the time," said Nicky.

"Well why not take Dora there tomorrow? You've got wheels, haven't you? West Sussex isn't so far," said Emily. "What do you say, Dor?"

"Yes, why not? I've never been to any Roman sites," said Dora. "Why don't you come with us, Em?"

Emily rolled her eyes. "You won't catch me playing gooseberry!"

After the long journey Dora took Wilf for some exercise and later when she went to find Nicky at the site he was waiting by the entrance. With him was an elderly, white haired gentleman whom he introduced as Professor Cummings, the curator. Only a handful of visitors had arrived that morning and the Professor was evidently glad of the opportunity to expound on his extensive knowledge of the excavations that had taken place since the villa's initial discovery.

They followed him past the crumbling walls and columns that had once formed the villa's courtyard and into one of the rooms that housed the mosaics. "And now I will leave you and return home for my luncheon," said the Professor, bidding them a courteous farewell.

"This floor is amazing," said Dora, staring at the intricate design of the colourful mosaics.

"Hard to believe when you look at it now but most of the tiles were scattered or broken," said Nicky. "Just imagine the hours of painstaking work to match up the fragments and then fit them into the pattern?"

"Hmm, like a very complex jigsaw."

He glanced at Dora and smiled to himself; at that moment her earnest expression was so endearing. Her receptiveness never failed to surprise him. There had been other girls in Nicky's life but none of them would have considered the idea of spending a Sunday visiting Roman antiquity, certainly not Camilla, the beautiful debutante he'd once been in love with. Dora was like no girl he had ever known.

Later, as they were finishing their sandwiches a sudden chill wind blew across the field where they were picnicking.

"I think we've seen the last of the sunshine today," said Nicky, looking up at the gathering clouds. "Time we were on our way."

He noticed her shiver as she bent to tidy up the picnic debris and he took off his jacket, draped it over her shoulders and wrapped his arms around her. Dora's head reached the top of his shoulder and with a contented sigh she rested it there.

"What a joy it is to be with you again," he whispered in her ear.

She looked up at him and smiled, wishing that this perfect day could go on for ever. He tipped her face towards his and covered it with gentle kisses and then his mouth found hers. He kissed her deeply and she kissed him back with a passion she didn't know she possessed.

Minutes passed before they drew apart. She released her hand from his and as she turned to finish her interrupted task he suddenly grabbed her around the waist and swung her off her feet.

"Stop! Put me down!" she giggled.

Nicky chuckled and before she could make further protest she was spinning round in circles.

When he dropped her back on the ground she fell against his chest, breathless with laughter.

Chapter 17

It was Monday morning and Madame looked irritable as she came out of her office. "Where is Miss Jamieson?" she asked Miss Gates.

"She's having her tea break, Madame," said Miss Gates.

"Then get her, immediately!"

Dora appeared a few minutes later looking contrite. She'd been chatting to Feathy and knew her break had been overlong.

"I have told you before that I won't have my employees wasting their working hours in idle gossip. You can do that in your own time."

"Yes, Madame."

"Now where are those invoices? I told you I wanted them on my desk first thing."

"They'll be ready directly," said Dora.

"Well, don't keep me waiting again," said Madame.

As Dora walked across to the office, she noticed the smirk of Miss Gates's face.

"Tiresome girl!" said Madame.

Miss Gates sighed. "Girls these days can be so flighty."

Madame looked at her sharply. "Is there something I should know about, Miss Gates?"

"Well, I don't like to tell tales but Miss Jamieson did leave work early on Saturday, a good forty-five minutes as I recall," said Miss Gates.

"As my most senior and responsible employee it's your duty to report such lapses, Miss Gates. Make sure it's entered in the day book," said Madame.

Miss Gates smiled ingratiatingly. "Yes, Madame."

"It's good to know there is someone I can rely upon," Madame nodded. "In the coming weeks I shall be out more often, what with my aunt being laid up in the hospital, and in my absence I should like you to act as my deputy. You may inform the others of my decision."

The following morning when Dora appeared ten minutes late Miss Gates wasted no time in asserting that authority.

She stepped forward as Dora walked through the door. "You are supposed to be here at eight thirty sharp, Miss Jamieson."

"I had to go to the pharmacy, Miss Gates. My mother has one of her migraines," said Dora.

"Personal errands should take place outside working hours, Miss Jamieson."

Feathy was seated in front of the sewing machine when Dora entered the work shop. "Miss Gates is certainly asserting her authority," said Dora, hanging up her coat.

"If she wants to lord it over us, let her be, Dor. She's not got much else in her sad little life," said Feathy with a chuckle.

When Dora went into the shop front afterward, Miss Gates was checking an order that had just arrived. "Would you like me to help?"

Miss Gates nodded and pointed at the pile of creased blouses. "You can take these to the work room and give them a good press."

She stepped across to the door and turned around the placard to 'open'.

"Oh, by the way, Miss Jamieson, Mr Armstrong passed by just now. He wasn't his usual self at all, didn't even look in."

Dora said nothing. Jack's habits were not her concern.

"It's no wonder really. What gentleman would take kindly to being stood up by a chit of...by a young woman as he was?"

"What is it you're trying to say, Miss Gates?"

"Come now, Miss Jamieson, you know very well that it was you."

"I don't think it's any of your business, Miss Gates," said Dora, picking up the blouses and striding off.

Feathy glanced across at Dora as she slammed down the iron on a silk sleeve. "Steady there, girl, you'll burn a hole in it!"

"But Feathy, how on earth does she even know?"

"Oh, that's easy. Her mum and his are thick as thieves."

"So Mrs Armstrong read my note. What a nerve!"

"And old Mrs Gates loves a bit of gossip."

"Oh, dear, I'd better go and talk to Jack; I didn't mean to offend him."

"'Course you didn't. Still, you'd best watch your back, love; looks like Priscilla Gates' has got it in for you."

Dora went to see Jack before going home that evening. Mr Humphries was leaving the shop as Dora entered and greeted her with a smile. Jack was bent over the reception desk sorting through some papers.

"Hello, Jack. How are you?"

Jack raised his head and looked her up and down. "Good evening, Dora."

"I'm so sorry about last Saturday."

Jack nodded. He didn't mention that his client had proved elusive and he had gone to great lengths to acquire the tickets for that evening and he didn't intend to let her off too lightly.

"Yes, Dora. I was disappointed you couldn't come. You missed an excellent show."

"I'm sorry that it was such short notice."

"Yes. That was regrettable."

"I thought you might have invited Miss Gates."

Jack frowned. "Miss Gates?"

"You know Miss Gates, Jack. She works with me in the shop."

He grunted. "Should I have wished to invite Miss Gates I would have done so in the first place. It was you Dora whom I chose to invite."

Dora paused a moment. "Well, um, perhaps we could go another time?"

He appraised her silently; from the top of her head to the tip of her shoes. "Maybe, so long we can guarantee your availability on the next occasion."

A few days later a letter from Nicky awaited Dora in the padlocked mail box. He said he was shortly returning to

Cambridge and wanted to make plans for their next meeting, then went on to say that an old school friend called Jonathan had invited them for a week-end at his parents' home in Sussex and, if she was agreeable, he'd drive over and collect her on the Saturday.

On her next half day off, Dora took the bus to Petticoat Lane Market in the East End to buy fabric to replenish her autumn wardrobe. Nicky's friends would be smart and she didn't want to look too provincial. She pushed her way through the bustling market until reaching her favourite stalls and having selected her fabrics she was on the way to catch the bus home when she was caught in a sudden downpour of rain. She rushed for shelter under a cafe awning and with the rain continuing to fall heavily she went inside for a cup of tea.

Immediately she spotted Madame Morel in one of the booths seated opposite a balding middle aged man. She was about to make a hasty retreat when someone pushed past her and she ducked down into the adjoining booth. She was close enough to overhear their conversation and judging by its intimacy the couple were well acquainted. The man's voice was deep and guttural and he spoke in a mixture of cockney and a foreign accent that Dora couldn't place. Madame's speech was peppered with cockney colloquialisms and sounded quite alien to the careful diction she employed in the work place.

She heard a shuffle as the pair got up and walked toward the exit. As they passed she noticed the man aim an affectionate slap on Madame's ample bottom and heard her exclaim. "Oh, you saucy bugger! Just you wait till I get you back!"

Tears of laughter poured down Feathy's face as she listened to Dora's account of the incident. Dora had kept Madame's secret to herself until she and Feathy were away from the shop and walking together along the street.

"Doesn't surprise me, not one bit," said Feathy, mopping her face with a handkerchief. "The sudden appearance of an ancient aunt cut no ice with me!"

Dora was surprised that Madame didn't contest her request to take the Saturday afternoon off and she speculated as to whether Madame's magnanimity could be attributed to her foreign suitor.

"You off somewhere nice come Saturday, Miss Jamieson?" inquired Miss Gates, smiling at Dora for the first time in weeks.

"Yes, Miss Gates. I'm seeing a friend," said Dora.

"A young man, eh?"

Dora nodded.

"Well, I'm glad to hear that, Miss Jamieson. Mr Armstrong is a very nice man but he is a little old for you, don't you think?"

Chapter 18

Once again Dora was heading towards West Sussex seated beside Nicky in his smart green Austin. Their destination was a Tudor manor house on the outskirts of Arundel and by the time they located it Dora had become adept at map reading.

He glanced at her as he turned into the driveway. "By the way, Johnny's parents aren't here for the week-end so we'll have the house to ourselves," said Nicky, turning into the gravel driveway.

"That's good news," Dora smiled. She dreaded meeting a mother as intimidating as Clarissa Ainsley.

There was a lot of jovial back slapping when the friends with reunited. Jonathan had raffish dark looks and an engaging smile that reached his twinkling hazel eyes. Dora took an instant liking to Rachel, his girlfriend, a slender girl with large soft brown eyes and alabaster skin. While the two men were catching up on their news the girls found plenty to talk about, particularly on the topic of fashion.

When tea was served by a maid in the drawing room they were seated together and discussing Parisian trends.

"Of course, Coco Chanel is all the rage these days," said Rachel. "I went to see one of her shows with my mother when we were last in Paris, it was really spectacular."

"Oh, lucky you, I've seen her designs in Vogue; they're so innovative," said Dora. "Paris to me is like a dream."

"My mother insists upon at least one visit a year. She says that English women have no sense of style," said Rachel with a grin. "I'm sorry; I hope that doesn't sound offensive."

"No, I expect your mother's right," Dora laughed. "I assume that your family aren't English then?"

"My family are Jewish. They were originally from Berlin but I've lived here all my life."

Rachel was so open and easy to talk to that Dora was soon confiding about her job.

Rachel looked admiringly at the short skirted dress that Dora wore. "If you hadn't told me I'd have assumed that frock came from one of the Bond Street boutiques," she said.

"You're very kind," Dora smiled.

"I realise it must be jolly hard work but I'm rather envious of your independence."

"Then don't be, I only took the job out of necessity. I have to support my mother and myself."

"And I must seem like a very spoiled girl to you," she said with a grin. "But you know, Dora, wealth and privilege like mine may cushion one's life but it does have its drawbacks."

Dora was curious. Rachel's pretty oval face was framed by a sleek black bob, and with her looks alone, Dora had imagined that Rachel would have the world at her feet. "What sort of drawbacks?"

"Choice to lead your life as you want. Once I hoped to follow a career in journalism, but all I've written to date are a couple of banal articles for the Jewish Chronicle. That must be the limit of my ambitions, as far as my father is concerned."

"I thought attitudes to women were changing."

"Unlikely in my case; I'm a well brought up Jewish girl, you see, and I have to pay obeisance to my parents' beliefs. Unfortunately, my love of a gentile goes against the rules."

"So they don't know about you and Jonathan?"

She shook her head. "Johnny and I have been meeting illicitly. This week-end my parents think I'm staying with Miranda, a chum from my school days. You can't imagine the subterfuge it's taken for us to spend time together."

Dora watched Rachel's brown eyes gaze adoringly across the room to where Jonathan sat chatting to Nicky and hoped him worthy of such unconditional love.

"I'm sorry, Dora. We've only just met and here I am inflicting you with my problems."

After dinner that evening Jonathan produced some jazz records that he said came hot from America and put one on the gramophone. They pushed back the furniture and rolled up the Persian rug and then Jonathan and Rachel began dancing. Dora had heard jazz playing on the wireless but she had never seen the Charleston danced and she loved it, tapping her feet to the rhythm.

"Come on, you two. You must join us," Rachel called out to Dora and Nicky.

"But I don't know the steps," said Dora.

Rachel came over, took Dora by the hand and led Dora on to the parquet floor. "Here, let me show you."

Dora smiled at the sight of her nightdress the maid had laid out on the bed and was relieved she had thought to buy a new one. It was after midnight when they left the drawing room and after two hours of dancing Dora was tired, but just as she had settled into the comfortable bed, there was a knock on the door.

"Just came to check you were all right," said Nicky, standing in the doorway.

"Yes, I'm fine. Do you want to come in for a moment?" said Dora, sitting up.

She and Tom had always shared confidences at bedtime and without thinking she patted a space beside her and it wasn't until Nicky was making himself comfortable on the bed that she was suddenly abashed by the impropriety of her invitation but by then it was too late.

"I hope you enjoyed yourself this evening," said Nicky, slipping off his shoes and throwing them on the floor.

"Oh, yes, it was enormous fun. I really like your friends, particularly Rachel; I felt I had known her for ever."

"Yes, Johnny is crazy about her."

A strand of hair had fallen over her face and he reached across to tuck it behind her ear.

"Oh, God, how beautiful you are," he said, moving his hand to the back of her neck and running his fingers through her hair.

With his eyes were fixed on hers he drew her head towards him. It wasn't the first time they had shared a kiss but this time it was different. This had heat and weight and urgency. Through the thin fabric of her night gown his hands began caressing the contours of her body, arousing sensations so intoxicating that Dora lost all sense of time or place.

He had wanted her from that first day they met and the feel of her soft, responsive body beneath him made him shudder with desire and before all reason left him he wrenched him himself away. This wasn't what he had intended, not yet anyway and certainly not in this house where they were guests.

*

Dora reached out her hand to take his arm. "Nicky?"

"I should go," he whispered.

Through half closed eyes she saw him sit up and walk to the door.

"Sweet dreams, my love," he said and left.

The following morning Nicky was seated alone at the dining room table reading the Sunday Times. The door was ajar and for several minutes Dora stood looking at him from the doorway, her emotions in turmoil. She cringed at the memory of her brazen behaviour and was fearful of losing his regard. She turned to retreat but he spotted her and went across to the doorway.

"Good morning, my love," he said, kissing her cheek, and putting his arm around her waist he led her across to the array of breakfast dishes set out on the sideboard.

"Sorry we're late, folks. Hope you haven't been waiting," said Jonathan, walking jauntily into the room. "I'm afraid I couldn't get this young lady out of bed."

Rachel came up beside him and prodded his chest playfully. "That's so untrue," she laughed, seemingly unabashed by his blatant lack of discretion regarding their sleeping arrangements.

As they took their seats at the table, Mason, the manservant, came in with fresh pots of tea and coffee. He put them down on the table and turned to Jonathan. "Will that be all, Master Jonathan?"

Dora watched him walk away, impressed by his and the other the servants' unobtrusive presence. Apart from Smithson, the maid who had served tea the previous afternoon, there were other semi-invisible servants attending to the smooth running of the establishment and it was a revelation to Dora that Jonathan's parents would employ so many staff in a household they visited only sporadically.

Through the open French windows came a soft, warm breeze and Jonathan suggested they should take advantage of the fine weather by playing a game of tennis on the grass court. Neither of the girls had come prepared and when Dora heard him mention that there were stables on the estate she asked whether they might go there instead.

"Do you like horses, Dora?" Rachel asked as they walked across the orchard.

Dora nodded. "Yes, very much; I used to ride a lot."

"Then I daresay Johnny's mother would approve of you," said Rachel with a chuckle. "Apparently she's a very keen horsewoman. She keeps her own horse here; the others we'll meet are bred for racing."

As they approached the stable block a man came out of the tack room. He was a wiry and middle aged with a narrow whiskery face and dressed in a tweed jacket with corduroy trousers.

"Good morning," he said. "I'm Mike Rawlings, Mrs Delaware's trainer."

Rachel nodded. "I'm Rachel Klein," she said, reaching out a hand. "We're friends of Jonathan's."

He shook her hand, his steely gaze scrutinizing her face. "So you're staying at the house, are you, Miss Klein?" he said.

Rachel nodded and turned to introduce Dora. "Miss Jamieson has a great interest in horses so I've brought her along to see them."

"I'm not usually here on a Sunday but we've got the vet coming to look at a lame horse," he said. "But seeing as I'm here I'll show you around."

On either side of the yard's well-scrubbed brick flooring were rows of stalls, most of them occupied by thoroughbreds and Dora stopped to stroke several of the handsome heads as she strolled between Rachel and Mike down the yard. The stable block was impeccably maintained and appeared to contain every modern convenience for a horse's well-being.

Mike Rawlings was not a man for small talk though when Dora inquired about a particular horse he was more forthcoming and willing to impart his in-depth knowledge. As they reached the end of the block a young man with a tall black horse on a leading rein appeared in the yard and made his way towards them.

"Ah, here comes Dark Invader," said Mike and turned to the boy. "How did he go, Billy?"

The boy halted in front of him and stroked the horse's muzzle. "He was grand, sir. Just grand," the boy said, smiling.

"Old Dobbs will be along shortly. I'll get him to check up on the Invader's fetlock whilst he's here," said Mike.

A stable lad appeared from the other end of the yard and led the horse into his stall.

Dora turned to Mike. "Has he raced yet, Mr Rawlings?"

He shook his head. "Nope, not yet; we intend to enter him at Goodwood next season. We have high hopes for the Invader."

Dora thought of Archie and Mrs Jennings's rustic stable yard and smiled to herself, observing and memorizing everything she saw and learned. Mrs Jennings would want a full account of this visit and she herself would willingly have remained there for the rest of the day but then the vet arrived and it was time to leave.

They took a path through the woodland, its foliage tinged with golden hues, and had been walking some while when they came upon a rustic bench at the intersection and Dora suggested they take a rest.

Rachel sighed wistfully as she sat down.

"You look thoughtful Rachel, is there something you want to talk about?" said Dora, sitting down beside her.

Rachel nodded. "I'm ending it with Johnny, Dora."

Dora turned to her in surprise. "What?"

"I made a promise to myself that this would be the last time."

"Have you told him?"

Rachel shrugged. "He doesn't believe I'll do it. He thinks we should elope and to hell with the consequences."

"Is that such a bad idea?"

"Not if there wasn't so much at stake. Johnny has too much to lose; I don't think he understands quite how much."

"But I thought it was your family that stood in the way."

"Do you honestly imagine that his illustrious parents would welcome a Jewish girl into their family, no matter how rich her Papa might be?"

Dora stared at her a moment. "I'm so sorry to hear that."

"They'd cut him off, Dora."

"Surely it's the same for you?"

"To be honest, I think I could adapt better to a more modest lifestyle and so on, but what if later he had regrets? How could I compensate for the sacrifices he'd made for me? It could destroy his life."

She picked up a copper leaf and turned it over in her hand. "And I can't go on living with all the lies. I hate the way I've had to deceive everyone, particularly my parents. When I told my mother I was visiting my school friend Miranda again, she gave me a very strange look. I know she suspects something."

"Does Miranda know about Jonathan?"

"She does. Apart from you, Miranda's the only person I've confided in," said Rachel, picking off a leaf that had fallen on her arm. "She also knows that this is the last time she'll have to be involved in our little conspiracy."

Dora rested her hand on Rachel's for a moment.

"It isn't my first visit to the house, you know."

"Oh?"

"We usually find some discreet place in London to meet but Johnny does love coming here."

"The staff don't tittle-tattle?"

"Oh no, Johnny can do no wrong in their eyes. Most of them have known him since he was a child. Anyway, his parents don't mind him bringing friends here; it's only me they don't know about!"

She slipped her arm through Dora's as they began walking back along the woodland path.

"And what about you and Nicky?"

"I'm not sure. We haven't known each other very long."

"That isn't much of an answer!" Rachel laughed. "I knew Johnny was the man for me the day that we met."

"Then I confess, I am in love with Nicky."

"It's obvious that he's in love with you, too, the chemistry between you is palpable."

"It feels safer to live in the moment."

"That's how I've played it for over a year but life has a habit of nudging you forward."

Jonathan and Nicky were waiting for them at the house. "You've been gone for ages! We were beginning to think you'd got lost," said Jonathan.

Rachel laughed as he took her in his arms and until Dora and Nicky left that afternoon her mood remained buoyant with no hint of the momentous step she was about to take.

Nicky glanced at Dora seated in the passenger seat. "You're very quiet, sweetheart. Is there something the matter?"

He looked thoughtful as she repeated her conversation with Rachel in the woods.

"Oh, poor fellow!" he said as she finished. "This is going to hit him pretty hard."

"It's so terribly sad."

"Yes, it is, I wouldn't want to be in Johnny's shoes right now."

"Rachel says she wants us to keep in touch. Actually she's suggested I break the journey to Cambridge and spend the night with her in London."

"But that's a brilliant idea. God Bless Rachel!"

Chapter 19

Jack was walking past Madame Morel's shop as Dora came out of the door. "Oh, Dora. Good to see you again," he said.

Jack was smiling and seemed in a more amiable mood than at their last encounter. She thought she must be forgiven.

"Please would you join me at the coffee house?" he said.

"I should be getting home, Jack."

"There's something I'd like to discuss with you. It won't take long."

"Just half an hour then."

As they waited for their coffee to be served Dora gave an account of her visit to Arundel.

"Well, well," said Jack, smiling indulgently. "So you learned how to dance to the Charleston, did you?"

"Let's say I got the hang of it. Rachel's really good."

"The Jewish girl?"

"Yes."

"You know, it's probably just as well she's put an end to that relationship."

"I think it's a terrible shame."

"In the long run it's best to stick to your own kind. Personally I've no time for the race."

"Why's that, Jack?"

"You can't trust a Jew, Dora, everyone knows that."

Dora frowned. "If I'd known you were so prejudiced I'd never have told you about Rachel."

The coffee arrived on the table and he handed Dora the sugar bowl. "I didn't mean to upset you, Dora," he said.

She scowled at the sugar bowl.

"I'm sorry, Dora, if I spoke out of turn."

"Yes, Jack. You did."

"Well, forgive me. I've no doubt this young woman is an exception."

Dora stirred her coffee cup and shrugged.

"Now look, let me explain the reason I invited you here. My book-keeper's moving away, you see, and until I can replace him I was hoping you might help me out."

"Oh?"

"With the two shops to run, I just don't have much time. It could mean a little extra cash in your pocket."

Dora nodded, thinking of her trip to Cambridge and the expense that it would incur.

"It will only be a few hours a week, and if it's more convenient you could always take the books home with you."

"Yes. That might be best. My mother gets fretful if I leave her for long in the evenings. There's Wilf, too. I see so little of him."

Jack raised his eyebrows. "Wilf?"

"My dog."

Jack chuckled. "Oh, I thought you were referring to a young man! But yes, now I remember. You mean that little mutt who nipped at my ankles."

The following afternoon after work Dora went over to his shop and Jack showed her into the office and directed her to the seat behind the desk.

He pulled up a chair beside her and opened the ledgers on the desk. "I'll show you the system we use."

As he lent over he was so close that Dora could feel his breath on her neck and she edged away so that she could focus on what he was saying.

"Hmm, Yardley's Lily of the Valley, if I'm not mistaken." he said, as Dora was getting up to leave.

She glanced at him, surprised. "Um, yes."

"Very nice. It suits you."

"I could take the ledgers now if you like."

"Then the least I can do is to drive you home."

As Jack's car pulled up in Dora's street, Mrs Simmons came hurrying out of her house and walked towards the car.

"Is there something the matter, Mrs Simmons?" said Dora, getting out quickly.

"I don't want to alarm you, Dora, but this morning your poor Mum had one of memory lapses and took herself off to that street where you used to live," she said.

"Is she all right?"

Mrs Simmons nodded. "This good lady, someone new to the street, saw her standing outside the old home looking ever so confused so she called the police. Fortunately, the constable recognised your mum and brought her back."

"Oh, thank God for that," said Dora.

"Sarah was going to come and get you but once I got her settled into bed I thought it best to wait until you got back."

"That's very kind of you, Mrs Simmons. Thank you so much."

"To tell you the truth I feel I'm to blame 'cause instead of visiting her mid-morning as usual, I had to go over to see my sister-in-law," said Mrs Simmons.

"My mother isn't your responsibility, Mrs Simmons, and I can't thank you enough for your trouble."

Dora felt a hand on her arm. "Is there anything I can do, Dora?" said Jack.

"No, thank you, Jack," said Dora. "The important thing is that my mother is back, safe and sound."

"Our Sarah's down the park with young Wilf. I'll get her to bring him back later, once you've had a chance to sort yourself out."

"Thank you again, Mrs Simmons. You're a good friend," said Dora.

"Oh, it's nothing, Dora. I just try to be a good neighbour," said Mrs Simmons, turning to leave. "Well, you know where I am if you need me."

"I'll carry these in for you, Dora," said Jack.

Dora glanced dubiously at the ledgers he held, wondering when she would find the time for them.

Before work the following morning, Dora went round to Dr Morton's surgery and was fortunate enough to find him there before the arrival of his other patients.

"I'm glad you're here Dora, I had intended to visit you today," he said, looking up from the notes on his desk. "You see, I've just received the report regarding the results of the tests that were conducted on your mother."

170

"Oh?"

"I'm sorry to tell you that your mother is suffering from a form of senility."

"Will she get better?"

"I can't promise that."

Dora nodded. Her face was now ashen.

"Now, what about Tom? I think he should be made aware of the situation."

"I'll write and tell him."

"Good. You shouldn't have to shoulder the responsibility alone."

Dr Morton stood up as Dora got up to leave. "Try not to worry too much, Dora. I'll be keeping a good eye on your mother."

"Thank you, Dr Morton."

He gave her a hug. "Remember that my wife and I are here for you any time you need us."

*

Over the following weeks and much to Dora's relief there were no further incidents and Enid's mood remained relatively stable. Dora made an effort to spend more time with her, often whiling away an evening with the card games she liked. Looking after Jack's books was not such an onerous task and once or twice a week, after Enid was settled for the night, she worked on the books at the kitchen table.

Nicky's letters expressed his impatience to see her again and Mrs Simmons suggested to Dora that Sarah could stay with her mother for the week-end she wanted to go away. Once she had saved sufficient funds, Dora wrote to Rachel and purchased a train ticket to Cambridge.

Rachel met her at Paddington railway station and they took a cab back to her home in Highgate. Her pale, gaunt appearance was testament to the strain of recent weeks, which Dora would learn about later that evening. Rachel's parents had gone to celebrate the Shabbat with relatives and as the girls sat in the dining room eating the meal prepared by the family cook, Rachel related the events of the last weeks.

"When I came home that Sunday evening, I confessed everything to my mother," she said, "It was just as well too, because one evening two days later Johnny appeared on our doorstep. My father had just returned home and by then he was conversant of the situation and invited Johnny in. I was upstairs supposedly in my room but I hovered on the landing and heard raised voices coming from the drawing room. About ten minutes later there were footsteps in the hallway and I glimpsed Johnny walking out of the front door."

Rachel picked up her glass and took a large gulp of wine. "The offshoot of it is that I'm leaving for New York next week."

"New York!" Dora gasped. "But Rachel, that sounds like banishment. Does Johnny know?"

"Not yet. I've been forbidden to make any contact. He's sent me several letters that I managed to retrieve from the post box before my parents could intercept them. Perhaps I shouldn't have, they were agony to read." She looked across at Dora with dark anguished eyes. "He won't accept that it's over."

For a few moments they sat in silence. Dora toyed with the stem of her glass. "Why New York, Rachel?"

"My uncle and aunt live in Manhattan and my father wants me out of the way. To tell you the truth, it won't be so bad to leave this house. Even my brother Benjamin won't speak to me and we used to be close."

"Maybe Johnny will follow you there?"

"What, to New York?" said Rachel. "No, Dora. He won't know how to find me. New York is a big city."

"Won't you write to him?"

Rachel shook her head. "I promised my father to give it a year. I'm being a dutiful daughter, you see," she said, smiling ruefully.

Rain drizzled down when Dora embarked the train and by the time she reached Cambridge it was falling heavily. Nicky, armed with an umbrella, met her on the railway platform.

"I was planning to take you for a stroll round the city but I think we'd better head straight for the restaurant," he said, guiding her over the puddles and into his car.

He had booked a riverside table at a popular local restaurant for lunch and was greatly disappointed that the usually excellent view of the River Cam was obscured by the incessant sheets of rain. Dora was so happy to be with him that the state of the weather was of little consequence. He ordered a bottle of wine and as the waiter poured it into their glasses he told her that Jonathan had been to see him.

"We spent the evening in a pub and both got blind drunk. Johnny was pretty cut up. Apparently, Rachel's father telephoned his home and spoke to his father and then all hell broke loose, particularly after Johnny's mother learned from her horse trainer that he had entertained Rachel in their home."

"Oh, what a Judas! And to think I took a liking to the weasel!" said Dora indignantly.

She swore Nicky to secrecy before telling him about Rachel's imminent departure to New York.

"Maybe it's for the best," said Nicky.

"How can you say that?" said Dora.

"Don't take this so personally, sweetheart."

"It's difficult not to, it seems so unfair, Nicky."

"But who knows what may happen in a year's time?"

Dora was impressed by Nicky's spacious and well-appointed accommodation. "What a beautiful apartment!" she exclaimed.

"Yes, I was lucky to find it," he said, carrying her bag into one of the bedrooms. "I'll probably sub-let while I'm away."

Dora followed him into the room. "Away where?"

"That's something I want to talk to you about. Let's go and sit down."

She followed him into the living room and seated herself beside him on the large squashy sofa. "You remember that I applied to join Carter's excavations in Egypt?"

Dora nodded. "Oh, yes, the tomb of Tutankhamen, how could I forget that!"

"Well, at last I've been given the go ahead."

"Oh, Nicky; you must be thrilled."

"Yes, I'm really pleased," he said, then turned to face her. "The downside is that I'll be away for three months."

"Three months?"

"Yes, I'm afraid so." He took her hands in his. "But, look sweetheart, I won't be leaving until the New Year and once I'm back in London for Christmas we'll have lots of time to see each other."

"And then you'll be gone!"

He reached out his arm and pulled her closer. "And I'll miss you, my love; miss you more than I can say."

Tears had welled in her eyes and she pulled out a handkerchief to blow her nose.

"Three months is hardly a life-time; it'll pass in a flash."

She nodded and smiled, not wanting to spoil the precious time by telling him about the terrible sense of foreboding that had gripped her. As he gently stroked her neck and kissed her damp cheeks she abandoned herself to the magic of the moment, and to all those that followed.

"Oh, my God, what time is it?" Dora heard Nicky mutter.

She opened her eyes and saw him get off the bed and walk across to the window. Outside it was dark and the rain continued to lash at the windows. He sat down on the bed and looked down at her.

"Is it night already?" she said. "I must have fallen asleep."

"You just stay where you are. I'm going to get us something to eat."

He kissed her lightly on the forehead and disappeared. She stretched languidly in the bed with a sigh of contentment.

He chuckled at the sight of Dora coming into the kitchen wrapped in his over large dressing gown.

"Oh, my! What a feast!" she said, staring in surprise at the tempting collation laid out on the pine table; cold meats, pies, cheeses and a loaf of crusty bread.

She sat down on the chair Nicky held out for her. "I've a suspicion you had all this planned."

"If I'd had the foresight it would have been champagne and caviar," he said, taking a seat opposite. "As it happens, the housekeeper, Mrs Desmond, takes rather good care of me. She keeps the larder very well stocked."

"My goodness, you're spoiled!" Dora grinned, and helping herself to a slice of game pie.

"Yes, I probably am spoiled, certainly more than I deserve," he chuckled. "Though having a housekeeper is no real substitute for a wife."

Dora looked at him quizzically. "You want to get married?"

"Of course I do. I've had to wait long enough to meet the right girl."

"Are you saying that you've found her?"

He reached across and clasped her hand. "Yes, Dora, I am, and all I'm praying is that she'll wait for me. Three months isn't such a long time, is it?"

It wasn't until mid-morning that the rain had finally cleared and they set off on a brief a tour around the ancient cloisters and courtyards of King's College. Dora had seen photographs in library books but they didn't capture the mystic ambiance, nor the timeless grandeur of the Gothic architecture.

Later, they walked down to the Cam and stopped for a few minutes on Clare Bridge.

"It's so beautiful here," said Dora, watching the gently flowing river.

He put an arm around her. "Next summer we'll go punting. I think you'd enjoy that."

"You'll be here next year?"

"With any luck. I think my future lies here and I hope you'll come to love it as much as I do."

Chapter 20

Feathy's impending wedding created a cheerful buzz in the shop and though she wanted to keep things simple there was a great deal to plan and organize. Dora was in need of the distraction. Nicky was a regular correspondent and though his letters were full of tender messages, his New Year departure loomed like a dark cloud on the horizon. It wasn't until her design for Feathy's wedding outfit came to fruition that Dora's spirits lifted and she began to plan a garment that would befit her role as the bridesmaid.

Glancing through the list of wedding guests she was surprised to see Jack Armstrong's name and when she commented on it, Feathy chuckled. "My Arthur loves his Rotary socials, you know, seems half the members are going to turn up."

When she saw the throng gathered at midday outside the town hall, Dora wondered whether Arthur had in fact invited every single member. Earlier that morning when she had walked over to Feathy's house she found the bride looking very nervous, though pretty as a picture in her lavender ensemble.

It began to snow around midday and when she and Arthur walked smiling out of the registry office snowflakes fluttered in the air, mingling amongst the confetti like tiny diamonds. When Feathy threw her bouquet of Christmas roses up in the air it landed in Dora's path and she reached out to catch it. Feathy glanced at Dora and winked.

Following a few jocular speeches, the band struck up and Dora was partnered on the dance floor by the police constable. Although the young man danced with more verve than technique Dora was caught up in the gaiety and Jack, who was seated with two other men at a corner table, watched in amusement.

Later, when she was walking past Jack's table he called out to her. She turned and smiled at him. "Hello, Jack. I didn't see you there."

Jack stood up and gestured to the vacant chair beside him. "Let me get you a drink, Dora. You look as though you could do with one."

He returned a few minutes later and handed her a glass of punch. "You and that young constable put on quite a spectacle!" he chuckled.

"It was great fun," she laughed.

"Well, don't go breaking his heart."

"What, Dennis? Don't be daft, Jack."

"He gazes at you like a puppy dog though I can't say I blame him. You do look very fetching in that dress."

"Thank you," said Dora, smoothing the skirt of her taffeta skirt. "I designed it myself."

"Did you really?" said Jack, looking impressed.

"Yes, I designed Feathy's, too."

"I remember you talked about being a designer but I had no idea you were so gifted. Do you design frocks for the shop, too?"

"I'm afraid Madame's taste is very conservative."

"Then it's time you were set up in your place."

Dora nodded. "Yes, that's what I aim for."

He looked at her thoughtfully. "Seems a shame to waste a talent like yours though I must confess I believed that these days you had other aspirations."

"Other aspirations?"

"Yes, like marriage to that chap who's been courting you?"

How could he have guessed her secret? She had made no mention of it to anyone. She blushed in annoyance and stood up. "It's time for me to go and see Feathy off."

Dora's dress had received many compliments that day and she hoped it would pass muster in the more rarefied society of Belgravia. The prospect of staying with Nicky's parents was daunting but Nicky had been insistent. "It's important to me that my family get to know you and love you," he had written in his last letter. And so, on the Saturday before Christmas, the dress was wrapped in layers of tissue paper and arranged on top of the other items in Dora's suitcase.

"You'll meet my sister this evening, she's here with the boys," said Nicky, ushering Dora through the front door of the Ainsley home.

A man servant appeared in the porch way, took Dora's suitcase from Nicky and told him that his parents awaited him in the drawing room.

"Thank you, Johnston," Nicky nodded. "This is Miss Jamieson."

"Yes, sir. Your mother said you were bringing a young lady." He turned to Dora. "Good evening, Miss Jamieson."

"Johnston will show you to your room, sweetheart. I'll meet you downstairs when you're ready."

The formality was intimidating and Dora sank gratefully into one of the armchairs that furnished the comfortable bedroom, glad to have a little time to adjust but within minutes a maid arrived to unpack her suitcase.

Soon afterwards she stood at the foot of the staircase wondering whether to turn left or right and it was a relief to see Nicky appear from a doorway.

"This way, sweetheart," he said, taking Dora's arm and escorting her into the drawing room.

His parents got up from their chairs by the fireside and came across the room to them. Clarissa gave Dora a wintry smile. "Ah, Dora, how nice to see you," she said.

Charles greeted Dora with a kiss on her cheek, and she noticed how tired he looked as he sank wearily into his chair.

Clarissa took Nicky to one side and as they began talking a tall, attractive young woman approached Dora. "I'm Lettie, Nicky's sister," she said smiling warmly as she took Dora's hand. "I'm glad to meet you at last."

Johnston came forward with a tray of cocktails and Lettie picked up two glasses and handed one to Dora. "Nicky's letters have been full of you, you know," she said with a grin.

At that moment two fair haired young boys burst unceremoniously through the door and rushed toward Lettie. "And these little rascals are my babies, Jamie and Robbie." she said.

"I'm not a baby!" said Robbie, the youngest boy.

"You'll always be my baby, Rob," she said, ruffling his red hair. "Now boys, say hello to Miss Jamieson."

Each boy turned to Dora. "I'm seven, you know," said Robbie, as Dora shook his small outstretched hand.

Dora laughed. "Well, you're a very big boy for seven!"

Jamie glanced up at his mother. "Is Papa coming?"

"No, poppet; I told you before," said Letitia.

"But he didn't come yesterday, either," said Jamie.

"I told you before Jamie, your father's very busy at the moment," said Lettie, a small frown crossing her brow.

Clarissa walked across to them. "Isn't it time the boys went to bed, Letitia?"

"Yes, Mother. I'm about to take them up," said Lettie.

"Good. They may be away from home but it's best to stick to a routine, particularly in the current circumstances. Less unsettling for them, Letitia."

When Dora descended the stairs later she was more familiar with the layout, Nicky having shown her where the dining room was located, but as she walked along the passage she heard voices in the library. The door was slightly ajar and she caught a glimpse of Nicky and his mother inside.

"Why did you invite her here?" said Clarissa.

"I want to marry her if she'll have me, Mother," he said.

Dora's heart leaped with joy and she stopped in her tracks.

"Marry her! You can't be serious."

"I most definitely am."

"But she's not one of us, Nicholas; you can't possibly marry a shop girl!"

"I'm in love with Dora."

"Oh, really, Nicky, you've really chosen the worst moment to spring this upon me," said Clarissa. "Your father's ill with worry over the failure of his business investments and as if that weren't bad enough your sister now wants to sue for divorce."

Dora caught a glimpse of Nicky getting up and pace across the room.

"If you ask me, Lettie should divorce the bounder. How many affairs is she supposed to forgive?"

"It may not bother you, Nicky, but I'm deeply concerned about the scandal."

"Divorce isn't such a stigma these days, Mother. People may gossip for a while and then it all blows over. Lettie deserves better than that philandering bastard she married, I think you should be more concerned about Father, he doesn't look at all well."

"It's no wonder; he stands to lose a great deal of money."

"How bad is it?"

"Suffice it to say, we will have to make some serious adjustments. Now that you're home he can tell you himself."

"Yes, of course."

"I'm afraid your allowance may have to be cut."

"That won't be a problem. I've got my eye on a teaching job."

Clarissa gave a sigh. "Well, you know my feelings about that."

"Yes, Mother. We've discussed this a hundred times before. You wanted me to study law and enter the bar like your brother and I'm sorry to be such a disappointment but, unlike you, Father has always encouraged me to follow my own path."

"More's the pity."

"If you want me to cancel the trip to Egypt, I'll do so."

Clarissa paused a moment. Three months abroad could be of benefit, by the time he returned this whole business

182

with the girl might have blown over. "No, Nicky, there's no need for that."

Dora heard voices approaching and bent to pick up her handkerchief.

"Oh, poor Dora, you look a bit lost," said Lettie.

"I was looking for the dining room," said Dora.

"This way," said Lettie, taking her arm.

During dinner Dora kept her eyes averted from Nicky's mother and due to the arrival of her brother. Henry Bellingham Q.C. and his wife Jane, the evening turned out to be surprisingly convivial.

"Oh, I'm sorry, old boy," he said to Charles, entering the dining room just as Nicky and his mother were taking their seats at the table. "And my apologies to you too, dear sister; I warned you that we might be late but little did I realise just how long the hearing would go on. It's a devilish case."

Henry was a man large in height and girth and with a personality to match. He was an excellent raconteur and his wealth of interesting and often risqué stories kept the diners well entertained. Jane, a small, softly spoken woman, sat opposite him, nodding and smiling, as though hearing these anecdotes and opinions for the first time.

Towards the end of the meal Henry and began talking to Letitia about her marital affairs and the evening took on a more sombre note. As they were talking Jane turned to Dora, seated beside her, and asked where she and Nicky had met. Jane had often stayed on Jersey with Nicky's parents and began to reminisce on those visits.

"Lettie was such a bossy little minx, you just can't imagine! She had her young brother so in her thrall that she'd instigate some mischief then plead such innocence that it was usually Nicky who got the blame," she said with a chuckle.

Dora laughed. "Did he mind?"

"Oh, no, not a bit; he never held grudges, the dear boy," she said, gazing fondly at Nicky across the table. "And look at them now, all grown up and the best of friends. Oh my, how time flies, I hate to think how long ago all that was."

Dora was grateful that she hadn't been obliged to give an account of herself and warmed to the gentle, self-effacing woman. "Do you have children, Mrs Bellingham?" she asked.

"No, my dear. We haven't been so blessed. That's why our nephew and niece are so special to us."

That night Dora lay awake a long while, that overheard conversation preying on her mind. Clarissa's disdain weighed heavily on her heart. From somewhere in the silent house came the distant chimes of a grandfather clock and when she heard it chime twice she turned over and drifted into sleep.

During the night it had snowed heavily and outside the dining room window at breakfast the virgin snow sparkled in the winter sunshine. The boys were transfixed by the white winter land and when Letitia promised them a trip to the park Nicky proposed that he and Dora should accompany them.

"There's something so romantic about freshly fallen snow," said Letitia, as they trudged through the deep snow that blanketed the London streets.

"It's the silence that makes it so magical," said Nicky.

At that moment Robbie slipped over and let out a shriek. Dora, who was closest, and wearing the stout boots that Letitia had loaned her, reached out a hand and pulled him up. "Slippery, isn't it?" she said, laughing.

Robbie looked up at her uncertainly, unsure whether to cry or laugh.

"Come on, little man," said Nicky, picking up the boy and hoisting him up on his shoulders.

Compared to the empty streets the park was a hive of activity. There were children with adults building a huge snowman; others throwing snowballs or skidding along on toboggans. Jamie and Robbie were delighted with the old sledge that Nicky had unearthed from the cellar and upon their insistence Dora found herself seated on the sledge behind them at the top of a slope. With a sharp push from Nicky it skidded downwards at speed and when it reached the bottom the three of them were thrown off and fell laughing into the snow. After several more runs Dora went to join Letitia who sat a park bench watching.

"Those boys of yours are inexhaustible," she said, sitting down.

"Oh, yes, don't I know it!" said Letitia, laughing. "I'm glad my brother's so patient."

"Look at him! He's loving every moment," said Dora.

"Yes, he's really good with children. He'll make a great father one day."

Dora was charmed by the boys. "Those two are a real credit to you, Lettie."

Letitia smiled. "Oh, I wouldn't be without them. Children can be a great solace when your man lets you down. I suppose you've heard about my errant husband?"

"Yes, I'm sorry."

"It's hard for the boys, they know there's something going on and they miss their father but this time Dominic's gone too far. Imagine having the gall to sleep with his best friend's wife? This time he's destroyed two marriages, the cheating swine!"

Robbie came running up to the bench, rubbing his sleeve across his face. "He hit me with a snowball!"

Letitia took out a handkerchief and wiped his face. "There we are, all better. Now you go and tell the others it's time to go back for lunch. Grandpa and Grandma will be waiting for us."

On the way back to the house, Robbie held Dora's hand. "Can Dora come for Christmas, Mummy?" he asked.

"Great idea, Rob. Well, what do you say, Dora?" said Nicky.

She was touched by little boy's invitation and smiled down at him.

Nicky winked. "I think she said yes."

The car journey home that evening was the first time he and Dora had the chance to be alone. "I'm afraid you got thrown in the deep end, sweetheart. I didn't realise that Lettie and the boys would be staying."

"Oh, but I enjoyed them; your sister's lovely and the boys are adorable."

"So what about Christmas then? You made a promise to Robbie, remember?"

Dora glanced at him. "What about your parents, Nicky? I'm not sure your mother approves of me."

"Mother's a bit tetchy at the moment; she's got a lot on her mind. Look, sweetheart, why don't we stop at a pub and talk it over, make a plan?"

"I'd love to, Nicky but I really ought to get back."

"Right, then we'll have to talk on the phone. Oh, damn it, I forgot, you don't have one!"

Dora thought of the telephone in Jack's office and promised that she would phone him.

After settling her mother for the night, Dora went to check the mail box and found a letter from Tom. She took it to the kitchen table and ripped open the envelope. She read the letter and gasped with pleasure. Tom and Kitty were coming to see her on the twenty-seventh of December and had booked rooms at Hillersdon House, the smartest hotel in the area. Dora smiled, knowing that it was Kitty who had instigated this visit.

After work the following day Dora went round to the opticians to use the telephone. George Humphries was in the shop, busy fitting a customer's spectacles. He listened to Dora's whispered request, then nodded toward the office. As luck would have it, Nicky was at home and answered the phone in person. He sounded disappointed that she wouldn't visit his home at Christmas but then surprised her by saying that instead he'd make a booking for himself at the hotel where Tom was to stay. For the next ten days Dora was in a flurry of excitement; she couldn't remember a time when there had been so much to look forward to.

*

Hilary Morton invited Dora and her mother to come to their annual party on Christmas Eve but Enid pleaded a headache and Dora went alone. Apart from Ian, who was working at his newly opened school in Kenya, the Morton children had returned home in force. Emily was very pleased to see her friend again and monopolised Dora for most of the evening and told her about her research into mental disorders.

"You mustn't despair, Dor, your mother's illness isn't that uncommon. Nowadays we have a greater understanding and psychiatric hospitals have much better resources than they had in the past; your mother would be well taken care of."

Dora knew that Emily meant well but she wasn't in the mood to consider such an option; she intended to wait and unburden her anxieties to Tom.

It was Tom's first visit to the house and he came alone. He and Kitty had arrived at the hotel the previous evening while Dora and Nicky were having a drink in the bar, and during a festive meal in the hotel's dining room it was Kitty who had insisted that he should bring his mother for tea.

Dora led Tom into the parlour where Enid was snoozing in her armchair. She looked up in bewilderment.

"Hello, Mother," he said, bending to give her a peck on the cheek.

"Thomas, what are you doing here?"

"Mother, I told you that Tom was coming to collect us," said Dora. "We're going out for tea."

"That will make a nice change," she said, getting up stiffly from the chair.

Dora helped her to her feet. "We'll have to get you out more, Mother. You need the exercise."

Kitty and Nicky were waiting for them in the hotel's conservatory, a large, airy room with large potted plants arranged amongst the tables and braziers to keep the guests warm.

"You're Dora's young man, aren't you?" said Enid, taking Nicky's hand.

Kitty stepped forward to meet her. "This is Kitty, my fiancé," said Tom.

"You didn't tell me you had a fiancé, Thomas," said Enid.

Dora glanced at Kitty. "Mother is a little forgetful, these days," she whispered apologetically.

Kitty seated herself next to Enid and began telling her about their wedding plans. A waitress came to take their order and after she left Enid turned to Kitty, "And where is this wedding taking place? Will it be local?"

"No. We're having it in Jersey. That's where I live," said Kitty.

"Jersey, you say? My daughter's been to Jersey, you know," said Enid.

Tom and Dora exchanged glances.

"My parents would like you and Dora to stay with them when you come over for the wedding," said Kitty, looking at Enid expectantly, but Enid's eyes were now roaming the room.

"I've been to this hotel before, you know. I came here with my late husband," said Enid. "It was a long time ago but I remember it rather well," said Enid. "Some clients of my husband invited us for dinner and very good it was too."

She related that evening in detail, even remembering the menu they chose.

Enid continued reminiscing, her mind straying back to the early days of her marriage until Tom could stand no more and gestured to Dora that it was time to take their mother home. When Kitty came to say good-bye Enid turned to Dora irritably. "Who are these people? What do they want?"

While Dora took Wilf for a walk Tom made up the fire in Enid's bedroom.

"I do feel the cold, you know. This house is like an ice box," said Enid.

"It's a very bitter winter, Mother," said Tom, striking a match and lighting the fire. "Well, this should warm you up."

She eyed him suspiciously. "Who are you anyway, young man?"

"I'm Tom, your son."

"No, you're not. Thomas is away at sea."

"Is she always like this, Dor, or have we caught her on a bad day?" he asked Dora as he drove her back to the hotel.

"No. You could call this one of her better days," said Dora, grinning wryly.

"I tell you, Dora, I've never been so embarrassed. God knows what Kitty must think."

"Don't worry about Kitty; she'll be full of compassion."

"Well, something's got to be done. I don't know how you put up with her."

Dora glanced at him. "I don't want to see her institutionalized, if that's what you mean."

"Surely it's the only solution?" said Tom.

"Look, Tom, I'm used to her and I'd prefer to keep her at home for now."

He patted her hand. "You're more than she deserves."

"She's all I've got, Tom."

"Well, I'm really sorry you've had to deal with this by yourself."

They were silent for a moment and then Tom spoke again. "I vowed I'd never come back here, you know."

"Yes, Tom, I remember."

"Father should never have left, it was unforgivably selfish, but I'm afraid I feel no loyalty to her. She never liked me anyway. I know that."

"I don't think that's true. She was very pleased when I told her you were coming to see us. She's softer now."

"Huh, soft in the head more like, she didn't even know who I was. Seeing her again has brought up things that I'd rather forget. It was only to see you that I agreed to come in the first place."

"It's all right, Tom. I do understand. Mother's always been her own worst enemy."

"Well, we'd better buck up," he said, patting her knee. "Let's go and have a great evening and enjoy the time we've all got together."

For Dora those last days of the old year were a bubble in time. The shop was closed and she spent every possible moment with Nicky and the others. They went on walks in the countryside and took full advantage of the hotel's amenities; enjoying the restaurant's excellent cuisine and the comfortably furnished lounge with its warming log fires.

When Tom and Kitty retired for the night Nicky and Dora slipped discreetly up to his room and they made love. Whether the management noticed the comings and goings no-one referred to it. Dora entered into the gaiety of the New Year celebrations with as much enthusiasm as she could muster. By the morning Nicky would be gone.

Chapter 21

The Annual Sale began as usual of the first day of January and the shop was inundated with customers. The weather had turned colder, turning the snow into ice, and though many of the clientele had come in for the warmth, within three days the sale merchandise had vanished from the shelves.

Enid complained about the freezing temperature of the outdoor lavatory and Dora bought a second hand commode and installed it in her bedroom. As the temperature plummeted Enid preferred to remain there, warmed by the fire that Dora lit before leaving for work with instructions to keep it stoked with the coal from the scuttle beside it.

After the rush of the sales the shop was exceedingly quiet and allowed Dora more time to dwell on Nicky's absence and the tears she had shed at their parting threatened to engulf her again. Due to the upturn in her fortune Brenda had resigned from her job and Dora missed her as a workmate. Due to the popularity of his dolls' houses, Terry's business was expanding and he had now taken a lease on a work shop with his younger son working as his apprentice.

Brenda had been replaced by a young woman called Susan, a niece of Miss Gates. Susan bore such an uncanny resemblance to her aunt, both in looks and temperament that Dora found it hard to warm to her. Like her aunt, Susan lacked humour and without the camaraderie of Feathy and Brenda to brighten the day, the working hours were long and monotonous.

One evening as she walked home from work Dora was pulling up her coat collar against the icy wind when she heard a fire engine approach, its siren blasting as it sped past her along the street. Praying that no-one she knew was in danger Dora quickened her pace but as she turned the corner into her street smoke was billowing in all directions.

A man hurried toward her. "Best not to go any further, love. There's a house on fire," he said.

She ran the rest of the way and bumped into Arthur who was standing on the kerbside outside her house. Together they stared in disbelief at the leaping orange flames that engulfed it.

"It's all right, Dora," said Arthur, taking hold of her arm. "They managed to get to your mother before the staircase went."

The crash of falling masonry and acrid smell of burning were overwhelming as the firemen made a valiant effort to contain the blaze.

"Move back, move back," called Arthur to the crowd of bystanders.

"But Wilf, where's Wilf?" yelled Dora.

"He's here, Dora. I've got him," said Sarah, pushing through the crowd with Wilf in her arms.

"Oh, thank God!" Dora cried, taking hold of Wilf and smothering him with kisses.

An ambulance appeared through the fumes and pulled up behind the fire engine. Dora looked up and saw a fireman come out on to the pavement carrying Enid's inert body in his arms. Two medical orderlies jumped out of the ambulance and moved her on to a stretcher.

"You'd best go with your Mum, Dora," said Mrs Simmons, coming up beside her. "Don't you worry about Wilf; we'll take him home with us."

She handed Wilf back to Sarah and was watching the stretcher being carried to the ambulance when she felt a hand on her arm.

"Let me come with you, Dora," said Jack.

She nodded. She was trembling so much that it was an effort to walk the short distance across the road, then Jack's arm reached out around her waist and supported her up the step into the back of the ambulance.

That evening Dora sat in Jack's sitting room with Feathy and Brenda and drank the cup of hot, sweet tea that Feathy had made. Jack walked across the room with a decanter of brandy and poured a slug into Dora's cup. "This should put the colour back in her cheeks," he said with a smile.

Dora turned to Feathy sitting beside her on the sofa. "Did they get the fire under control? I was so worried about our poor neighbours."

"Those fireman are heroes," said Brenda, who sat on the wing chair opposite "The Hoskins' house will need a bit of gutting work but considering the power of those flames the damage wasn't so bad as it might've been."

"'Course, the real hero of day was little Wilf," said Feathy with a grin.

Dora turned to her questioningly. "My Wilf?"

"Yes, love. It was your Wilf who alerted the Simmons," said Feathy. "He set up such a racket outside their front door it would've woken the dead."

Dora laughed. "Wilf did that!"

"Beats me how he got out the house," said Feathy.

"Must have been that flap Terry put in the back door," said Brenda.

"Well, thank God for your Terry," said Feathy.

The three anxious hours that Dora had spent with Jack at the hospital had left her drained and it was a relief to feel the tension seep from her body.

"That little fellow saved your Ma's life, Dora, reckon he deserves a medal!" said Brenda, laughing.

"And how is your mum, love?" asked Feathy.

"She's been sedated and they say she's stable. It's her lungs that they're worried about," said Dora.

"Smoke inhalation is very damaging; the doctor has given her a broncoscopy," said Jack. "We won't know much more for a few days yet."

"Thank Heaven's you were there, Mr Armstrong. All that medical jargon's ever so confusing," said Brenda.

Dora glanced at Jack who was now seated in one of the easy chairs. "Yes, Jack. Thank you. I don't know how I'd have got through it all without you."

"It was the least I could do," said Jack. "And, as I said, you can have the use of this flat for as long as you want it. I'll stay with my mother when I'm in town."

"That's very kind of you, Jack. I do appreciate it," said Dora.

Brenda glanced around the small but comfortably furnished sitting room. "It's good to know that poor Dora will have a roof over her head. You're a good friend, Mr Armstrong."

Over the following week Jack took time off work to drive Dora to the hospital. It was another two weeks before Enid was ready to be discharged and in the meantime Dora remained in Jack's flat and returned to work; though she took time off when eventually Tom arrived, his trip having been delayed by bad weather.

"It's a wreck, Tom. I was devastated when I came to look at it the next day," said Dora, as they approached the burnt house.

"Hmm, I see what you mean," said Tom, staring in dismay at the remains of the roof and damaged brick wall at the front of the house.

"And it's all my fault this happened," said Dora. "I should never have allowed her to have a fire in her room. She must have over-stoked it and then fallen asleep."

He put his arm around her shoulders. "No, Dor. You weren't to know it would end up like this."

The glass was missing from the front window and Tom peered inside though the charred frame. "Looks like it'll have to be gutted. I'll talk to the insurance people later and then we'll get on to a builder." He turned to her and smiled. "Don't you worry, Dor, within six months you could have a brand new home with even an indoor bathroom installed. Just think of that!"

Dora was feeling a great deal more cheerful when they arrived at the Morton home for lunch.

"Now you eat up, Dora. You need to keep up your strength," said Hilary Morton.

Dora smiled at her. "With all those tasty casseroles you've brought over; I think I'm starting to gain weight!"

"This is delicious, Mrs Morton," said Tom, tucking into the crusty meat pie. "It was very good of you to invite us."

"That's my pleasure, Tom," she said. "I've told Dora to come over for a meal any time she likes. I offered her refuge here but Mr Armstrong had already arranged to accommodate her in the flat."

"Mr Armstrong seems a very good sort," said Tom. "When I talked to him yesterday he suggested that when Mother comes out of hospital she should stay at the flat with Dora."

"Did he really?" said Hilary, ladling another portion of pie on to Tom's plate. "That seems like a good plan, don't you think?"

Tom nodded. "Yes, indeed."

"Hmm; I'm not sure I want to be beholden to Jack," said Dora.

"Well, it's not like it's for ever, Dor," said Tom.

"I'd feel better if I could afford to pay him some rent," said Dora.

"I proposed that to him yesterday but he wouldn't hear of it," said Tom.

"Well, that's very generous; God Bless him!" said Hilary.

"But we'll be living on his charity, Mrs Morton," said Dora.

"He says that your taking care of his books is sufficient payment, he seems to appreciate that," said Tom.

"Now, tell me Dora, how is that nice young man of yours?" said Hilary. "I hope he's a good correspondent."

Dora's face brightened. "Yes, Mrs Morton. Nicky is living the fulfilment of his dreams. The post is slow but I did have a long letter from him last week and his descriptions of the terrain were so graphic that I was transported into the heat and sand."

Hilary got up and Dora helped her to gather up the plates then she carried them off to the kitchen.

"Does Nicky know about the fire, Dor?" said Tom.

"No, not yet; I'm not sure that I should mention it. It would only worry him," said Dora.

"Well, I think you should."

They were silent for a few moments before Tom addressed her again. "What's the situation with you and Nicky? Has he asked you to marry him?"

Dora shrugged. "His mother's not keen on him marrying a shop girl. That's what she calls me."

"I suppose that's not surprising. Kitty say Clarissa Ainsley's a terrible snob. Still, you shouldn't let that put a spanner in the works. Once she gets to know you I'm sure she'll change her mind."

*

"Ah, Miss Jamieson, you've deigned to honour us with your company?" said Miss Gates, looking up from the counter with a smirk.

"Good morning, Miss Gates," said Dora, ignoring the sarcasm and walking through to the work room where Kathleen was hanging up her coat.

"Morning, Miss Jamieson," said Kathleen, smiling. "Any news of your poor Ma?"

"She's improving, thank you Kath."

"I'm working in the shop front today, suppose I'd best be getting along."

Dora was tidying her hair in the small mirror when Madame appeared. "So you're back with us, are you Miss Jamieson?"

"Yes, Madame. My brother left yesterday evening."

"Whilst I have made allowances for your absence due to the unfortunate circumstances, I don't expect it to become a habit. I have a business to run."

"I'm afraid I may need to take a little time off when my mother comes out of hospital."

"Hmm, I see. Well, in the meantime there's plenty here to keep you busy here."

"Am I assigned to the work room then?"

"Yes, I should like you to take over Miss Sullivan's work while she gains some sales experience. Miss Gates will tell you what needs to be done."

A few moments later Dora went out to the shop front where Miss Gates was whispering to her niece.

"Here you are, Miss Jamieson," she said, gathering up the garments laid across the counter. "I'd like you to take these and give them a good press."

Dora hadn't seen Jack for a few days when he turned up at the flat that Friday evening. She got up from her chair and went out to the kitchen to make a pot of tea.

He followed and took a seat at the table. "Well, how was your week, Dora?"

"Horrible!" said Dora, filling the kettle.

"Why? Whatever made it so?"

"It seems I've been demoted and sent to work at the back of the shop."

"Surely that's just temporary?"

"Temporary or not, it's mortifying to see that vile Gates woman gloating; if she had her way I'd be scrubbing the floors!"

Jack chuckled. "I expect it's just jealousy."

"Whatever her reasons, Miss Gates is so insufferable I just wish I never had to see that smug smile again."

"The old girl needs you to do the book keeping, don't forget."

"Who knows!" said Dora bitterly. "Do you know, Miss Gates is virtually running the place these days and Madame has even allowing her to select new stock for the shop, I can hardly believe the drab clothes that are ordered. Before I left today I glanced at the ledgers and profits are down by almost fifty per cent."

"Perhaps it's time you looked for another job, Dora."

"But what, Jack? I've worked there since I left school."

She poured out the tea and took the cups to the table.

"You could come and work for me; I need an assistant to replace Mrs Brown. She got married last year and now she's expecting a baby."

"Doesn't your mother work in the shop?" said Dora, recalling her meeting with the formidable matriarch. That was one person she wouldn't wish to work with.

"No, she only helps out on rare occasions such as an employee being absent."

"When is Mrs Brown leaving?"

"She'd like to go by the end of next week though she says she'll stay on until the employment agency has found me a suitable replacement."

"I see."

"So what do you say?"

Dora looked at him thoughtfully. "What would I have to do, Jack?"

"You'd take care of the appointments, look after the clients and see to their fittings, Humphries would show you how to take the measurements. The job does require some typing skills, invoices and that kind of thing but you know your way around an office so that shouldn't be a problem. I don't believe you'd find the work too taxing."

"It's a tempting offer, Jack."

"Well, think it over, just let me know your decision by Monday so that I can cancel with the agency. And if you do decide to accept you can tell Madame what she can do with her job!"

Dora laughed. "That would give me great satisfaction!"

Miss Gates was staring through the shop window when Dora arrived on Monday morning. She turned to Dora and glanced meaningfully at the clock on the wall.

"Is Madame in?" said Dora.

Miss Gates nodded and gestured to the office door.

Madame looked up in surprise as Dora walked purposefully into the room. "Miss Jamieson!"

"I've come to tell you that I'm resigning, Madame."

"Resigning?"

"That's right, as from today."

Madame stared at her in amazement. "You can't resign Miss Jamieson, not until you've served out your notice."

"I think you'll find that I can," said Dora, turning to leave.

"Please wait a moment. You're a most valued member of my staff Miss Jamieson and I have no desire to lose you," said Madame, her tone conciliatory. "Close the door and come and sit down."

"There's really no more to be said."

"Then if that's your game you'll get no reference from me, girl!" said Madame, rising from her chair in anger but Dora had already left.

Dora almost laughed out loud at the sight of Miss Gates's open mouthed astonishment. She opened the street door and turned in the doorway.

"I wish you good day, Miss Gates," she said haughtily before closing the door firmly behind her.

That evening Jack came round to ask for her decision and was amused hear Dora's account of her visit to the dress shop. "Well, you certainly handled that with aplomb!" he chuckled. "I hope it was cathartic."

She nodded and smiled but she now had something else on her mind. She picked up the letter she had received in the afternoon post and handed it to him.

"What's this?"

"The insurance company won't pay up for the house renovation. They say I'm behind with the premiums."

He glanced over the letter. "Are they correct?"

"Yes, I'm afraid so. What with all the excitement and expense of the trip to Jersey I must have forgotten."

Chapter 22

He glanced at the letter again. "Looks like the house will have to be sold as it is. You'll get something for that."

"But where will we live? Oh, Jack, what am going to do?" said Dora, and burst into tears.

Jack got up and went to put his arms around her. "There, there now. We'll work something out."

He put a glass of brandy in her hand and settled her on the sofa while he made up the fire. She watched the kindling catch light, sipping the fiery amber liquid and feeling its burn as it slipped down her throat.

Once the fire was blazing in the grate he went to sit down beside her and topped up the glass. "A little better now?"

"Yes, much better," she said, sniffing as he wiped her tears with a handkerchief.

"Tomorrow I'll go and see the bank manager, see if I can raise a loan," he said.

Dora took another sip of the fiery liquid. "Why would you do that for me?"

"Why do you think?" he said, chuckling.

He reached his arm around her and she snuggled up against him. The texture of his tweed jacket against her cheek was evocative, lulling her senses into the comfort of that long ago place of safety. She closed her eyes with a contented sigh barely aware of the hands now roving over her body and creeping up her legs. The feel of his touch on the tender skin at the top of her of stockings was arousing and she gave an involuntary moan but when his fingers began probing between her legs she was suddenly alert and recoiled in shock, begging him to stop. The next thing she remembered was being pushed to the floor and the weight of his body pinning her down as he thrust himself into her.

Chapter 23

Three Months Later

Dora opened the door to the dispensary and poked in her head. "I'm just off for lunch, Mr Humphries. I'm meeting a friend."

Mr Humphries looked up from the work bench and smiled. "Very good, my dear. No need to hurry back, I can hold the fort. You just have a nice time."

He watched Dora's departing figure with a frown of concern, wondering what could be wrong. She carried out her work efficiently but in recent weeks her demeanour had changed and the light had gone from her eyes.

Emily was waiting at their usual table in the tea shop.

"Hope I haven't kept you waiting, Em," said Dora.

"No, I only arrived a few minutes ago. I've been looking out of the window and watching the world go. Funny the way people remember how to smile the moment the sun comes out."

She took a good look at Dora as she sat down. "You don't look so sunny, Dor, are you ill or something?"

Dora fidgeted in her chair, she had dreaded this moment. "I'm not ill, Em, I'm pregnant."

"Pregnant!" Emily paused a moment. "Are you sure?"

Dora looked down at the table and nodded.

"Does Nicky know?"

"It isn't his."

"No, of course, he's abroad, isn't he? Then who is the father?"

"Jack Armstrong."

Emily stared at her in shock. "What!"

"I know," Dora muttered, too embarrassed to say more.

"Only this morning Mother was singing his praises and telling me what a great support he's been," said Emily, angrily. "Oh God, I'm so sorry. What a swine!"

A waitress appeared at the table. Emily glanced over the menu and gave her their order.

"I've ordered two 'toad in the holes'," she said, turning to Dora. "I know you like that."

She looked out of the window for a moment then turned back to Dora. "I take it he'll marry you?"

Dora nodded mutely.

"Have you been to see Pa?"

"I wanted to tell you first."

"Then promise me you'll see him this week. You ought to be checked over."

"Yes, Em, I promise," said Dora.

Their meal arrived and they began eating in silence. "Glad to see you haven't lost your appetite," said Emily.

Dora felt a sense of relief now that at she shared her shameful secret. "No. The morning sickness is hell and then suddenly I'm ravenous."

"So is Jack Armstrong still living with his mother?"

Dora nodded. "Ma's in the spare room. She's got a cold and I left her dosed up with medication plus a dose of laudanum to help her sleep."

They finished their meal in silence and after the waitress had cleared away the plates Dora felt her friend's eyes upon her. "What is it, Em?"

"Nicky. You were in love with him, weren't you?"

"I still am, Em. I did write to him," said Dora, thinking of all the hours she had agonized over that letter. "I told him I was getting married and wouldn't be able to see him again."

"How did he respond to that?"

"He didn't write back."

Dora was desperate to hear something from him even if they were angry words of rebuke and then, a few days after that conversation with Emily, she learned the reason for his silence in a most unforeseen manner.

It was a Wednesday half day and she was in the kitchen washing up the lunch dishes when an unexpected visitor arrived.

"Hello, Dora," said the woman standing on the doorstep.

Dora gasped in astonishment. Nicky's aunt was the last person she expected to see. "Mrs Bellingham!"

"I hope you'll forgive the intrusion," said Jane.

"Yes. Please come in," said Dora hesitantly, and led her into the sitting room.

"So this is where you live," said Jane, glancing around the tidy room. "It took me a while to find you."

Dora nodded, glad that her mother was resting in her room. "Please have a seat," she said nervously. "May I get you some tea?"

"No, thank you, my dear. I've just paid a visit to your charming little tea room," she said, taking a seat on the wing chair.

Dora perched on the edge of the sofa, wondering what was going on.

"I've been staying with a cousin in Godalming and thought I'd take the opportunity to visit you. I wanted to see how you were and to talk to you about Nicky. You see, he's been laid up in a hospital in Cairo."

Dora turned pale. "What's happened to him?"

"He was unlucky enough to have contracted typhoid fever."

"Oh, no, poor Nicky! How is he, Mrs Bellingham?"

"I'm glad to say he's making a good recovery. My sister-in-law went out to Cairo to see him and hopes he'll be well enough to come home soon."

"Thank God for that!" said Dora with a sigh of relief.

Jane cleared her throat. "I hope that you'll forgive the impertinence but my nephew wrote to tell me that he's worried about you, he says he's heard nothing from you for a long while."

Dora bit down on her lip, too distressed to speak.

Jane looked at her kindly. "I'm sorry, my dear, I realise that it's none of my business."

Dora got up and walked distractedly across to the window. "I have written to Nicky, Mrs Bellingham, and I explained my changed circumstances. He must have been taken ill before he received it."

"I see." She paused a moment. "I'm very sorry to have upset you. My husband told me I shouldn't interfere."

Dora turned a tear stained face to her. "No, it was very good of you to come. You see, Mrs Bellingham, I will always love Nick but a lot of things have happened since he's been away."

"You know, I think I'd like that cup of tea after all."

"I expect Nicky will come to stay with us when he returns," said Jane later, now seated at the kitchen table. "He'll need a period of convalescence."

Dora pulled up a chair and sat down. "With you?"

Jane nodded. "His parents are moving at the end of the month and Clarissa will be up to her eyes."

"Where are they going?"

"A mews house in Chelsea. It's very charming but much smaller than they're used to so Clarissa will have a lot of furniture to dispose of. My poor sister-in-law's had such a lot on her plate; she's a shadow of herself."

The back door opened and Jack strolled into the kitchen. "Ah, there you are, my love," he said, kissing Dora's cheek.

Dora was irritated by the unfamiliar term of endearment but had no choice but to introduce him.

He took a seat at the table and looked across at Jane. "Dora didn't tell me she was expecting a visitor."

"This is something of an impromptu visit, Mr Armstrong. I was in the area and thought I'd call in."

Dora poured another cup of tea and put it in front of Jack. "Thank you, sweetheart," he said, looking up and catching her hand. "Good news, Dora. I've just been to see the registrar; he can fit us in on Saturday."

"Well, it's time I was off," said Jane, gathering up her bag.

Dora followed her out of the door and down the stairs to the pavement. Much to her surprise she saw Jane take out a key and unlock the door of the small car parked outside. She gave the roof an affectionate pat and grinned. "This girl is a gem, you know, she takes me wherever I want to go and never divulges my secrets!"

She turned to Dora and gave her a peck on the cheek. "Good luck, my dear."

Dora watched wistfully as the car moved off down the street and disappeared round the corner, her heart so full of yearning to be a passenger that she thought it might burst.

*

Mr Humphries was a thoughtful, courteous man and under his guidance Dora had quickly adapted to the new job and appreciated the convenience of having her mother in residence in the flat upstairs, where she could keep an eye on her. It was a few months since Enid's return from hospital and though she hadn't recovered her former strength she seemed content, happy to potter about the flat or sit by the window with her knitting.

When the weather was clement Dora took her to the park with Wilf and she seemed to take pleasure in these outings. One warm summer's day Dora prepared a picnic lunch and as they sat eating it on a park bench Enid's mood was unusually reflective. She often had moments of clarity but rarely spoke with the candour she did that day.

"I know that I haven't always been easy but you've been a good daughter to me, Dora, and I want to you to know that I'm grateful."

Dora handed her some tea from the thermos flask. "I've done my best."

Enid sipped her tea thoughtfully. "I wish I'd been kinder to Thomas; I should have been more tolerant. It was having the boy there, so loud and boisterous when my poor Edwin was cold in the earth. Edwin was so quiet and gentle; you couldn't find brothers more different."

Dora had loved her elder brother and admired him for enlisting but she hadn't been blind to his faults. Doting on her first born as she did, Enid was unsparing in her devotion and sometimes Dora wondered whether Edwin resented the arrival of his younger siblings. Edwin might have been obedient but he could be sly, often allowing Tom to take the blame for a misdemeanour of which he had been the culprit.

Enid patted Dora's belly. "I'm looking forward to being a grandmother."

Dora glanced at her in surprise. "Are you?"

Enid smiled ruefully. "I might be better at that."

Wilf went to retrieve the ball that Dora had thrown across the grass then ran back and dropped it at her feet. Dora smiled; it always cheered her up to have Wilf with her. Jack would only allow him to stay at week-ends and during the week his home was with the Simmons.

"That little chap must be getting on now, surprising he still has so much energy," said Enid.

Dora picked up the ball and sent it spinning through the air.

Enid suddenly put a hand on Dora's arm. "Shouldn't you be at work?" she said anxiously.

"No, Mother. I've been off work for three months, the baby's due soon."

Enid nodded. "Oh, yes, of course, you are to have a baby."

"Well, it's time we took Wilf home and got back to the flat."

"Very well," said Enid, getting up and brushing the crumbs off her skirt. "I'm glad that you married that nice Mr Armstrong, you know. It's so good to see you happily settled."

That autumn Enid caught another cold and couldn't shake it off. Her mental faculties had deteriorated alarmingly and their exchange in the park was the last coherent conversation that Dora would share with her.

One Saturday morning after Dora returned home from collecting Wilf for his week-end visit, Enid's cold had turned feverish.

Dora changed the damp bed clothes and tucked Enid back into bed with a hot water bottle. By bedtime she seemed a little better but a few hours later Dora was roused by her groans and, alarmed by the sudden escalation in her temperature, she telephoned Dr Morton. He arrived twenty minutes later, took one look at Enid and sent for an ambulance.

It was almost dawn before Dora came home from the hospital and she went to sleep in the spare room with Wilf. A few hours later she heard Jack rustling around in the bedroom next door. He'd had little sleep and his mood was testy as he came out of the bedroom. Dora's door was ajar and needing to relieve himself outside, Wilf rushed out to the staircase crossing Jack's path as he was about to descend. Jack didn't see him and almost tripped, and grabbing at his cane he let out a curse and kicked out with his good leg. With a shrill cry of pain Wilf went hurtling down the stairs.

Within seconds Dora was out of the bedroom and flying downstairs. She picked up Wilf's limp body and wrapped him gently in a towel, carried the bundle in her arms and still wearing her nightdress she ran outside to the pavement.

Jack came up behind her, threw a coat across her shoulders. "Calm down, Dora. We're taking him to the vet," said Jack, bundling her into the car.

Her heart was pounding as she cradled Wilf in her arms and begged Jack to drive faster.

The vet turned to Dora, shaking his head. "I'm sorry Mrs Armstrong but there's nothing we can do. He's broken his pelvis."

"No, no, you must do something!" she shrieked hysterically.

"He's not a young dog, Mrs Armstrong. It really would be kinder to put him to sleep," said the vet.

"No, absolutely not! How can I live without him?" Dora cried.

The vet glanced down at Dora's large belly then gestured to Jack and they left the room. Wilf lay on his side on the surgery table as though nothing was amiss while Dora stroked his head but when his eyes looked trustingly up at hers she thought that her heart would break.

She jumped at the touch of a hand on her arm and turned around to see the kindly middle aged veterinary nurse standing beside her. "I know how you're feeling, love. Last year my little Trixie got run over by a motor car, the poor little thing," she said.

Dora looked at her imploringly. "Did – did she survive?"

"No, love, I had to be brave and let her go. You can't argue with fate."

Chapter 24

THREE YEARS LATER

Dora climbed up into the bus and sat down heavily on a seat by the window. It trundled off down the road, passing rows of identical brick houses, their tidy front gardens and neatly clipped hedges proclaiming their new found gentility. The town had been sprawling into the countryside for many years, property developers having taken vast tracts of countryside and replaced it with a warren of modern housing that included the house where Dora now lived. Much as she appreciated the modern conveniences the house had to offer, its distance from the town created a sense of isolation and she missed the chumminess of the narrow street where she had lived with her mother.

Jack had built up the business in Hammersmith before buying into the local shop and he spread his working life equally between the two, attributing his success to a disciplined routine. Dora soon learned to adapt to his exacting standards and ensured that his evening meal was served promptly at six thirty each evening and a hot drink ready on the bedside table when he retired to bed at ten o'clock. Fortunately for Dora the baby was docile and was usually asleep in his cot before Jack returned home. Once every month Jack would announce he was taking a business trip and would disappear for several days. Dora never asked him where he went, she was only too glad to have some respite from her duties and from his demands.

The new pregnancy was taking its toll and she had only agreed to go into town because Mr Humphries was off sick and Jack wanted her to check how Desmond Clarke, the new dispensing optician, was managing in his stead. Mr Clarke was attending to a client when Dora entered the shop and she went to talk to the new receptionist.

She listened to the young woman's grievances about Mr Clarke's high-handed attitude and later she remonstrated with him in the office, reminding him that this wasn't the first complaint and that two former receptionists had resigned due to his overbearing manner. Mr Clarke stared back at her with an insolent smirk and told her that she was not his employer, then turned and walked out of the room. Dora knew that unwittingly she had made an enemy and it was no surprise to learn subsequently that the arrogant young man was Miss Gates's cousin.

Dora boarded the bus home with a sigh of relief and began thinking about the job applicants she would interview on her return. The employment agency had assured her that they had on their books several suitable candidates looking for a live-in position.

The first to arrive was a prim middle aged spinster called Miss Briggs and Dora had high hopes of her. Miss Briggs had formerly worked as a nanny and was highly recommended by the agency. However, Miss Briggs's air of condescension as she entered the house did not bode well.

"I haven't of course worked in suburbia before but doubtless it has its own charm," she had said with a short laugh.

Dora had prepared a list of questions but Miss Briggs had so many of her own that Dora began to think that she was the one being interviewed. Dora's home did not contain the variety of modern appliances that Miss Briggs was accustomed to and Dora listened with growing impatience to her account of the illustrious households by whom she had been employed.

Dora rose from her chair and stared down at the woman. "It seems to me that my home falls short of your requirements, Miss Briggs," she said with firm civility. "I can therefore see little point in continuing this interview."

The look of astonishment on Miss Briggs's face was almost comical. "As you wish, Mrs Armstrong," she said, getting to her feet and making the most dignified retreat she could muster.

In the family room Matt sat in the middle of the carpet, bored and grizzling. Dora sighed in irritation and turned to look at Marlene, the girl seated on a chair by the window, her eyes focused on the magazine she was reading. "Isn't it time for his walk, Marlene?"

The girl jumped up guiltily. "Yes, Ma'am. We were just going."

After they left Dora began to gather up the toys strewn across the floor then suddenly she felt weary and sat down on the chair that Marlene had vacated. Matt was over three years old yet still wasn't talking.

Matt, or Mathew Thomas, as he had been registered, had been a very premature baby and despite the hospital medics' assurances at the time Dora believed that his early arrival as well the complications at his birth were responsible for the boy's slow development. She knew that there had been speculation about her lack of interest in the new born baby. "She's grieving for her mother," she had heard someone whisper; unaware that Dora was still in shock from the trauma of Wilf's sudden death and the birth that followed so quickly afterward.

Enid had died in the same hospital where Dora gave birth and the news was withheld until the obstetrician believed her to be strong enough to accept her loss.

"Mrs Jamieson was fully conscious and looked happy when we told her about the birth of her grandson. I believe the news provided great joy," said the doctor, smiling benignly. Enid had in fact been detached from reality for some while but he hoped that the lie would bring comfort to the bereaved young mother.

The doctor had turned to the doorway as a nurse wheeled in the baby's trolley and parked it beside Dora's bed. "Ah, now here he is, Mrs Armstrong. The nurse has brought baby Mathew to see you. He's making good progress, you know, and feeding much better, isn't he, Sister?"

The nurse had nodded and smiled. "Yes, doctor. He's just managed a four-ounce bottle."

"Would you like the little chap to stay with you for a while?" the doctor had asked.

Dora had glanced at the puny baby for a moment then turned to the doctor with listless eyes and nodded her assent.

The front door bell rang and Dora heaved up her bulky body, praying that the new applicant would not turn out to be another Miss Briggs.

"My name is Ruth Gibson, I answered your advertisement in the Lady for a mother's help," said the woman in a soft North Country burr.

Dora looked at the woman standing on the doorstep in a buttoned up coat and dark felt hat pulled low on her head. "Oh, yes, Mrs Gibson, please come in."

Ruth was a slight woman in her forties and when she removed the hat it revealed once reddish hair now streaked with grey and pinned into a roll at the back of her head. There were traces of former beauty in her thin lined face.

"I apologise for the lack of references Mrs Armstrong but as I mentioned in my letter I haven't had this kind of job before," said Ruth, perching on the edge of a chair in the sitting room. "But I am hard working and I like to cook and can turn my hand to most things. I'm also very fond of children."

"Well, that sounds like sufficient recommendation," Dora smiled, liking the woman's unaffected manner. "I understand you're a widow Mrs Gibson."

"Yes, Mrs Armstrong, that's correct," she said, pulling down her cardigan to cover the frayed sleeve of her cuff. "And if it's acceptable I'd be happy for you to address me by my first name."

Dora explained what her duties would entail and realising that Dora was expecting a response Ruth nodded.

"I hope the hours and wages are satisfactory," said Dora. "You would have your own room at the top of the house and the bathroom's on the first floor."

"Yes, thank you."

"Do you have any questions you'd like to ask me?"

Ruth shook her head and glanced around at the smart re-upholstered furniture, the neatly arranged books on the shelves and at the floral paintings that adorned the cream walls. "You have a very nice home, if I may say, Mrs Armstrong."

The compliment was gratifying. Dora had been upset when Jack had vetoed the cost of renovating her former home and had chosen instead to move them out of town. The modern semi-detached house was identical to the others in the leafy suburban road but its bland interior was spacious and employing her natural flair Dora had transformed it into a stylish, comfortable home.

"Perhaps you'd like me to show you around and introduce you to Matt, my son," she said, getting up.

Marlene had returned from her walk with Matt and was preparing to leave as they entered the family room behind the kitchen.

"You can come along with me, Marlene, and I'll get my purse," said Dora and turning to Ruth she said she'd be back shortly.

When Dora returned to the room Ruth was sitting on the carpet with Matt, his play bricks arranged to form a bridge in front of them.

"I'm afraid you won't find him very responsive," said Dora.

"You're just a bit shy, aren't you, Matt?" said Ruth, picking up his toy car and demonstrating how it could drive across the top of the bridge.

Matt tried it out for himself and smiled then reached forward and sent the bricks flying.

Ruth laughed. "I know your game, you cheeky monkey! You want us to make that all over again, don't you?" she said, and gathering up the bricks she began re-building the bridge.

Later, when Ruth got up from the floor Dora noticed how Matt's solemn gaze followed her around the room.

"When could you start?" Dora asked.

Ruth glanced at her in surprise. "Just as soon as you wish, Mrs Armstrong," she said. "My suitcase is at the boarding house."

Chapter 25

Jack was a man with a highly developed libido and it was due to the advice from the Marie Stopes clinic that Dora had avoided another pregnancy sooner. When she had told Jack the news his smug smile had been galling. He took little enough interest in the child they had.

As she rested her swollen ankles on the sofa Dora thought of their wedding night and how Jack had wiped away her tears and assured her that love would grow but Dora knew that all she could ever offer him was a grudging affection. There were occasions during the first years of their marriage when she railed against his overbearing ways but her plans to leave him came to nothing. She couldn't inflict herself upon Tom and Kitty, especially not with a child in tow, however willing they might have been to accept her. They were already the doting parents of two babies and Tom's letters glowed with contentment.

The advent of Ruth was the best thing that had happened to Dora for a long while and when the new baby arrived, Ruth more than proved Dora's faith in her. It had been a long, hard labour before the large baby girl emerged, bright red and squalling.

On the day after the birth Ruth brought Matt to the hospital to meet his new sister.

"Oh, what a beauty!" she gasped, peering into the cot beside Dora's bed. "May I hold her?"

Ruth picked up the baby and held her tenderly, her eyes lit with love as she gazed into the plump pink face. She glanced over at Matt who had settled himself on the floor and was playing with his new toy train. "Come on, Matt. Come and see your baby sister."

"I want boy, not want girl!" he said and returned his attention to the toy.

Dora watched from her bed in amusement. It was a relief to hear Matt beginning to form sentences.

Ruth looked across at her and smiled. "Have you named her yet?"

"Jack has suggested Pamela; it's his mother's second name."

"That's a lovely name. I think it really suits her."

"Then Pamela it is," Dora nodded with a smile.

The arrival of the new baby could have caused a major upheaval in the household but in Ruth's capable hands a new routine was quickly established. Dora had been persuaded by the intimidating hospital Sister to breast feed the baby, a feat she'd been unable to accomplish with Matt. She didn't much relish the experience but it was rewarding to see the pounds falling off and her figure return to its former size.

At feeding times Ruth took baby Pam to Dora and watched as she suckled, and when she was finished Ruth smiled fondly and whisked her away. Dora's relief at handing her back was usually tinged by guilt.

Whilst Ruth looked after the children, Dora took over in the kitchen and began to enjoy creating new recipes from the cook book that Feathy had given her for Christmas.

Every day Ruth was busy with a new load of washing and, despite her protests, Dora insisted upon sharing the myriad tasks associated with a new baby. The two women were comfortable in each other's company; Ruth went about her tasks unobtrusively and her conversations with Dora usually revolved around the children though, as they became better acquainted, they discovered a mutual love of literature. One or other of them made regular visits to the local library and the novels they selected provided some lively discussion.

Each week Dora took a trip into town to shop and would often drop in to see Feathy or Brenda and catch up on their news but since the birth of the baby she hadn't visited Janet Jennings for almost a year. When the recently installed telephone rang it was usually Jack and Janet's voice on the line was unexpected. Dora accepted her invitation to lunch and was intrigued by the little surprise that Janet said she had in store.

After the long months of hum drum domestic routine Dora set off on her visit with anticipation but without Wilf beside her she took little pleasure in the familiar walk. Her memories of Wilf had not dimmed though she could now think about him without her former gut wrenching sense of loss. Feathy had meant well when she suggested that she should get another dog and was taken aback by Dora's sharp retort. A replacement for Wilf was unthinkable.

Janet clasped Dora in her arms as she walked into the hallway. As a rule, she wasn't demonstrative and Dora was touched by this display of affection.

"Oh, my dear girl, it's so good to see you here again and looking so well, too!" smiled Janet. "And how is that beautiful baby?"

"She's thriving and quite enormous, Mrs Jennings!" Dora laughed.

"I'm glad to hear that. Nevertheless, motherhood is no excuse for neglecting old friends. Dear old Archie will be so pleased to see you again."

She took Dora's arm and pulled her to one side. "Now I have a young man here who's dying to meet you. His name is Simon Holmes."

Dora frowned. "What, you don't mean Marian Holmes's son?"

"The same."

Dora stared at her in shock. She wasn't sure that she wanted this surprise after all but at that moment Henry Jennings came out into the hallway with a tall good looking young man beside him. He shook Dora's hand warmly and then he introduced Simon.

During lunch Dora eyed Simon covertly across the dining table. He and Jeremy, Janet's younger son, had been friends as children and there was a great deal of rowdy ribbing as they recalled their boyhood escapades. When Simon looked up laughing he caught Dora's eye and there was something in his expression that reminded her of that pretty dark haired girl laughing up at her father's face. She turned away, rankled that this stranger had been such a big part of his life.

Later, she was standing at the fence nuzzling Archie's head when Simon walked up beside her. "This must be the old fellow that Mrs Jennings was telling me about," he said.

"This is Archie," said Dora, taking a mint from her pocket.

Archie reached out his head and took it from her hand. "He's just reached the grand old age of twenty-two."

"Could I give him one?" said Simon.

Dora turned in surprise and gave him a mint but he held out his hand so tentatively that she couldn't help laughing. "Just keep it flat, he doesn't bite!"

Simon's open, affable manner was disarming and by the time they left the field and walked back to the house Dora's reservations had diminished. He wasn't after all responsible for what had happened all those years ago.

"Are you staying for long?" she asked.

"I expect I'll be around for a week or two. I'm here to sort out my grandfather's estate and I'm temporarily living in the old house."

"I see."

"I was hoping we might meet up again, Dora," he said diffidently.

There were suddenly a hundred questions she wanted to ask him and her face broke into a smile. "Yes, I'd like that," she said.

"Perhaps I could come and collect you and take you up to the house. It hasn't been lived in for a while and I'm afraid it's a bit musty but we'd get some privacy there."

*

Dora stared in dismay at the clothes thrown haphazardly across the bed and wished she had time to buy something new but then she spotted the cream linen dress left hanging in the wardrobe; Feathy had made the dress for her trip to Jersey and it was one of the garments found in the suitcase she had salvaged after the fire. The dress looked at bit dated now but with a few nips and a shortened hemline, it would have to do.

Two days later, wearing the dress and with her hair arranged into a flattering chignon she popped into the kitchen to tell Ruth she was leaving. Baby Pam was sitting in her high chair banging a spoon on the table whilst Ruth was bent over Matt, coaxing him to eat up his lunch.

She looked up at Dora with a grin. "Oh, my, Mrs Armstrong, you look like a fashion plate!"

"Thank you, Ruth." Dora smiled. "I'm not sure what time I'll be back but I won't be late. Simon will bring me back in his car."

"Don't worry about that, you enjoy getting acquainted with your new step-brother," said Ruth.

The façade of Bingley Hall was built in the classical style of the early Georgian period though the back of the building bore traces of a much earlier period. Simon greeted Dora at the entrance and led her along a wood panelled passage and into a large beamed kitchen with an aged brick floor. Dora took a seat at the rustic oak table and as he opened a bottle of chilled white wine he told her that the house had come to the family a few generations ago when his ancestor had won it at the card table.

"The story goes that my great-great-grandfather had a reputation as a cardsharp as well as a rogue before his reinvention as a gentleman of means," said Simon as he busied himself around the kitchen.

Dora watched him take eggs and oil from a cupboard and then break the eggs into a bowl.

"Is that mayonnaise you're making?" she asked in surprise.

"Yes, I like to practice my skills in the kitchen, when I was a boy I wanted to be a chef."

"I've never met a man who could cook!" said Dora, laughing.

"I learned from my mother, she's an excellent cook," he said, lifting a large salmon from a pan and on to a serving dish, arranging sliced cucumber around the perimeter.

"Well, it's nice to know my father was well fed," she said with a grin.

He glanced across at her. "My mother was devoted to him, you know."

"And what about you and your brother?"

Simon stopped for a moment. "Your father was extremely good to us boys and we had a lot of respect for him. Except from those low moods he had Uncle Gerald was always very genial."

Dora looked puzzled. "I don't remember my father as moody."

"It didn't happen often but when it did he just withdrew into himself, I guess it was a form of depression. My mother said that he needed time to himself and to leave him in peace; and it wasn't until I was older that I understood the guilt that he lived with, it was his children he grieved for. Before he died Uncle Gerald confided in me, he talked a lot about you and Tom but most of his remorse was centred on you. He'd been planning to come to England to see you both but then he caught this infection and it went to his chest."

"When did he die?"

"Last year, the fifth of August, that's why I didn't come back for my grandfather's funeral. My mother needed my support."

"How strange, that was the day that my daughter was born."

"To tell you the truth, Dora, I wasn't sure that you'd agree to meet me. After all, you've every right to resent me."

"So that's why you involved Mrs Jennings?"

"Afraid so," he said sheepishly.

"I think that was clever," said Dora with a chuckle. "Seriously though, I don't imagine it was easy to lose your father and then have another man take his place."

He lifted her hand and pressed it to his lips. "I'm so glad we're going to be friends."

Dora smiled at the old fashioned gallantry and watched him carry the food to the table.

While they drank coffee Simon began describing their life in Canada and of how her father had encouraged him to study law.

Dora looked impressed. "I didn't know you were a solicitor, Simon."

"The reason I'm back is to take up a job with a firm in the city. My Godfather was responsible for my acquiring the position. I'll be working in the litigation department, an excellent career opportunity for an ambitious colonial, and of course it has the bonus of bringing me back to the old country."

"Goodness, you are full of surprises!"

He chuckled and topped up Dora's coffee.

"And what about your brother? Is he still in Canada?"

He nodded. "I doubt Oscar will ever leave. He's four years younger than me and he doesn't remember England so well. Oscar's a lumberjack, a real outdoor boy. He says he'll come and visit once I've got settled."

Before he drove Dora home he took her on a tour of the old rambling house. Most of the furniture was shrouded in dust sheets and when she lifted them back some fine antiques were revealed. What really caught her attention was a painting that was hung on the drawing room; it reminded her of one she had seen in Aunt Hettie's house.

She stared at the beautiful landscape in awe. "Is that by Whistler?"

Simon glanced up at the painting. "I'm afraid I've no idea. My knowledge is art is somewhat rudimentary."

"All this must be worth a fortune, Simon. Do you plan to sell it?"

"Yes, my brother wants to invest in a lumber yard and I'm hoping to raise him the cash. I'd like to hang on to the property if I can."

"There's a shop called the Fine Arts Emporium at the end of the high street," said Dora, thinking of the many times she had stared through the window at the exquisite merchandise inside. "They have an excellent reputation; you could go and talk to them."

"Yes, that could be very helpful, particularly if you'd be good enough to come with me."

Jack was away for most of that week and she told him about Simon at supper on the Saturday evening.

"Fancy him turning up out of the blue, that must have been a shock," said Jack.

"Actually it's been really interesting to learn about the last chapter in my father's life, cathartic too."

Jack finished his meal and pushed aside his plate. He had something else on his mind.

"What do you know about Ruth Gibson?" he said unexpectedly.

"Ruth? Not much. Why do you ask?"

"I'm sure I've seen her before, certain of it in fact. You know me, I never forget a face."

"Well, if she knew you she'd have mentioned it."

"I hope you checked her references?"

Dora nodded; Ruth's circumstances were none of his business. "Of course I did," she lied.

"Does she talk about her life before coming here?"

"Ruth's not that talkative."

"Well I want you to find a replacement."

"What? Get rid of Ruth? That's out of the question. Ruth's wonderful with the children."

"I don't trust the woman, Dora."

"Then that's your problem, Jack! I like Ruth very much and I shan't get rid of her, whatever you say!"

Jack shrugged and decided to indulge her, for the moment. Dora looked particularly desirable that evening. Her breasts had filled out since the birth of Pam and they pressed enticingly against the thin fabric of her blouse.

"Is that something new you're wearing?"

"Yes, I bought this blouse last week. It's been a long time since I had anything new."

She stood up to clear away the dishes but then sat down again. "Jack, I'd like to get a job."

He stared at her in surprise. "Why on earth do you want to do that?"

"It would be nice to have a little cash in my pocket; the housekeeping money doesn't go far."

She didn't tell him that Mr Clifton, the owner of the Fine Arts Emporium, had mentioned that he was looking for a part time assistant when he had visited the Hall. Dora had listened with rapt attention to Mr Clifton's expertise and when he apologised that his clerk was away with influenza and he wouldn't be able to take an inventory until the following week, Dora had suggested that she and Simon could do so.

Jack looked affronted. "If you have time on your hands you can come back to the shop."

"But I already do the book-keeping, isn't that enough?"

"I won't have you working in another establishment."

"Don't be so unreasonable, Jack."

"Well, that Dora is my final word. There will be no further discussion on the matter."

Dora told Simon about her disappointment when she returned to the house to work on the inventory. She rarely aired her grievances outside the home but this time she was so angry that she had no compunction. The mundane domestic tasks that filled her days were making her restless and the idea of working amongst beautiful objects inspired her with an enthusiasm that she hadn't felt in years.

"Your husband sounds a bit controlling," said Simon.

"That's putting it mildly," she said bitterly. "Jack is an obdurate man."

"Would you like me to have a word with him?"

"No, thank you, Simon. I don't think it would make any difference. I know him too well."

The last thing she wanted was an encounter between the two men. She never allowed Simon near the house when Jack was there. Jack's moods were too unpredictable.

One afternoon of the following week Jack arrived home unexpectedly while Dora was out in the garden with Ruth and the children. Ruth had suggested she do some work on the neglected borders and flower beds and subsequently had discovered a great aptitude for horticulture. She had cleared a small area where Matt could learn how to grow things and that afternoon they were sowing seeds while little Pam chuckled happily in the sand pit. Nearby Dora sat in a deckchair reading a book about antiques that she had found in the library and she looked up startled when Jack called out from the terrace.

She groaned inwardly as she watched him settle purposefully in the wing chair. There was something amiss.

"Well, Dora, there's gossip about you in the town."

She felt his piercing eyes upon her. "What gossip?"

"It's been reported to me that you and that Canadian fellow have been swanning about town together."

"But I've told you all about Simon."

"But you never mention how often you see him, do you? You've been seen together on more than one occasion."

Dora remembered seeing Miss Gates when they went to buy coffee beans and had just been coming out of the shop when she felt Miss Gates's sharp eyes upon her from the other side of the street.

Dora's eyes flashed angrily. "Are you saying you don't want me to see my step-brother?"

He looked at her a moment. Recently he had observed in her a radiance that he hadn't seen for years. He had also noticed the careful attention she was paying to her wardrobe. He had no doubts about the person responsible.

"No-one makes a laughing stock of me, Dora."

"Oh, don't be ridiculous, Jack."

"Well, I tell you now, Dora, you are not to meet that whore's son again. I forbid it."

Shortly afterward Jack left. Out in the garden Pam was screaming in the perambulator and Ruth went over to pick her up then called over to Matt who was playing in the sandpit and told him it was time to come in for tea. Dora stood at the French windows watching the little domestic scene with detachment. Sometimes the children were sweet and appealing, especially when fresh from a bath. She liked to see them well cared for but that potent maternal connection that she saw in other mothers had not taken hold.

Ruth popped her head around the door. "Do you fancy a cuppa, Mrs Armstrong?" she asked.

"Yes, thank you, Ruth," Dora nodded and followed her out to the kitchen.

Later, as the two women sat together at the table, Dora confided her thoughts.

"Sometimes I feel like his captive," she said.

Ruth looked at her with sympathy. "Perhaps it's his war wounds that trouble him, make him difficult. Women often say how their husbands came back changed men."

"Oh, how Jack likes to be seen a war hero!" said Dora with a small mirthless laugh. "But the truth is he never fought in the war."

She remembered her shock at seeing his withered leg for the first time. "He had infantile paralysis as a child and almost died. He says he was kept in an iron lung for ages and for most of his youth his legs were in braces."

Dora refilled their cups with tea. "I hope your marriage was a happy one, Ruth. You never mention it."

"My husband was a religious fanatic, Mrs Armstrong. He had us down on our knees praying for most of it," said Ruth. "Joshua was a pillar of the church and a scourge to his family."

"That must have been hard."

"At least the monster now lies in his grave."

Dora rested her hand on Ruth's. "Isn't it time you called me by Christian name, we're friends now, aren't we?"

"Yes, I'd like that but not with him around I shan't," said Ruth with a grin. "Now why don't I prepare the supper tonight and you go and take a nice hot bath, it always makes you feel better."

Dora got up and smiled at her. "I really don't know what I'd do without you, Ruth."

After Jack left the following morning Dora phoned Simon to tell him that she couldn't meet him again.

"Yes, I know," said Simon. "Your husband was here yesterday."

Dora was aghast. "Oh, no, how dare he?"

"Jack Armstrong's not a man to be reasoned with, is he?" said Simon with a low chuckle.

"Oh, I'm so sorry, Simon. I suppose he behaved badly?"

"Think nothing of it; I know how to take care of myself, Dora."

He didn't say how riled he'd been by Jack's abusive remarks about his mother but he did agree that it might be wiser not to meet again, at least for the time being.

They didn't see each other again for almost six months, not until Simon was sufficiently established in his work place to take a few hours off and they arranged to meet on the forecourt of the National Gallery.

Neither of them had visited a major gallery before and after studying the floor plan they agreed to make the Impressionist rooms their first port of call but they lingered there so long that it was lunch time before they were ready to leave.

The meal served in the dining room was mundane fare but there was so much to talk about that what was served on their plates was of little consequence. Hettie had been responsible for Dora's introduction to art history and it was from her that she had learned about the work of the Impressionist school. She could talk about the paintings they had seen with an insight that impressed Simon and forced him to confess to a woeful ignorance on the subject of art.

"Well, you have no excuses now, do you?" Dora laughed.

"Absolutely not and let me assure you Dora that I shall be taking full advantage of all the culture this capital has to offer."

"Ah, how I envy you that."

"Don't envy me, Dora, come and join me on my journey of discovery."

It was this conversation that prompted their visits to a variety of galleries and museums over the following months.

Chapter 26

Dora drove up to Matt's school in the Model T-Ford that Jack had bought cheaply off an impoverished client, parked it on the curb outside and prized out her protesting three year old, a strong willed child with a great deal to say for herself.

Dora glanced down at her round plump face with its small pouting mouth. "Come on now, Pam, and take my hand, we're already late."

Unlike her brother Pam had learned to speak early and Dora knew that Ruth could take credit for that, she was devoted to the child.

Under the supervision of a teacher the children stood about in the school yard, chatting and giggling. Matt as usual was alone, looking very small and vulnerable in his grown up school uniform. As soon as he caught sight of Dora his earnest little face brightened and he rushed towards her.

"Ah, Mrs Armstrong. Good afternoon," said Miss Gilchrist, his teacher, stepping forward. "Might I have a quick word?"

Dora liked Miss Gilchrist. During the last year they had met on several occasions to discuss Matt's progress and Dora was impressed by the conscientious young teacher's unflagging efforts with her introverted young son.

"I'm afraid that young Matt's been bullied again," she said apologetically. "He was pushed over in the playground and he's got a nasty graze on his knee. The boy responsible has been reprimanded and his mother informed."

She glanced down at Matt clutching at his mother's leg. "You'll have to learn to stand up for yourself, won't you Matt?" she said gently. "You know, Mrs Armstrong, I usually find it's the fathers who can teach that best."

Jack had no patience with children and Matt's stammer grew worse when he was around. Of the two he tended to favour Pamela though even she wasn't immune to his criticism and learned to keep out of his way.

On their way home, Dora drove down the high street and saw a Lease for Sale board attached to Madame Morel's shop. On an impulse she turned into the street where Feathy lived.

"Madame Morel is taking retirement, and about time too," said Feathy as she sat with Dora in her comfortable kitchen. "That shop's been going downhill for ages."

Tim and Charlie, or Feathy's boys, as Dora had come to think of them, had taken Matt and Pam off to play. Although they were now strapping young teenagers they could always be relied upon to keep the little ones entertained and a lot of laughter could be heard from the room next door.

"I'd like to take it over, Feathy," said Dora.

"Thought you might be thinking that," said Feathy with a chuckle. "And if that's what you're after, why not? Reckon you'd make a grand job of it, too."

"I've always wanted my own shop and this could be the moment to make it happen."

"Seriously though, Dora, it's a big undertaking."

"Yes, but I think I'm up to it. The major hurdle would be finding an investor."

"Couldn't you ask Jack? Persuade him of the potential, he's a business man after all."

Dora nodded. Jack was the obvious choice however beholden that would make her.

Feathy sat back in the Windsor chair and looked at Dora thoughtfully. "And how are things at home, love? Jack treating you right?"

"You were never taken in by him, were you Feathy?"

"Jack Armstrong's a very charming man but there was always something I couldn't put my finger on, something I didn't trust."

"Pity you didn't warn me."

"Fat chance of that with him all over you, day, noon and night."

"Yes, I remember. After the fire Jack took control of my life and then everything happened so fast."

"Ruth's day off, is it?"

Dora nodded. "Funny you know, she leaves really early in the morning and doesn't come back before dark but she never says where she's been."

"Likes to keep her business to herself, can't blame her for that."

"Oh, I don't. Ruth is a treasure and I know how lucky I am to have her. The only problem is that Jack's never taken to her and that's putting it mildly. He'd have had her out ages ago but where Ruth's concerned he knows I won't budge."

"And what about her?"

"Ruth takes it all in her stride, even the overt hostility. Sometimes I see her looking at him like he's an over indulged child."

Feathy chuckled. "Well, she's spot on there. His Mum spoiled him rotten as a youngster, so I've heard."

"That doesn't surprise me," Dora nodded. "The only time she telephones the house is when he's at home; sometimes I wonder whether they have a telepathic connection!"

"Can't be easy having her as an in-law."

"We so rarely see her that it's really no problem. Even when she comes at Christmas she doesn't stay long and everything she says is directed to Jack."

Feathy got up and called out to the children to come in for tea.

"Look at me!" shrieked Pam gleefully as Charlie came charging into the room with her on his back.

Dora turned in surprise to see Matt sitting on Tim's shoulders and laughing his head off.

"Right, that's enough or you'll have something over. Put them down, boys," said Feathy, cutting into a big chocolate cake.

Dora glanced in the car's rear-view mirror and saw that the children had fallen asleep. She slowed down towards the end of the high street to get a better look at the recently refurbished exterior of the Fine Arts Emporium. Every time she passed by she thought about Simon and how Jack had knocked that relationship on its head.

It was now a year since that day he had taken her to tea at Fortnum & Mason as a joint celebration of their birthdays; Simon was her senior by a year but they shared the same month. It was the last time that she had seen him. Jack had made sure of that.

"I know all about your illicit meetings, Dora," he had challenged her a few days later.

"What are you talking about?"

"Your liaison with the Canadian."

"Yes, I do see Simon from time to time, he's a friend and I see nothing wrong in that."

"Except I forbade it."

She had looked at his angry face and suddenly remembered that man lurking outside the store's smart entrance doors. She had only noticed him because of his cheap department store suit, an incongruous figure amongst the fashionably dressed clientele going to and fro through the glass doors. It would be no surprise to discover that Jack had employed a private detective to trail her.

"Have you had me followed, Jack?" she asked.

"No need of that. You obviously don't appreciate what a spectacle you make walking brazenly on to the railway platform dressed up to the nines."

Dora had been puzzled for a moment. She was usually so vigilant about not being detected when she went into the station and boarded the London train but perhaps she had become too complacent.

"You can't stop me going, Jack."

"I think I can, Dora. You see, the senior partner of the company he works for is a God fearing man who happens to be a friend of a client of mine."

"Surely you're not referring to Simon's boss?"

Jack nodded. "What if this gentleman hears about his employee's proclivity for married women? A smear on his reputation might be the least of his worries."

"You wouldn't dare!"

"Try me."

Whether or not there was truth in Jack's connection to the man she knew what he was capable of and the risk had been too great.

Chapter 27

Dora had gone to bed early and didn't see Ruth until her return from taking Matt to school the next morning.

"Not going into work then?" said Ruth, surprised to find Dora in the kitchen.

"No, I wanted a lie in, they can manage without me today," said Dora, lifting out jars from the cupboard. "I thought I'd have a good clear out instead."

Ruth filled up the kettle and put it on the gas ring. "That fellow in the shop still giving you lip, is he?"

"Worse than ever now he's got his diploma, the annoying thing is that Jack thinks Desmond Clarke is an asset to the business and refuses to get rid of him," said Dora.

"Good thing you've taken the day off; you haven't looked yourself for days," said Ruth.

"That's because my period was over a week late and I've been imagining the worst."

"You've taken contraception advice, I suppose?"

"I was fitted with a diaphragm but when Jack discovered it in the bathroom he hit the roof. And Jack likes to exact punishment, you know."

Ruth looked at her with concern. "Do you mean he knocks you about?"

"He's careful to find places where bruises don't show."

"Oh, the brute!"

"You'd think that at Jack's age his sex drive would have diminished but the only time I get a good night's sleep is when he's away and I don't have to listen to him snoring beside me afterward."

"And you live in dread of another pregnancy?"

Dora nodded. "I would never have told him of course but I'd already planned on having a termination, illegal or not."

Ruth blanched and a hand flew to her mouth. "Oh no, that's too dangerous, you must never do that! A botched abortion is what killed my daughter."

Pam toddled in from the back room and pulled on Ruth's skirt as she was pouring hot water into the teapot. "I'm hungry, Roofs!"

"All right, my poppet. Go back and play with your toys, I'll bring you a drink and a biscuit in a minute."

Pam pulled on Ruth's skirt again. "But I want it now!"

"Just do as Ruth says," said Dora, her tone sharper than she had intended.

Pam glanced at her mother with a scowl and did as she was told.

Dora took a drink of tea and looked across the table at Ruth. "I'm so sorry about your daughter, Ruth, that must have been a terrible time for you," said Dora.

"It was all her father's doing. Had he not discovered about the pregnancy and knocked the living daylights out of her, Mary would never have run away and got into the clutches of that wicked old hag. Two days later I found my girl collapsed on our doorstep. By then it was too late to save her and when I got back from the hospital and told Joshua, he said it was God's just retribution for her sin. That was the last time he ever shoved God down my throat!"

Dora was shaken by Ruth's revelation but when she went to give her a hug she was gently pushed away. "Nay, lass! Don't fuss. I've come to terms with the past and I won't let it break me."

"You're a very brave woman, Ruth."

"Well, I still have my son Christopher, even if he's on another continent. Thank heavens he had the sense to escape before his father could destroy him, too."

Ruth filled a glass with milk and put some biscuits on a plate then carried them out of the room. When she returned Dora was standing on a chair emptying the contents of one of the high cupboards.

"Here, let me give you a hand," said Ruth, coming up beside her.

Dora reached into the back and pulled out a bottle. "Good Gracious! An unopened bottle of laudanum, what on earth's it doing in here?"

"I was going to ask you that same question. I noticed it the first time I tidied that cupboard."

"This is the stuff my mother used to take, it must have got packed with the other things when we moved."

"Well, don't look a gift horse in the mouth!" Ruth chuckled, taking the bottle from Dora and inspecting the label. "A few drops of this would cool your husband's ardour."

After Ruth left to take Pam into the garden Dora went to collect the post that had just been pushed through the door. She was pleased to find a letter from Rachel and took it off into the sitting room to read. Over the years their correspondence had been sporadic but when they did arrive

Rachel's letters were always long and interesting. The first time she had written was a few months after her arrival in New York and she said how she had fallen in love with the lively cosmopolitan city and had just found a job on Vogue magazine. Her subsequent letters described her gradual climb from general dogsbody to a coveted position in the editorial department. Rachel was apparently focused on her career and had never referred to her private life; it was a surprise to learn that she had just accepted an offer to work on Vogue in London.

Dora was thinking about Rachel's return as she sat at her dressing table combing her freshly washed hair when she heard Jack's heavy tread on the landing.

"You're usually in the kitchen at this time of day," he said, coming into the room and standing behind her chair.

"You're early," she said, tugging on a tangle. "It's really time that I had this cut; a nice bob would be so much easier."

"No, Dora. You know how I prefer long hair on a woman."

He spotted the envelope lying beside her brush and picked it up. "Who's writing to you from America?"

"It's from Rachel, an old friend of mine. She's coming back to London soon."

"Rachel? Ah, I remember now, that's your young Jewish friend. You didn't tell me you kept in touch."

She was about to tell him to mind his own business but thought better of it. She wanted to keep him in a good mood.

"Jack, did you know that Madame Morel's shop had come on the market?"

"Yes," he said, resting his hand on the back of her chair. "Why do you ask?"

"Because I'd like to take over the lease."

"You, Dora? And how do you think you'd pay for it?"

"From the money I put aside from the sale of Mother's house."

"But that would barely cover the lease. You'd need a great deal more than that if you wanted to reopen the shop."

She glanced at him in the mirror. "Couldn't you help me, Jack? Both the businesses are doing well, you said so yourself."

He looked back at her. With her hair dishevelled she looked so young and lovely that he felt an urge to take her across to the bed. "No, Dora, not at the moment. I've just invested in new equipment," he said.

"Jack, do you remember once telling me that I shouldn't waste my talent, you even said that I should be set up in my own shop. Have you forgotten that?"

"No, I remember but times have changed, Dora. It was a long time ago."

She swung around in the chair and looked up angrily. "The difference is that now you've got me where you want me!"

"I've done what?"

"First you trap me into a loveless marriage…"

"You stop right there, Dora, and listen to me. There aren't many men prepared to take on soiled goods like I did; you should count yourself lucky that I did the honourable thing."

Dora glared at him in fury. "What, like raping me?"

He gave a coarse laugh. "You were gasping for it, girl."

She got up, picked up the dressmaking scissors from the table and held them out threateningly. "Get out, Jack, get out before I do something I might regret."

That night when Jack came to bed he ignored her feigned sleep and pulled Dora toward him. Without speaking a word, he reached between her legs and pushed himself into her.

For days afterward Dora treated Jack with such icy disdain that it made him uneasy. She had never been as pliant as he would have liked but recently he had noticed a steeliness in her that he hadn't seen before and he wondered at how that adorable girl he once knew had been transformed into this spiky young woman.

One afternoon as Dora was reading in the sitting room Jack came in and offered her the pretty bouquet of flowers he held.

Dora nodded her thanks and took them out of the room.

Later, when she came back to retrieve her book Jack looked up from the newspaper he was reading.

"Do come and sit down. You can't go on sulking for ever."

She picked up her book but before she could retreat Jack was on his feet.

"Just sit down, woman," he said, taking hold of her arm.

"Please let go of me, Jack."

"I need to talk to you, Dora. That's why I came home early."

Dora turned and perched on the edge of the nearest chair. "Well?"

"I think you should know that we've been harbouring a fugitive in this house," said Jack, sitting back in his chair.

"A fugitive! What on earth are you talking about?"

"Ruth Gibson is an imposter. I've been having her investigated over the last weeks and some curious things have come to light."

Dora was suddenly alert. "What kind of things?"

"If my man is not mistaken her name is actually Constance Hardacre, ring any bells?"

"No, should it?"

"Five years ago Constance Hardacre was accused of murdering her husband but she disappeared before they could arrest her. It was all over the papers."

"Then it must be a question of mistaken identity."

"No, Dora, there's little room for doubt and I'll shortly have the evidence to prove it."

"And what do you intend to do with that?"

"Hand her over to the police authorities, of course. The Lancashire constabulary will certainly be interested."

"Is that where this murder took place?"

"Yes, that's where the trail has taken him."

She thought of Ruth upstairs putting the children to bed, perhaps at this moment reading their bedtime story, oblivious to the threat hanging over her. Everything that Jack said was plausible and it filled her with dread.

At supper that evening Jack was pleasantly surprised to find Dora's mood so convivial; perhaps secretly she too had suspicions and would be glad to see the back of Ruth Gibson. The woman had not been a good influence on Dora he ruminated and, as far as he was concerned, she was largely responsible for Dora's taciturn moods. The way that Dora smiled when he complimented her on the excellent meal was encouraging and he felt the familiar stirring in his loins. When this whole affair with Ruth Gibson was over he might suggest they took a holiday together. That would invigorate him and take care of the annoying fatigue he was beset by these days.

He retired early to bed and leafed through the Reader's Digest while he waited for Dora to come up. Jack was a man of habit and he enjoyed the ritual of the night time drink that she brought him before she herself came to join him in the bed. Downstairs in the kitchen Dora ladled the extra spoons of sugar into the hot chocolate, thankful for his sweet tooth. The few drops of laudanum that she added could do him no harm. On the previous occasions she had resorted to the subterfuge he had fallen asleep almost instantly.

Chapter 28

Jack was still sleeping when she went downstairs in the morning. It was Ruth's day off but she had already given the children breakfast and was tidying up the kitchen. As soon as she left, Dora bundled the children into the car and dropped Matt off at school then drove to the nursery that Pam now attended.

Later that morning, Dora sat tensely in the silent kitchen drinking coffee. The minutes ticked by and she felt time closing in... Her faith in Ruth had not wavered and she would do anything in her power to protect her but first she needed to know.

She glanced around at the tidy room and neatly made bed and though at first recoiling from the task ahead she sifted quickly through the wardrobe and bedside cabinet before turning to the chest of drawers. For a few moments she studied the photograph of the boy and girl displayed on top before inspecting the contents stored beneath. Inside one of the two top drawers and secreted under some undergarments was a small bundle of press cuttings tucked into an envelope. She picked them up and took them across to the bed.

A few of the articles had been cut out from national newspapers but the majority were from local press reports and contained long missives about the deceased, Joshua Hardacre, respected civil servant and revered church elder. She glossed over them and picked up the two articles that featured a photograph, one of a family group and the other of an attractive young woman standing alone beneath a tree.

The hair might be darker and differently styled but there was no mistaking Constance Hardacre's likeness to Ruth.

The next article she read was taken from the national press and stated that Joshua Hardacare had been stabbed through the heart with a carving knife and that his wife Constance Hardacre, who had fled soon afterward, was under suspicion of murder. The police had instigated a nationwide search but as yet Mrs Hardacre had not been apprehended.

There was another article dated one month later that described how the body of a middle aged woman had been dredged from the River Yarrow, but after lying in the water for over ten days the body was too decomposed for formal identification. However, the police had good reason to believe the body to be that of the murder suspect Constance Hardacre and have now closed the case.

The rest of that day passed in a blur as Dora went through the familiar routine of collecting the children from school, giving them tea and preparing supper for Jack. Both children were tucked up in bed by the time Jack returned in the evening.

"Any news from your private detective today, Jack?" said Dora casually as she cut into the crust of the steak and kidney pie.

"Yes, he's coming down on the train to see me, should be here by the end of the week. Hitchings has now obtained photographs and police statements taken at the time," he said with a satisfied grin.

Dora was about to serve him a portion of the pie when she felt it slip from the serving spoon. "Oh, Dammit, how clumsy!" she muttered, and hastily retrieved it from the table cloth.

"You seem a bit agitated, Dora," said Jack.

"Yes, I suppose I am. It must be this dreadful business about Ruth."

"Well, try not to worry too much, it'll all be over soon," said Jack, tucking into his meal. "By the way, I was wondering today whether we need bother finding another live-in help. It won't be too long before Pamela is in full time school and with you only working part-time I'm sure you could manage with just a cleaner a few times a week, couldn't you?"

Dora nodded. "Yes, I expect so."

"I have a surprise for you, Dora," said Jack, picking up his napkin and wiping his mouth.

"Oh, what's that?"

"Well, I talked to a travel agent today. It's time we had a holiday."

"A holiday?" said Dora, startled. Her mind was elsewhere and she was finding it hard to focus on what he was saying.

"Yes. Torquay or Brighton is where I was thinking, what do you fancy?"

"But we never go on holiday, Jack."

"Well, that's about to change. I intend to ask my mother to take care of the children; it's time she got to know them better. We can find a girl to help her out."

"So you're serious about it, are you?"

"Of course I am. Now tell me which destination you would prefer?"

"I'm not really sure, Jack. Why don't I leave that to you?"

Dora was re-reading George Elliot's Middlemarch and was so struck by its resonances on her own life that she didn't at first notice when Ruth opened the sitting room door.

"Oh, Ruth, you're back!" she said, looking up startled.

"Hmm, just got in," said Ruth with a smile. "He's gone up, has he?"

"Just a few minutes ago, it's time I went to make his cocoa."

"I can take care of that, I know how he likes it. You just stay put; I can see how you're enjoying that book."

Dora stared after Ruth's departing figure, the novel erased from her mind. She should warn Ruth about what Jack had been up to and then let her decide on the best course of action, but she feared that Ruth would take flight and she might never see her again.

A little later, she handed the mug of chocolate to Jack and went off to the bathroom. By the time she returned to the bedroom the mug was empty and Jack was asleep. He didn't like the light left on so she put on her dressing gown and went downstairs to lie on the sofa. Ruth had now gone to bed and, having decided to talk to her first thing in the morning, Dora picked up the novel. She didn't expect to sleep that night but after an hour or so she drifted off and didn't wake up until daylight came streaming in through the gap in the curtains.

The bedroom was silent and still in darkness when she crept in to fetch her clothes and later, when she returned from the bathroom, Jack hadn't stirred. She pulled back the curtains and went across to the bed, then reeled back in shock. Jack lay motionless on his back, his eyes open and staring.

Dr Hargreaves, a young doctor from the local surgery she hadn't met before, arrived fifteen minutes later.

He came solemnly down the stairs and took Dora to one side in the hallway. "I'm afraid it was a heart attack, Mrs Armstrong."

Dora swayed and held on to the balustrade at the bottom of the staircase.

"I think you need to sit down," said the young doctor solicitously. "This must be a terrible shock."

In the kitchen the children stood beside Ruth, Matt dressed in his uniform and ready for school. Dora glanced at her and went to sit down.

"Well, we'll be off, Mrs Armstrong," said Ruth, taking the children by the hand.

"There's fresh tea in the pot."

Dora nodded and was about to get up when Dr Hargreaves took her arm. "Let me do that but first I need to use your telephone."

"When did you first notice that something was wrong, Mrs Armstrong?" he asked later, stirring his tea.

"Not till I went up to rouse him this morning."

"And what about last night? Was he out of sorts?"

"No, he seemed all right."

"And nothing seemed out of the ordinary?"

Dora shook her head.

"And during the night?"

There was no need for him to know that she had spent the night on the sofa in the sitting room. "No."

The doorbell rang and he got up. "Ah, that will be the ambulance."

He stopped in the doorway and turned to her. "Is there someone you'd like me to telephone, Mrs Armstrong, someone to come and be with you?"

"No, that's very kind but Ruth will be back soon. She lives in."

Dora was reeling in shock and by the end of that day she was so exhausted that she fell asleep instantly in the bed that Ruth had made up in the spare room, and it wasn't until the next morning that she was struck by the full implications of Jack's death. Ruth had just brewed the tea and the children weren't yet up when Dora went down to the kitchen and she gave her a wordless hug. The household routine commenced as normal but Dora was so elated by the sudden release from her marriage that nothing seemed real that day.

It was the arrival of Inspector Fairchild the following morning that sobered her mood.

"The reason I'm here, Mrs Armstrong, is that I'm investigating your husband's death as a possible murder case," he said, taking a seat opposite Dora in the sitting room.

He took out his notebook and glanced across at her. "There is no history of heart problems in Mr Armstrong's medical records but a great deal of laudanum has been found in his system. Can you explain that, Mrs Armstrong?"

"Yes, Inspector, I can. My husband was a habitual user of the drug, you see. He said it calmed his nerves."

"Oh?"

Inspector Fairchild paused for several moments. He often used this ploy to ruffle the respondent. Should they have something to hide, the unexpected silence usually made them uneasy and put them off guard but this young woman said nothing and appeared entirely composed.

"And for how long was your husband a user of this drug?"

"I've no idea."

"So what you're saying is that your husband was dependent upon the drug. Can anyone else testify to that, his mother for instance?"

"It isn't something that we talked about."

"Your husband must have kept a supply in the house, in the bathroom cabinet for example?"

"Not that I've noticed, Inspector, but then my husband is or was what you might describe as a secretive person."

The Inspector looked down at his notes. "I understand that your husband was a great deal older than you, Mrs Armstrong?"

"Yes, he was, Inspector."

"And did this age gap cause any problems?"

"Why should it?"

"So you would consider your marriage to have been a happy one, Mrs Armstrong?"

"I suppose we had our ups and downs, like any other married couple."

Inspector Fairchild had been a detective for twenty-five years and believed he had enough experience to judge a person's veracity but whether or not this young widow was dissembling he couldn't say.

"And when did you and Mr Armstrong get married?"

"Almost eight years ago."

"So that would have been 1925," said the Inspector, making a note. "Had Mr Armstrong been married before?"

"Married before?" Dora repeated, puzzled by the odd question though when she thought about it she realised how little she knew of Jack's past. "Well no, Inspector, I don't believe so."

"Very well, Mrs Armstrong; I think that will be all for now."

Dora had just risen to her feet when the Inspector raised his hand. "Ah, there is just one more thing, Ma'am. It's about your employee, Ruth Gibson."

For a moment Dora froze then forced herself to sit down again. "What is it you wish to know, Inspector?"

"How long has she been in your employ?"

"Oh, Ruth has been with us for years."

"Can you be more precise?"

"She came to work for my mother some years before I was married, perhaps ten or eleven years ago now."

"And what can you tell me about her?"

"Mrs Gibson is a war widow, Inspector. I believe her husband was decorated for bravery in action, I know she's very proud of him," said Dora, embellishing her story as she went along.

"And what about her family?"

"I don't believe she has anyone left. She and her husband had no children."

Feathy jumped up from her chair as Dora came into the kitchen. "Has he gone then?" she said.

Dora nodded and went to sit down.

"So what was all that about?"

"He said he was here to make inquiries about Jack, just routine police procedures, I believe," said Dora.

"Hmm. Arthur's told me that often happens in cases of sudden or unexpected death. Still, it's not as though he got murdered!" she said.

Ruth retreated through the door. "I'm just going to check on little Pam."

"Time I was off then," said Feathy, getting up. "I'm glad to see you're all right Dora and don't forget, if you need any help with the funeral arrangements, you just let me know."

*

As soon as they all left Dora reached into the kitchen cupboard to remove the evidence but the bottle of laudanum was no longer there. Emily was due to arrive that afternoon and Dora was tidying away the toys in the family room when the doorbell rang. Instead of Emily, an odd looking little man dressed in an over-size mackintosh and trilby hat stood on the door step.

"My name is Oswald Hitchings and I should like to speak to the lady of the house, if I may," he said.

"I'm Mrs Armstrong," said Dora.

"My condolences, Ma'am," he said, removing the hat. "I know this must be a difficult time and my apologies for the intrusion but I've recently been working on an assignment on behalf of your late husband and there is an account to be settled."

Dora told him that she was aware of the matter, ushered him into the kitchen and began thinking fast. She knew that from time to time Jack would deposit sums of money into the safety box that he kept at the back of the airing cupboard, cash that he siphoned from the two businesses and that did not appear in the ledgers. It was a relief to find the box had not been moved and the sum of money it contained far exceeded her expectation. The collection of five, one and ten shilling notes and coins were arranged in separate bags and she grabbed it all up and shoved it into her handbag.

Mr Hitchings pocketed the money Dora handed over without comment, then took out a file from his briefcase and placed it on the table. "This is the dossier that I have compiled."

Attached to the front of the dossier was a photograph that Dora recognised from the press cuttings in Ruth's drawer. "Thank you, Mr Hitchings," she said, about to get up. "And now that I've settled your account I trust that is all."

He removed his spectacles and began polishing the thick lenses with his handkerchief. "This dossier should be lodged with the authorities, Mrs Armstrong."

"That won't be necessary, Mr Hitchings, I'm afraid my late husband was mistaken. The lady in question has been known by me and my family for many years and she is of exemplary character."

"But I've been most diligent in my investigation and have the evidence here to prove it," said Mr Hitchings, reaching for the file.

"That I don't doubt, Mr Hitchings, nevertheless it is a question of mistaken identity," said Dora firmly, taking hold of the file.

He stared at her a moment, his expression dubious. "This case has taken a great deal of my time and effort, Mrs Armstrong."

The obnoxious little man seemed unwilling to leave and was testing her patience; she needed him gone before Ruth's return.

"I don't doubt it, Mr Hitchings, and for that I'm willing to offer you a bonus of two guineas," she smiled and taking the money from her bag she placed it in front of him.

Dora didn't see the Inspector again until Jack's body was released for burial ten days later. She was walking up the path toward the church when she caught sight of him amongst the crowd waiting outside. His presence was unsettling; perhaps the investigation wasn't over, after all.

Jack was a well-known figure and a large congregation was already assembled when Dora entered the church with Tom and Kitty. She noticed Jack's mother seated at the back with a grey haired middle aged woman whom Dora didn't recognise and wondered why she hadn't taken her rightful place on one of the front pews.

Later, at the burial site, Jack's mother kept her distance from Dora and only stepped forward when it was time to throw a handful of earth on to the coffin. Afterward she returned to stand beside the same woman she had sat with in church and with them were a well-dressed young man and woman. Dora noticed Miss Gates and her mother standing nearby and hovering behind them was Desmond Clarke, looking dapper in his hired mourning suit.

*

It was two days after the funeral that Tom and Kitty had arranged to meet Simon in London and after seeing them off at the railway station Dora went to keep her appointment at the offices of Campbell & Pembury, the trustees of Jack's estate. They were the solicitors who had once employed her father though Roderick had now retired and it was his son Cedric who came to meet her at reception. Cedric, an earnest looking man in his thirties, broke into a smile as he shook her hand and reminded her how many years ago they had met at her parents' home.

As soon as they entered his office Dora noticed a subtle shift in Cedric's demeanour. For a few moments he sat behind his desk shuffling the papers in front of him then looked across at Dora with an air of apology before finally clearing his throat, he was extremely uncomfortable with the news he had to impart.

Dora drove directly home afterward and retreated to the bedroom she used to share with Jack. She lay fully dressed on the bed assessing the implications of what she had just learned and would have remained there longer if Ruth hadn't tapped on the door.

"Whatever is the matter, Dora?" said Ruth coming into the room.

Dora sat up and swung her legs off the bed. "Jack Armstrong was a bigamist, Ruth. I was never married to him and my children are bastards!" she said and burst into laughter. "Now I understand why Inspector Fairchild continued to take an interest in us!"

Ruth frowned. The laughter had become hysterical. She put her hands firmly on Dora's shoulders. "Stop this, Dora. You've got it all off your chest now and we're going to talk this through calmly."

They sat talking long into the night, drinking endless cups of tea whilst doing so.

"I hate to say this Ruth but you'll have to start looking for another job. I have no money to pay you," said Dora.

"No, Dora, I won't be leaving you and the children, not unless you order me to do so."

"But we'll have nowhere to live, you know. We won't be able to stay here."

"So you get nothing?"

"No, everything goes to his legal wife. Estranged or not they were never divorced."

"Who is this woman?"

"Her name's Evelyn and she lives in Somerset. She's the woman I saw with Jack's mother at the funeral; I imagine that young man and woman are his children."

"Do you think she knew about you?"

"I doubt it. Apparently he visited her from time to time, remember those mysterious trips he went on? Cedric was extremely well informed."

"Do you know how long we can stay here?"

"They've given us six weeks and then to all intents and purposes we're out on the street!"

Chapter 29

Within the month Dora had moved the family into the vacant flat above Madame Morel's shop. The flat was in a poor state of repair but Dora and Ruth rolled up their sleeves and, with the help of Feathy's boys, Tim and Charlie, the walls were soon coated with fresh paint. Simon had arrived with a bag of tools on the week-end that they moved in, and with his surprising talent for carpentry the renovations were soon completed. Janet Jennings donated a comfortable sofa and chairs for the living room and the bed and other furniture came from Mr Wiggins, proprietor of the huge dusty junk shops on the outskirts of town.

"You strike a hard bargain, Mrs Armstrong," he chuckled as Dora haggled over the price of the mahogany dining table, recalling how he had succumbed when she demurred over the price of a pretty but badly damaged walnut bureau.

Much as she admired the bureau, Dora had considered it a luxury that she could live without and it was extremely gratifying when eventually Mr Wiggins let it go for a song.

After Brenda's husband had restored the bureau in his workshop, Mr Clifton of the Fine Arts Emporium had come to make an appraisal and, having attributed its fine craftsmanship to the William and Mary period, he immediately wanted to buy it. By now, Dora had decided to re-open Madame Morel's shop and needing every penny she could muster. She waited a few weeks until Mr Clifton increased his original offer to a figure that she couldn't refuse.

News of her bigamous marriage had been leaked to the press and there were certain members of the community who were still relishing the scandal. One day Dora went over to Jack's former shop to hand over the ledgers to Mr Humphries and later when she came out of the office Miss Gates and Mr Clarke were gossiping in the shop.

"Oh, how have the mighty fallen!" chuckled Miss Gates in glee.

"Serves her right, the haughty bitch," said Mr Clarke.

"But brazen as you please she moves into Madame Morel's flat and now word has it she intends to re-open the shop!"

"What, she's going into business?"

"Well, she's whistling in the wind if she thinks she'll get customers through that door!"

"I wouldn't bank on that, Priscilla, a bit of notoriety could work in her favour. People will be curious to meet the so-called widow!"

Dora stepped into the room and gave the couple a beaming smile. "Well thank you Mr Clarke for that sage insight. You may be sure that I shall fully exploit it!"

Over the weeks Simon had been such a regular visitor that he was almost part of the household, and whether he was sanding floors or putting up cupboards there was always laughter when he was around. The children eagerly awaited his week-end visits and when his green sports car pulled up on the kerb they would rush out to meet him.

One Saturday evening Simon took Dora to see the recently released film *The Private Lives of Henry VIII* starring Charles Laughton. Whilst having dinner at a local restaurant they discussed their favourable impressions, particularly of Charles Laughton's towering performance in the title role. They had also watched the newsreels of events taking place in Berlin and the anti-Semitic ideology was very alarming.

Rachel was now back in England and remembering that she had family there, Dora hoped that they weren't affected. They had spoken several times on the telephone since her return and Rachel had listened sympathetically when Dora told her about the planned launch of the shop and of how the bank manager had peremptorily dismissed her request for a loan.

"Sad to say but it's still the men who hold the reins, particularly where business is concerned; but don't give up the fight. From what you tell me you've devised a good business plan and there are still ways we can make it work. Give me a few days and I'll look into it," Rachel had said.

As they were finishing their meal Simon mentioned that he intended to embark on the renovations at Bingley Hall.

"I'm keeping the place for my retirement, you see," he said with a chuckle.

"But that's years away!" said Dora.

"Indeed it is, but in the meantime I shall let it."

"What a very good idea, Simon."

"I'm glad you approve," he said with a grin.

"Of course I do," Dora laughed. "Seriously though, Simon, it's been so good to have you around and I really appreciate all your help. Your friendship means a great deal to me."

"And I'd like to be more than a friend," he said earnestly.

"Are you saying what I think you are?"

"Yes. I'm in love with you, Dora."

"Oh, Simon!" she said, flustered.

He looked at her a moment, remembering that evening he had kissed her and the passionate way she had responded before suddenly pulling away. "I had hoped for some words of encouragement," he said.

"Oh, Simon," she said with a sigh. "You know I'm terribly fond of you; I'm sorry but this isn't good timing. The business is now my priority; it's all I can think about at the moment."

Simon had come to recognise that stubborn look on her face and wondered whether after her experiences with Jack she would ever be able to trust another man.

*

Jack would be turning in his grave to see how she had spent his stashed away cash in the airing cupboard, Dora thought ruefully, as she unpacked the first of the orders to arrive. She counted out the garments as she put them on hangers, and looking at the meagre merchandise she realised she would have to delay opening the shop and meanwhile find another way to support the family.

That evening Simon arrived unexpectedly and Ruth greeted him at the front door with a big smile. "Oh, Simon, it's good to see you again."

"I've just popped in to collect my tools," he said, following her into the kitchen.

"You haven't been round for a while; the children have been asking after you," she said.

He sat down on a chair at the table. "Where is everyone?"

"The children are upstairs, they've just had their bath and Dora's downstairs unpacking her orders."

"How is she?"

Ruth sighed, taking a seat opposite him. "Things aren't looking good, as far as I can tell. She may have bitten off more than she can chew."

He shrugged. "I'd give her a loan tomorrow if she'd accept it."

Ruth sighed. "You know how proud she is."

He nodded.

"Why don't you stay for supper, Simon?" said Ruth. "If anyone can talk any sense into her I reckon it's you."

He winked conspiratorially. "I'll do my best."

Later, he and Dora were having a glass of sherry in the living room when he made his proposal. "Why don't you let me invest in the shop? I know that you're doing it on a shoe-string."

The offer was exceedingly tempting but Dora was loathe to be beholden to anyone. The conversation was making her uncomfortable but just then the telephone rang and she hurried off to answer it. When she returned to the room five minutes later the children had come in dressed in their night clothes and were chatting to Simon.

"Time for bed, you two," she said.

Pam looked up and shook her head. "Just a bit longer, please Mama."

Simon got up and took her by the hand. "Come on; let's go, if you're very good I might read a story."

Matt took his other hand. "Could we have Treasure Island?"

"No, I want Rumpelstiltskin," said Pam as they walked from the room.

"Was that Rachel you were talking to on the phone?" asked Ruth, as she served the lamb stew.

Dora nodded. "She was a bit mysterious but she says she's found a way forward."

"That's good news, no wonder you're looking chirpier."

Dora turned to Simon. "Rachel is the friend that I told you about, the one who works on Vogue."

He nodded. "Sounds as though your friend has the right credentials."

"She's suggested coming here next week."

"Well, I intend to take a few days off and do some work on the house; why don't I bring her down in the car?"

"Thank you, Simon. That would be excellent."

*

The following Monday morning Ruth came into the kitchen just as Dora stepped through the back door with her shopping.

"Simon and the young lady are here, Dora. They arrived about ten minutes ago."

"Oh, Dammit, I won't even have time to change," said Dora.

"Well, you go and tidy yourself up and I'll put this lot away," said Ruth.

Later, when Dora entered her living room Rachel jumped up from her seat. "Oh, Dora, how marvellous to see again," she said.

"You, too," said Dora, giving her a hug.

It was more than a decade since she had met Rachel and the sophisticated young woman in her tailored monochrome dress and stylish kid leather shoes who sat beside Simon on the sofa bore little resemblance to the vulnerable girl Dora once knew.

"I'm so glad to meet your children at last, Dora," said Rachel, glancing towards Matt and Pam unwrapping the parcels she had brought them.

"Look what I've got, Mama!" said Pam in delight, holding up a large, golden haired doll.

"Oh, Rachel, how kind of you," said Dora.

"To tell you the truth I had no idea how big they were and if it wasn't for Simon taking me to the toy store I wouldn't have had a clue what to get them."

After Simon went off with Matt to unpack his Meccano set in the playroom Rachel turned to Dora. "You didn't tell me you had such a good looking brother, I couldn't believe my luck when he turned up on the doorstep!"

"He's my step-brother, Rachel," said Dora.

"Yes, Simon did explain the family history."

"Well, what's it like to be back home, Rachel?" said Dora, pouring out coffee from the pot on the table.

"It's great actually. The job's terrific; I've been promoted to assistant editor of our British magazine. It's been really nice to see the family again, especially to meet my new nephew. And would you believe it, I was welcomed like the prodigal daughter!"

"Your parents must be proud of what you've achieved," said Dora, handing her a cup.

"That's the funny thing, Dora, the way my father boasts about my career you'd think it was he who promoted it!"

She looked thoughtful as she took a packet of gold tipped cigarettes from her bag and fitted one into an ivory holder. "Mind you, I think my return is a welcome diversion. He and my mother are so desperately anxious about my uncle's family in Berlin. Have you heard how they've started to boycott Jewish businesses?"

Dora nodded. "I thought the Germans were a rational race until they elected to make that dreadful man Hitler their Chancellor."

"Yes, indeed, but he and his cohorts are making the Jews the scapegoat for the nation's grievances and their insidious propaganda machine has profound influence."

"Well, it certainly puts my problems into perspective," said Dora ruefully. "It's good of you to come, Rachel, when you've got so much on your mind."

"Life has to go on, don't they say?"

Later, when Dora escorted her around the premises Rachel's ideas and enthusiasm were just the tonic that Dora needed.

"It's good to aim at the higher end of the market," said Rachel, nodding approval as she inspected the garments that hung in the cupboard.

She pulled out a dress from the rail and held it out. "This is pretty."

"That's one of my own designs," said Dora.

"Then why doesn't it have a label? You should be promoting yourself." She put back the dress and turned to Dora. "It would be a good idea to get your name sewn inside like other designers do."

When they returned to the living room Rachel took a pad from her bag and began making notes whilst Dora went to check on the lunch that Ruth was preparing.

Rachel looked up as Dora came back into the room, tore a piece of paper from the pad and handed it to her. "I've sketched some ideas for the two window displays. Never clutter them, Dora. One elegant gown artfully arranged in the centre of a window always has the most impact."

She picked up her briefcase and withdrew some professionally drawn sketches that she handed to Dora. "Now I've been doing some research and found some fledgling companies, there are two here that may be of interest."

Dora liked the designs very much and nodded her approval.

"They're willing to supply stock on a sale or return basis, should I be willing to promote them in one of our issues."

"And you're prepared to do that?"

"Yes, happily, their designers are very talented, they deserve some exposure. What I suggest is that you meet me in London and I'll take you to see them."

"That sounds perfect."

Rachel lit up another cigarette. "By the way, I heard that Johnny got married to the Honourable Jessica Hamilton and has two children."

"How do you feel about that?"

Rachel shrugged. "That's all water under the bridge," said Rachel with a shrug. "But what about Nicky; have you heard what he's up to?"

"No, I've no idea."

"I sense a touch of wistfulness there."

"Perhaps, but I wish him well whatever he's doing."

Ruth had a newspaper spread across the table and was polishing the children's shoes when Dora went into the kitchen later. "Well, how was it?" she said, looking up.

"Very useful indeed; Rachel may yet save the day."

"Glad to hear it," said Ruth. "But you look tired, Dora. Why don't I make us a cuppa?"

Dora yawned and sat down. "That would be nice."

Ruth placed the shoes on the floor and folded up the newspaper. "I hate to remind you but Matt really does need a new pair."

"Is there anything left from the house keeping?" said Dora.

Ruth shook her head. "I have a little put by; I could take Matt to the shoe shop after school tomorrow."

"Leave it to me, Ruth. I haven't pawned my mother's wedding ring yet," said Dora with a grin.

For weeks now they had been living hand to mouth and with the meagre sums at her disposal each evening Ruth had contrived to provide a nutritious family meal. She rarely referred to the past unless in relation to the excursions she took to visit her daughter's grave. Sometimes she mentioned her son Christopher who was now working on a sheep farm in Australia, and Dora vowed that one day she would fund a passage for Christopher to visit his mother in England. Though they discussed most things of a confidential nature they never spoke of Jack, nor the manner of his demise. It wasn't a deliberate evasion, just a part of their history best left in the past.

Chapter 30

Dora stared apprehensively at the crowd gathered outside on the pavement, glanced at her watch and turned to her employee Sarah Simmons with a nod. With promises of a bonus system Dora had lured Sarah from her job as a sales assistant at Selfridges in Oxford Street. She was now a comely and competent young woman with the experience of sales that the shop needed.

Sarah turned the placard on the door to 'open' and gradually the customers filtered into the shop. The minutes ticked by slowly whilst the clientele appraised the merchandise and hovered over the price tags. Some just shrugged and went on their way and Dora was wondering whether her prices were too high when suddenly a young woman emerged from one of the changing rooms and told Dora to wrap her purchases, a total of six separate garments, two of which were Dora's own designs. As soon as the purchases were wrapped and taken off by the young woman's chauffeur, several other customers began jostling for a place in the changing rooms and the cash till was ringing up sales for the rest of the day.

One of the companies that Rachel had promoted was a particular success, the garments being of such high quality and style yet at an affordable price that they disappeared from the shop within days of their arrival. After a brief perusal of the balance sheets the bank manager had no compunction in granting Dora a loan to invest in more stock which gave her the chance to expand and to branch out into accessories. In the run up to Christmas the shop was so busy that Dora took on a second assistant and within a few months her reputation had spread, attracting a clientele who came seeking her expertise regarding a gown for a particular event. It was a bonus to discover that they could purchase a complete ensemble under one roof.

By the time that Whitsun came around Dora was in need of a break and she closed the shop for a brief hiatus.

"Will Simon be coming to join us?" asked Ruth, as Dora came into the kitchen one evening.

"Not that I know," said Dora, taking a seat at the table.

"We haven't seen him for weeks now," said Ruth, stirring a pan on the stove.

"I expect he's still busy working on the house though the last time we talked he said he was taking a business trip to Berlin."

"Berlin, eh? That's not a place I'd wish to go, not these days."

"Rachel told me he's going to pay a visit to her uncle and persuade him to obtain exit visas for him and his family."

"That sounds like a sensible plan."

Dora poured out a glass of sherry from the bottle on the table. "Would you like a glass, Ruth?"

"Perhaps in a moment, I need to get this pie in the oven first," said Ruth, pouring sauce over a dish of chicken and leeks, then folding a pastry crust over the top.

She put the pie in the oven and went to sit down. "Has something happened between you and Simon, something you haven't told me?"

Dora handed Ruth a glass of sherry. "This is beginning to feel like an interrogation, Ruth."

"Well, you can't blame me for asking, he used to be such a regular visitor and the children are missing him. Matt keeps asking when he'll be coming again."

Though she wouldn't admit it Dora was missing him, too. "Well, if you must know, Simon would like us to have a more intimate relationship."

"That doesn't surprise me a bit. I suppose you put him off?"

"Look, Ruth, the business is going from strength to strength and it needs my full time attention."

"Is that really all that matters to you, Lass?"

"I'm enjoying my independence, Ruth," said Dora defensively.

"I can see that. What bothers me is that by the time you are ready Simon might well have been snapped up, in fact I'm surprised it hasn't happened already. A fellow like Simon would be a fine catch."

Dora didn't mention how unsettled she'd been by Jane Bellingham's visit. It was about a month after the shop had opened when one afternoon Nicky's aunt walked through the door. Sarah was serving a customer at the time and after whispering a word in her ear Dora went off to the tea room with Jane.

"I'm afraid I can't stay long, Mrs Bellingham, the shop's very busy today," said Dora, taking a seat at the table she used to share with Emily.

"Well it certainly seems a great success and I take my hat off to you, Dora. I read about the shop in my cousin's local paper and recognised your maiden name, I couldn't resist coming to have a look," said Jane.

"Well, I'm glad you came, Mrs Bellingham."

Jane had ordered a pot of tea and cakes, then turned to Dora. "I understand you've been recently widowed, Dora. Please accept my condolences."

Dora had nodded, wondering whether she knew about the scandal of her bigamous marriage.

"I hear you have two children, too. That must be hard for you on your own."

"Fortunately, Mrs Bellingham, I have a wonderful woman to take care of them so I'm very well supported."

After a short pause Dora had looked across at Jane and asked after Nicky.

"Nicky is currently living in Madeira with his mother," she said. "After my brother-in-law passed away Clarissa bought a house there, you see. The mild climate suits her better than damp old England."

"So Nicky has moved there as well?"

"Yes, he's keeping his mother company."

"What about his academic career?"

Dora noticed a tremble in Jane's hand as she poured out the tea. "My sister-in-law is now his priority; she needs his support."

She quickly changed the subject, apparently more comfortable to talk about Lettie's new marriage and didn't mention Nicky again. Afterward Dora wished she had asked more questions. There had been no mention of a wife and believing that Jane would tell Nicky of her visit she waited expectantly for him to make contact. The weeks passed by and she was beginning to lose heart when one day three months later he telephoned to say that he was in London and wanted them to meet.

*

Dora had dreamed of this day for so long and could hardly contain her excitement as the train trundled toward London. However, when she arrived at the entrance to the chic French restaurant her confidence suddenly vanished. She was in two minds about entering when a young waiter caught sight of her through the glass door and ushered her inside. She followed him across the crowded restaurant to a table in an alcove and it took her a moment to recognise the tall, gaunt man who stood up to greet her.

"Dora, you look wonderful!" said Nicky, bending to kiss her cheek. "It's so good to see you again."

"You too, Nicky," she said, taking the chair that the waiter held out for her.

As they sipped at a cocktail he explained that he had come to London with his mother to settle affairs with their family lawyer, and as he began talking in his easy familiar manner Dora was pained to see how much he had aged, his hairline had receded and his handsome face was etched with lines.

Nicky brought up the subject of his aunt's visit, telling Dora how proud he was of what she had achieved.

"I always knew how clever you were, Dora, but as for acquiring a business of your own as well as raising two children, you have even surpassed my expectations," he laughed.

She had longed for him to know the truth, to describe Jack's perfidy and the dark days of her marriage yet too many years had elapsed and Nicky was almost a stranger to her now.

By the end of the meal he had spoken little about himself except to tell her of his guilt at not being there to offer his father the support that he needed. "My father took his own life, you see," he confided.

Dora reached across the table and touched his hand fleetingly. "How terrible for you, Nicky, I am so sorry."

They didn't discuss their former relationship, nor refer to the future that they had once hoped to share. It seemed best to leave all that in the past.

Chapter 31

It was Feathy's birthday and as it fell on a Wednesday that year, Dora closed the shop at lunch time and, armed with a large bunch of flowers and accompanied by Pamela, she went to pay her a visit.

"Ruth's in bed with a cold so I've brought Pam with me," she said, walking into the hallway.

"It's always a treat to see my Goddaughter. Hello, sweetheart," said Feathy, taking the card that Pamela handed over shyly. "Oh my, aren't you growing up fast!"

"She's tall for a six year old," Dora nodded, following Feathy into the kitchen.

Feathy took a box from the sideboard that contained an assortment of buttons arranged in compartments according to size and colour. "Now, here you are my love, I know you like playing with these," said Feathy, handing the box to Pamela.

She filled the kettle and began arranging the flowers in a vase. "So the business still flourishing, eh?"

"The turnover last month was the biggest yet, sometimes I have to pinch myself to make sure it's not all a dream," Dora laughed.

"You deserve it, girl. You've worked hard enough."

"I'd never have got it launched without you and Rachel."

"Well, that young woman was ever so helpful. How is she, by the way?"

"Rachel has got a lot on her mind; she has family in Berlin she's anxious about. They're Jewish, you see."

Feathy poured water into the teapot. "Hmm, that must be a worry."

"But it was you, Feathy, and all those patterns you cut that really got me started, you know."

"And it's your knack of being abreast them new trends that gets the customers coming back."

Dora grinned. "We certainly get a more fashion conscious clientele than in Madame Morel's day."

"That reminds me, I saw Miss Gates in the grocer's the other day," said Feathy.

"Oh?"

"Couldn't help feeling sorry for the woman. She lost her mother six months ago and now that cousin of hers is getting married, the one who went to work in the shop when you was still there, remember her?"

Dora nodded. "Don't imagine Miss Gates is too happy about that!"

"Poor soul needs a job by the look of her; she looked really down on her luck. She's had no work since Madame retired."

"Then why doesn't she go down to the labour exchange?"

"I reckon she's too proud. For some it's stigma to go on the dole."

"That woman was no friend to me, Feathy."

"I know that love, but you've got to let bygones be bygones."

"I hope you're not suggesting I give her a job?"

"Well, I thought you were on the lookout for another sales person and she was good at her job, you've got to give her that."

Dora was appalled by the idea. "For Pity's sake, Feathy, I don't run a charity," she said sharply.

Dora could see by Feathy's expression that she was hurt but then Pam, who was playing nearby, overturned the box and the buttons spilled out across the floor.

Dora turned to the child irritably. "Now look what you've done!"

Pam looked up at her mother and apologised.

Feathy went over and patted Pam's back. "Never mind, sweetheart, we'll have 'em old buttons up in a jiffy."

Once the buttons were back in the box and Pam was out playing in the garden, Feathy turned to Dora. "You can say it's not my business but don't you think you're a bit hard on the child?"

"Yes, Feathy, you're probably right, I think I'm turning into my mother."

"You're alright, girl, you work too hard, that's all."

Through the window they could see Pam bent over the pond entranced by the goldfish darting in the water.

"Time those youngsters of yours had a garden to play in again," said Feathy.

Dora nodded. "Yes, that would be nice."

"Well, what's to stop you? What with the money you're making you'll soon have enough to buy them a mansion," said Feathy with a chuckle.

Chapter 32

Dora had seen little of Emily over the past year and was astonished when one day she telephoned to say that she was engaged to be married and would be bringing her fiancé, Ephraim Fried, to meet her parents at the week-end.

"We're coming for Sunday lunch and I'd like you to join us. I may need your support, Dor," she said.

"My support?" Dora queried. Emily had never before made such a request.

"Well, to be frank with you, I'm not sure how Ma will welcome a foreigner into the family, particularly a Jewish one. You know what she's like about her faith."

Ephraim Fried was a neurologist of international repute whose family had fled Russia during one of the Jewish pogroms when he was still a boy. Now, at almost fifty years of age, his voice still betrayed a hint of his forebears, a fact he attributed to his mother's resistance to learn the language of her adopted country.

He was a tall, thin man with a goatee beard and, though of a serious demeanour, he kept them smiling with his humorous account of the family's departure from Odessa and his dear Mama's panic at the loss of her wig, an essential accessory for a respectable Jewish lady, he explained to them drolly.

Toward the end of the lunch he thanked his hosts for making him so welcome.

Hilary glanced at him across the table and smiled. "I understand you have two teenage daughters, Mr Fried."

"Yes, Mrs Morton I do indeed and I'm extremely grateful that your dear daughter is willing to adopt the role of step-mother."

He turned to Emily seated serenely beside him. "I'm also delighted though slightly amazed that this lovely, talented young lady is courageous enough to share her future with mine."

Emily's face glowed with joy and was imbued with a beauty that Dora had never seen before. Hilary Morton, despite her reservations at Emily's choice, dabbed at a tear.

*

Jenny Baldwin was a talented young seamstress recommended by Feathy, and Emily's bridal gown was one of her first commissions. Emily, as practical as ever, had insisted upon a garment that could be re-used and Dora designed a gown in blue silk crepe that lent curves to her angular frame.

It was during her first fitting that Dora learned of Emily's intention to give up her career.

"Don't look so surprised, Dor. Ephraim doesn't want a part time wife!" she had laughed.

"But Em, you always swore that no man would ever take precedence over your career."

"Well, my priorities have changed. There are his teenage daughters to consider and Ephraim believes that a feminine influence will be good for them. Mind you, once the girls are off to university I may consider working part-time."

*

On the evening before the wedding Rachel telephoned Dora to tell her that she would be attending the reception. "My parents and Ephraim's were neighbours and friends, you see, but my father's not well and I'm going in their stead."

"Nothing serious, I hope?" said Dora.

"No, just a bad cold; though all the worry about Uncle Samuel has taken its toll."

"What's the news there?"

"With any luck he and the family should arrive in England next week but I don't think my father will believe it until he sees them in the flesh."

"You must be relieved, Rachel."

"That is an understatement," she laughed. "And I'm very grateful to Simon, he's been such a support. Uncle Samuel has been a very outspoken critic of the new regime, you see, and we fear there will be reprisals. My father has begged him to get out of Germany as soon as he can and Simon says that that my uncle promised to apply for exit visas and come to us in England.

The following morning Dora travelled up to Highgate in Dr Morton's car, arriving in time to assist the bride with her personal preparations. All the family were to attend, except for Ian who was too busy at the Mission school to take off the time. The twins were now in their last year at university and making their own travel arrangements.

"Now, before you have dressed in your finery, we are going to apply a little make-up," said Dora, and much to her surprise Emily was willing to comply.

The reception was held in Ephraim's large Victorian house and shortly after they returned from the registry office the guests began to arrive. Dora was chatting to one of the caterers in the hallway when she saw Rachel walk through the front door and went over to greet her.

"It's good to see you, Rachel," she said, and just as she was kissing Rachel's cheek Simon came up beside her.

Dora stared at him in surprise. "Simon! I didn't know that you would be here."

"Simon kindly agreed to be my escort," said Rachel, turning to him with a proprietary smile.

Following the buffet supper, the drawing room was cleared for a concert of Russian folk dancing, the performers accompanied by a group of gypsy musicians, and afterwards Ephraim's daughters took over the floor and executed a traditional dance of great charm. As the guests were roaring their applause Ephraim took hold of Emily's hand and beckoned the others to join them.

Dora stood watching from the doorway when Donald Morton came up beside her.

"Whoever could have predicted that Em would be the first to tie the knot?"

The family, including Donald himself, had imagined it would have been him, but after a two year courtship Glenda had abandoned him in favour of an academic career and Donald had remained a bachelor.

"And doesn't she look happy?" said Dora, as she watched Ephraim lead his radiant bride across the floor.

"You know something, Dora, I would never have guessed that my sister had such a romantic soul, such a pity that Ian couldn't be here to witness this!"

Dora noticed that Rachel had dragged a slightly bemused Simon on to the floor and saw her laugh flirtatiously as he attempted to follow her footwork. Rachel appeared in her element, reminding Dora of the girl who had once taught her the steps of the Charleston.

Rachel caught Dora's eye and flashed her a smile. "What a stunning young woman! Is she a friend of yours?" asked Donald.

"Yes, that's Rachel, she's a fashion journalist. I met her years ago."

"Unmarried?"

"Yes."

"Is there something going on with Rachel and your step-brother?" he asked.

Dora glanced across at them thoughtfully. "Not that I know."

When the dance ended Dora took Donald across the room to meet Rachel.

As they were chatting Simon turned to Dora. "I've hardly seen you all evening, is there somewhere we can go and have a chat?"

He followed Dora into the library and was telling her about his planned trip to visit his mother in Canada when Rachel breezed into the room.

"So this is where you two have been hiding!" she laughed tipsily and draped herself on the arm of Simon's chair.

"I forgot to ask about your meeting with Nicky, Dora. How was it?"

"It was fine, Rachel," said Dora.

"Well, that sounds a bit lame!" said Rachel. "You know, I was telling Simon how romantic it is that you two have found each other again!"

At that moment Emily put her head around the door and told Dora that she and Ephraim would shortly be leaving on their honeymoon trip. Though the revelry continued well into the evening Dora left soon after the bride and groom's departure.

She was putting on her coat in the hallway when Simon appeared. "You're not leaving already, are you?"

"Yes, I've got a train to catch."

"Then let me drive you to the station," said Simon.

"No need, I have a cab waiting. Sorry but I really must dash. Bye for now," said Dora and hurried off out of the front door.

Ruth was still up when Dora arrived home and was waiting for her in the kitchen.

"I almost missed the last train home," said Dora, slipping off her coat and sinking on to a chair.

"I thought Dr Morton would be driving you back," said Ruth, putting on the kettle.

"No, they booked into a hotel for the night; it's been a long day for them."

"So, how did you enjoy yourself?"

"Very much. It was informal and fun and Emily looked radiant. I think even Mrs Morton enjoyed herself."

Ruth made a pot of tea and carried it to the table. "Oh, God Bless her. You can't blame her for wanting her daughter to do things the traditional way with a church wedding and all that."

Dora laughed. "Em would never follow convention! She was always full of surprises though reneging on her feminist beliefs has stunned us all. Em is as single minded about this marriage as everything else she does."

"Love changes everything," said Ruth with a chuckle.

"By the way, Simon was at the reception."

"Simon? What was he doing there?"

"He came with Rachel; she has a connection to Ephraim's family."

"I thought she might set her cap at him."

"Really?"

"You must have seen how she couldn't take her eyes off him."

"No, I didn't, too many other things on my mind I suppose. How did Simon react?"

"Don't know that he noticed."

Later, after Ruth had retired for the night Dora went to the cabinet where she kept a decanter of whisky for Simon; poured some into a glass and returned to her chair at the table. She sipped at her glass pensively, recalling her meeting with Nicky but resisted the temptation to dwell on it and grow maudlin. However, the image of Rachel draped over Simon's chair could not be as easily banished. She knew that they had been seeing each other but thought nothing of it. How could she have been so blind?

Ruth came quietly into the room. "I thought you'd gone to bed," she said, taking a glass to the sink and filling it with water. She looked across at Dora. "What's the matter?"

"You're right, Ruth. I've been a fool."

"Simon?"

Dora nodded. "Simon and Rachel."

"You've had an emotional day, expect you're over-tired."

"I thought I had everything I wanted, you see."

"Well, this won't do you any good," said Ruth, picking up the bottle of whisky and returning it to the cabinet.

"But I don't know what's up with me, Ruth. I even snapped at Feathy the other day."

"Well, it's no good sitting here brooding. Go and get a good night's sleep, things always look better in the morning."

But sleep didn't come easily that night. She was ashamed at the way she had spoken to Feathy; and resolved to make amends. She might have lost Simon but she didn't want to lose her friends, too. It was painful to confront the emotional barrier that she had erected around herself, especially in relation to her own children. She might have been a dutiful mother but duty wasn't enough. They were not responsible for their paternity and it was time that she let them into her heart.

Chapter 33

Over the months the shop's merchandise had begun encroaching upstairs and with boxes and packages stacked in every available corner the flat had become decidedly cramped. Ever since her conversation with Feathy, Dora had thought about buying a house but due to the boom in the property market she decided that for the time being they would move into rented accommodation.

A few days later Trevor Dunlop from the estate agents arrived to take Dora and Ruth on a viewing of the properties he had on his books. Of the selection he showed them was a pretty semi-detached just a few streets away that well suited their needs and when Dora informed him of their choice he begged her to make no decision until they had seen the last property on his list.

Dora stared out of the window of Mr Dunlop's car, surprised to see that they were driving out of town when she had specifically requested a location within walking distance of the centre. What was even more puzzling was that about half a mile later he turned into a lane she knew well.

"Why have you brought us here, Mr Dunlop?" she said. "I know Mr Holmes, the owner of this property, and I also know it will be way over the budget I mentioned."

Mr Dunlop pulled up in the driveway and turned to Dora seated in the back of the car. "This house only came on our books recently and the landlord is prepared to accept a very modest rental to the right tenant. It's a unique opportunity, Mrs Armstrong."

Ruth gave Dora a nudge. "Couldn't we just take a look, Dora? I'd really like to see it."

Dora sighed. "As you wish, Ruth."

Mr Dunlop pointed out that the house had been completely refurbished and Dora knew that it was worth double the rental figure he quoted. She paced around the garden whilst he accompanied Ruth on a tour.

"As I was saying, Mrs Gibson, the landlord is retaining the lodge house for his own use and his visits will be restricted to week-ends," said Mr Dunlop when they came out.

"I don't understand your reluctance, Dora," Ruth said as they sat together in the living room that evening.

"Mr Dunlop said that Simon will be a close neighbour," said Dora.

"Well, that's a bonus, isn't it? The children will love having him around."

Dora was thinking about living in close proximity to Rachel, and should Simon decide to marry her Rachel would certainly prefer to live in the big house.

Ruth was already planning what she would grow in the vegetable garden. "And you said yourself that the rent will barely make a dent in the bank balance."

"But what about Simon, shouldn't we wait until he returns?"

"And in the meantime the house will get snapped up."

"I still think he should be consulted first."

"You shouldn't worry about that. The agent will know how to contact him in Canada, that's his job."

*

The removal men had already taken their furniture and possessions and with a last look around the empty flat Dora shut the front door and went to meet Mr Dunlop who waited outside. Her visit to Simon's house had brought back memories and she was still ambivalent about her decision to move in. She wanted a few moments alone there to adjust to the idea of Simon being her landlord and was grateful for Ruth's offer to collect the children from school in the recently purchased Austin motor.

Most of the furniture and paintings had long since gone but what thrilled Dora was to see that the Whistler landscape had been restored to its former position on the drawing room wall. The removal van was parked on the driveway and the men were awaiting her instructions but her eyes were lingering on the painting when suddenly she was conscious that she wasn't alone.

Her head swivelled round and there was Simon leaning nonchalantly against the door frame, looking lithe and tanned from his forays on the ski slopes.

"Simon! What are you doing here? I thought you were still in Canada."

"I got back yesterday."

"So you knew it was us moving in?"

"Yes, I did."

"Have you come alone?"

"Who else were you expecting?"

"I thought perhaps Rachel might be with you."

"Rachel? Why would I bring Rachel here?"

"Well, I know you've been seeing a lot of each other."

"But that was months ago, I've hardly seen Rachel since that wedding and you dashed out of the door like a scalded cat!"

He was chuckling as he walked across the room to her. "Dora, I do believe you're jealous!"

His eyes were even bluer than she remembered. "Look, I know I should have talked to you about us taking the house. I hope you don't mind…"

"Oh, Dora, you silly goose!" he grinned, then suddenly adopted a more serious demeanour. "Though now I come to think about it, there is something I do mind about."

Simon stood a foot away and she could see that his eyes were twinkling. "Are you teasing me?"

"I'm totally in earnest when I confess my disappointment at the way you have pre-empted me."

"What do you mean?"

"It may seem like an old-fashioned notion but I had anticipated the day that I would carry my bride over the threshold."

The End